Perfect on Paper

GILLIAN HARVEY

ORION

An Orion paperback

First published in Great Britain in 2021
by Orion Fiction
an imprint of The Orion Publishing Group Ltd
Carmelite House, 50 Victoria Embankment
London EC4Y 0DZ

An Hachette UK Company

1 3 5 7 9 10 8 6 4 2

A CIP catalogue record for this book is
available from the British Library.

ISBN (Mass Market Paperback) 978 1 4091 9189 6
ISBN (eBook) 978 1 4091 9190 2

Typeset at The Spartan Press Ltd,
Lymington, Hants

Printed and bound in Great Britain by Clays Ltd,
Elcograf S.p.A.

www.orionbooks.co.uk

To my gorgeous children Lily, Joe,
Tim, Evie and Robbie

Chapter One

'And congratulations to Will for yet another win in court!' Nigel concluded, the harsh light of the meeting room bouncing off the sheen on his bald head, giving him the appearance of a haloed monk. 'Well done.'

The four of them clapped obediently as Will stood and gave such a smug little bow that it was all Clare could do to stop herself from leaping over the table and smacking him in the chops. His epic court battle over Mrs Jones's sprained ankle had netted the firm about two hundred pounds in costs – the sort of money her department made before breakfast. Yet for some reason, news of his win had bumped her presentation to the bottom of the meeting's agenda.

'So, I think that's it!' Nigel concluded. His leather chair let out a flatulent creak as he stood up, and he stared at it pointedly for a second to make sure everyone knew exactly where the sound had come from. Then, looking at his watch, he announced 'time, two p.m.' in such a formal way that she had to look around the table to make sure he wasn't pronouncing someone dead.

'Um,' Clare raised her voice slightly. 'Um, Nigel, I thought I was going to go through the last quarter's figures from conveyancing.' *After all, my department does make about seventy-five per cent of our turnover.*

Nigel glanced at her as if noticing her for the first time. 'Er, oh . . . yes, of course. So, all good?'

'Yes, we're, actually we've—'

'Great, great,' Nigel waved her away as if he was swatting a small fly, rather than dealing with one of his longest-serving members of staff. 'Do you want to jot it all down in a memo and I'll give it a proper look through?'

'Of course,' she replied, her knuckles whitening against the folder she was clutching.

Because the fact they'd smashed their target for the third time running was absolutely not as important as the fact that Will had won Mrs Jones's claim against the builder who'd left a plank of wood lying in the street for her to (lucratively) tumble over.

'It'll get better,' Ann said, once Clare was back in her office, adopting an American accent that made her sound like a character from a US law drama, 'when you start taking homeowners to court and *suing their asses* rather than help-ing them move from A to B.'

'Yep,' Clare grinned, 'I guess actually coming into the office and slogging away just isn't as sexy as strutting around the courtroom in a sharp suit.' She tugged at the edge of her washed-out blouse, rather self-consciously.

'Look, don't worry about it. They'll realise soon enough when they come to balance the books,' her friend said, rub-bing Clare's shoulder briefly.

Would they though? Clare wondered. She'd been ten years in the job, four years as associate, and still Nigel seemed to take her presence, her Saturday morning paperwork ses-sions, her endless evening phone calls, for granted.

Will had joined the firm six months ago, newly qualified and over styled – a man-boy who clearly imagined life as a lawyer would be just like TV drama *Legal Minds*. Tailored suits, high-profile courtroom drama, glamorous women offer-ing themselves up over tequilas in shady bars after work.

Maybe in Hollywood, or even Chicago, Clare thought; but things are a little different in the Home Counties.

Nigel, her boss, and a lover of litigation, had recently taken Will under his wing, evidently having earmarked him for greatness, or at least a future partnership in their small firm. 'He told me he sees me as the son he never had,' Will had remarked to her recently.

'That's lovely,' she'd replied, not really knowing what was required of her in the conversation. Or whether she should mention that Nigel actually did have a son, who was a successful accountant.

'It's not as if Nigel's even going to *read* my memo anyway,' she griped later to her husband Toby, as they shared an after-work glass of red in their kitchen. 'He's too caught up in the whole courtroom thing – he goes to watch Will *perform*, you know. His *rising star*.'

'Yeah.' Her husband stared at his reflection in the glass-fronted oven and smoothed a stray strand of hair back into place. 'Tricky.'

'Toby?'

'Yeah?'

'Can you maybe look at me when we're talking?'

'Sorry.' He turned towards her, his blue eyes looking slightly panic-stricken. 'It's just . . . well, I'm having such trouble with my fringe. It's hard to focus on anything else – you know?'

She'd started to wonder whether her husband's recent promotion was all it was cracked up to be. After a few comfortable years presenting a section of the breakfast show on regional TV, he'd recently been offered the chance to be a third wheel on the national programme.

This meant two or three days a week he'd disappear to

London in the early hours – sometimes picked up by a sleek black car, other times driving in himself to 'beat the traffic'. He'd become obsessed with what he referred to as his 'brand' and begun to ask himself 'what would *Toby* do?' out loud when he was making important decisions such as whether to wear daring red socks or stick to his habitual grey.

One day in three he might get a shot at doing a piece to camera. Last week, he'd interviewed a woman who believed she was in love with her pot plant.

'Don't you see?' he'd said to Clare when she'd made a joke about it. 'This is a foot in the door of serious TV journalism! There's talk of me getting my own weekly section.'

'Your fringe looks fine,' she said now, impatiently, as he continued to fiddle with it.

'Are you sure? It's not too nineties?'

'No! Anyway, what do you think I should do?'

There was a silence.

'Lasagne?' he said at last, his tone uncertain.

'What?'

'Lasagne.'

'Toby! I wasn't even talking about . . . I was talking about work for God's sake!'

'Sorry! Sorry,' his hand returned to his fringe. 'Look, I was listening. It's just . . .'

'But you weren't, were you?'

'Yes. You were worried about your, um, work problem. Well . . .' he paused for so long she thought he might have fallen into a coma. 'I think you should do what you feel deep inside, you know, what your gut tells you,' he continued eventually, patting his lower stomach for emphasis.

'Hmm,' she said, wondering what would happen if she really let her gut speak for her. Irritable bowel syndrome – a side-effect of being a successful but busy solicitor – meant that she was always acutely aware of exactly what her gut wanted to say, and was often desperately trying to prevent it from expressing itself in the middle of the office.

'Anyway,' Toby continued, 'try not to worry.' He patted her leg and began rearranging his fringe again in the reflection. 'It's only work.'

What happened, she wondered briefly, to the attentive, mildly ambitious man she'd married fifteen years ago? The boy with a guitar who'd wooed her when they were at university? The man who, until he'd been catapulted into the realm of Z-list celebrity, had been her soulmate?

In six short months he'd started a regime of 'self care' that would befit a top model. Special shampoos, endless face creams – she'd even caught him plucking his nose hair with the tweezers she reserved for her eyebrows.

'That's disgusting!' she'd said, grabbing them from his hand. 'Get your own!'

He'd looked at her, tears in his eyes. 'But I'm shooting tomorrow.'

'Oh, for God's sake, you don't have to cry about it!'

'I'm not!'

Now he had clearly been thinking so much about his fringe that he'd forgotten to actually pay attention to what she was saying. She wasn't even as important as a little bit of hair.

'What I feel inside about *what*?' she challenged.

'About, you know . . . the work thing.' His face – always an open book – registered almost pure panic.

'Toby,' she said, sitting forward slightly. 'You haven't been listening to anything, have you?'

'I . . .' he began indignantly.

Just then, the door slammed and Alfie arrived home from football practice. Looking taller than he ought to for his fourteen years, he loped into the room. 'What's for dinner?' he asked.

It wasn't even, Clare thought, as she furiously stirred the gravy, that she expected much of her family. Just vague acknowledgements from time to time that she was there, that she *existed*. Even their daughter Katie, who until she'd turned twelve six months ago had been Clare's little side-kick, seemed recently to have been flooded with the kind of hormonal indifference towards her that ought by rights to be reserved for girls who at least had the good grace to be in their teens.

Looking up now, Clare caught a glimpse of her reflection in the chrome of the extractor. A blur of beige skin, slightly red nose – which always seemed to happen when she was stressed – and limp brown hair that she'd spend ages volumizing every morning with mousse and a hairdryer just to have it gradually reduce over the course of the day like a disappointing soufflé, or a cake that had been removed too soon from the oven.

Toby wasn't the only one who needed to dial-up the self care. But she couldn't afford the time to groom herself! Who could slap on face packs or get manicures when they were juggling hundreds of balls? She wasn't Dynamo, or Houdini, or Angelina frickin' Jolie.

'Katie,' she called. 'Any chance of a hand with the cutlery?'

Silence.

Eventually Clare laid the table herself, flinging the knives and forks down with slightly more aggression than was probably necessary. As a small act of revenge, she gave Toby the dodgy fork; one of the prongs was bent after Alfie had tried to use it to press the reset button on an old mobile.

That'd teach him.

'Dinner's ready!' she said at last, and suddenly it seemed

the collective family deafness was cured as they all came to the table, carefully laying their phones next to their plates as a kind of shield in case they were actually expected to converse with one another.

'Well, this looks nice,' Toby said brightly as she plonked his plate of cottage pie and carrots down in front of him. 'Only ...'

'Only what?'

Clearly Toby hadn't sensed the tone, as he carried on talking.

'Only ... I'm sure you said you were going to make lasagne?'

Chapter Two

'Come on, come on,' Clare hissed and turned the key in the ignition again. Not even a flicker of life. She glanced at her watch and felt a wave of panic. She couldn't be late today — she barely had enough time to get everything done as it was.

Two minutes earlier, Toby had purred out of their driveway in the new silver Mercedes he'd insisted he needed to keep up with the others in the studio. 'They've given me my own parking space,' he'd said when making his case for the purchase a few weeks ago. 'It's got my name on it. Well, my initials . . . I can't park a Volvo next to Samantha's Bentley!'

The cost of the finance had meant Clare had had to delay upgrading her battered Scenic. ('It'll be fine,' Toby had told her knowledgably. 'There's plenty of life in the old girl yet . . . And the car too! Eh!')

Which was, of course, exactly the kind of joke that goes down well when you're trying to convince someone you need to sign up for forty grand's worth of credit.

While she was still reeling from the hit to their bank account, he'd then asked his PA at work to help him choose him an entirely new wardrobe from shops whose names Clare had never even heard of. 'I just can't wear my old stuff,' he'd said. 'It's not current enough, not *with it* enough!'

When she'd seen the receipt, Clare had nearly thrown up. She could have managed a reasonable second-hand car at least with the money he'd splashed out on what his PA had assured him were the 'latest trends'.

Clare wasn't too sure what she made of the floral shirts and pointed shoes his twenty-five-year-old PA, Hayley, had picked out, but she'd had to admit Toby looked pretty hot in his new ensembles. He'd lost weight recently: the trousers hung flatteringly on his bum and the shirts, when tucked in, accentuated the fact that the paunch she'd used to tease him about had all but disappeared.

In fact, although his head was somewhere else, the rest of him had begun to resemble the Toby he'd been when they'd first met – young, toned, energetic – only with fewer band T-shirts and more floral cuffs.

She'd probably have been flattered if any of it had been for her. But whenever she made a move, he seemed to almost jump away – as if she'd electrocuted him rather than pinched his bum. Yesterday she'd sidled up to him when he was pouring coffee and he'd nearly tipped the lot over his hand.

'Hey!' he'd said, a little too crossly for her liking. 'Not in the *kitchen*!'

For a man whose foreplay – back in the days when they'd used to have a normal amount of sex – had often involved coming over and dry-humping her bum when she was loading the dishwasher, this had seemed rather rich. She'd begun to get a little suspicious of Hayley, who seemed to have more say over Toby's life than she did these days.

The kids had left at eight this morning, both sloping off to the school bus. Both resisting a goodbye kiss. There had been a time, Clare thought grimly, when the little buggers could hardly be prised off her at the school gate. Suddenly the thought of even a quick peck on the cheek before they went off was not only undesirable but – as Katie had put it the other day when she'd actually managed to land one on her daughter before she'd left the house – 'disgusting'.

Clare counted to thirty and tried the key again. Still nothing.

It was quarter to nine. She'd been cutting it fine to get in for half past as it was. Now she was definitely going to be late. She stepped out of the car into the freezing air and grabbed her battered tote bag full of papers from the passenger seat.

One advantage of living on a main road, she thought as she walked along as best she could in her narrowest heels, was that there was at least a regular bus service into the town centre. The stop was only a five-minute walk, and if she was lucky there might be a bus along quickly enough for her to still make her meeting at ten.

As she rounded the corner, she saw three others waiting by the stop. Two youngish studenty types of the sort that invaded the town in droves between October and June, and a chubby, grey-haired man in a raincoat, from which protruded (rather worryingly) a flash of bare leg followed by a pair of wellies.

The papers strained against the bag and she moved it into her arms, cradling it like a child rather than letting it burst its seams and spew her work all over the pavement. Why wasn't she one of these women with an appropriate bag for every occasion? Why always the tote bags? she wondered briefly. The other day, she'd emptied one out on her desk and an old pair of bikini bottoms and a battered pair of goggles had fallen out along with her paperwork, two chewed pens and a scattering of sand.

She really needed to go shopping. Perhaps Toby's PA could pick her out something 'on trend'. If there was any money left in the kitty that was. Probably with Toby's attempt to keep up with the Piers Morgans of ITV draining their joint account, a decent bag was probably once again a distant dream.

She thought again of Toby's man-makeover, the fact he'd thought nothing of splashing the cash on himself, whereas she felt guilty buying a new pair of shoes and was carrying legal documents in a bag that was more suited to tins of sweetcorn. They'd used to be on the same page about everything but now it was as if they had completely different priorities.

Usually, when her 'work bag' was flung on the passenger seat, she didn't really think about it. But walking along the road clutching a bag bursting with important files made her painfully aware of just how unprofessional she must look. Even the potential flasher in his raincoat was holding a leather briefcase.

The traffic that passed her as she walked was constant, and little drips of rainwater began to pepper her tights as drivers flicked the edges of puddles and sent tiny droplets skyward. Suddenly she was aware that there was the noise of a larger vehicle approaching. She glanced over her shoulder and saw to her relief it was the town bus.

The stop was just a few metres away – she'd made it. Deftly stepping to the side as the vehicle hissed to a stop, she even managed to avoid the slightly larger slosh of water it sent up as it pulled over at the stop.

See? The day was beginning to turn around already.

The two students got on, waving their cards briefly at the driver before turning their attention again to their phones. Mr Flasher was next, his coattails flapping dangerously as he stood on the step in the slight breeze.

'Got a pass, mate?' the driver asked him.

'Sorry?' Mr Flasher leaned forward and cupped his ear.

11

'I need to see your pass, innit.'

'You . . . if you what?'

'Can see your PASS!' Clare said loudly, fed up with waiting.

'Oh, can you? I'm so sorry!' Mr Flasher pulled his coat more tightly around him. 'I thought the coat was covering everything.'

Then it was her turn. She lifted her foot towards the step, only to have the bus doors hiss shut so close to her face that the rubber seal almost touched her nose. 'Wait!' she said, smacking her palm against the door. Surely the driver had seen her?

The man in the driver's seat was in his twenties, hair slicked back under a cap and sporting a beard so bushy it could well be home to several endangered species of wildlife. He wore a pair of slightly tinted glasses, and as she banged on the door again, she saw the white of a music pod in his ear. 'Hey!' she said. 'Hey!'

Without even a flicker of acknowledgement, he pushed the gearstick forward and the bus pulled away, its heavy wheels sending a cold slug of rainwater into one of her shoes.

Gasping, she stepped back, nearly colliding with an elderly woman in a red jacket who had arrived while the others were boarding. 'Sorry,' Clare said, stumbling slightly and nearly dropping her bag. 'Can you believe that? He was wearing earphones too. Are they allowed to do that? Surely, it's unsafe!'

The old woman regarded her with a steady gaze. Buoyed by the attention, Clare leaned conspiratorially towards her new confidante. 'Well, he's got another think coming,' she said, feeling anger still bubbling inside her. 'Let's just say I've memorised his number plate and I'll be getting on the phone to his boss.'

The woman's watery blue eyes looked back at her for a moment, as if digesting what she had said. Then, seeming to realise that Clare was expecting some sort of response, she nodded sagely and raised a gnarled finger to tap the side of her nose. 'Spring onions!' she said, looking eagerly at Clare. 'Spring onions and a dash of red wine! That's the secret. That's the secret!'

Typically, Nigel was in reception when she arrived late, bedraggled, and twenty-two pounds fifty poorer after having to call a cab. 'I can't help the traffic,' the driver had protested when she'd questioned the fare. 'I have to make a living you know.'

'Everything all right, Carol?' Nigel asked as she entered the building, tote bag sodden, hair stuck to her head, tights a riot of muddy polka-dots.

'Yes,' she said, not bothering to correct him. 'Yes. I'm sorry I'm late . . .'

'Oh!' he said, glancing at his watch. 'I hadn't realised you were.'

Luckily, she managed to get to her office and slip her tights off under the desk (thankfully, she'd shaved a couple of days ago so although her legs felt like sandpaper, they looked smooth enough) before Stefan Camberwaddle arrived. Which, bearing in mind the way the day had started, was an almost inconceivable win.

While the bread and butter of her work was sorting out transactional minutia between ordinary homeowners, she'd begun to take on more and more commercial work in recent months. After ten years of purely residential conveyancing it was a relief to tackle some different issues and landing Stefan as a client had been a real boon. She'd handled his personal house move – involving a particularly complicated right of way – about six months ago and now he wanted to involve her in his business. His multi-million-pound property flipping business.

When he'd said the word *retainer* on the phone, she'd almost wet herself. Stick that in your pipe and smoke it, Will, she'd thought. It'd be a tidy bonus in her pocket and surely at last the chance of a promotion? Nigel had been hinting to her about a potential partnership for the past two years.

After a little bit of diligence with a comb and the hand-dryer in the work loos Clare had also got her hair to more or less behave, and had even applied a slick of slightly strange tasting lipstick from a tiny stump she'd found in the bottom of her tote, so by the time Ann showed Mr Camberwaddle in, Clare was looking almost entirely human.

'Hello Mr Camberwaddle,' she said, rising to her feet and extending a confident hand for a shake. 'How are you?'

'Stefan, please,' he said, then smiled, revealing teeth that were so shockingly bleached she jumped involuntarily. 'Is everything OK?' he said, no doubt feeling the jolt from her shaking arm travel up his. 'You look very white.'

'Ohhh, two million of business, ohhh, two million of business,' she sang under her breath as she strode confidently to her boss's room an hour later. Somehow the phrase had become set to the tune of the hokey-cokey and stuck in her head on a loop.

Nigel's door was slightly ajar, so she knocked lightly and stuck her head around the gap. Inside, Nigel was bent over his desk, his face so close to the notepad he was writing on that had she been in the chair opposite, she'd have been tempted to draw a second face on the top of his bald head.

Luckily, it was Will, not she, who sat in front of the boss.

And he seemed to have had no such temptation. Instead, he was talking about advertising. 'Business cards on reception desks in doctors' surgeries,' he was saying. 'And maybe something we can stick under windshield wipers in hospital car parks.'

'Um, Nigel . . . Mr Mann?' she said, raising her voice slightly.

Both men jumped as if they had been caught in an illicit act. Then Nigel cleared his throat. 'Clare!' he said, getting it right for once. 'What can I do for you?'

'Just thought I'd let you know that the meeting with Mr Camberwaddle, you know, the property tycoon, went really well.'

'Oh well done, well done,' her boss replied absent-mindedly.

'In fact, he's actually put us on a—'

'Sorry, sorry,' Nigel said, laying his pen down for an instant and pinching the bridge of his nose. 'This is all wonderful news of course, it's just that Will and I were in the middle of a session.'

'A mind-mapping session,' Will added, helpfully. 'Advertising strategies, you know. Trying to net some serious cash for the firm.'

'Oh, I see . . . well, I just wanted to—'

'Do you mind,' Nigel interrupted, smiling in the mildly strained way a grandfather might to a slightly irritating child, 'if I could ask you to pop back later with the details, or jot them down? It's just that you're not meant to break the um . . . the . . .' he looked at Will imploringly.

'The flow,' Will finished for him. 'It's one of the strategies of highly successful people I've been reading about,' he said, unbuttoning his suit jacket and shifting forward on his chair. 'Pour your ideas onto the page and genius will out!' He grinned, without a jot of self-consciousness.

'So, if you don't mind?' Nigel said, nodding at her as if he wanted to headbutt her out of the door from four metres away.

'Sure,' she said. 'Sure, no problem.'

As she closed the door she heard Will begin again. 'Defibrillators! We could put our number on defibrillator paddles!'

Chapter Three

Standing in the queue at the local independent coffee house that lunchtime, her thermal cup clutched in her hand, Clare waited impatiently for her cappuccino. She had ten minutes left on her lunchbreak – easily enough time, but for some reason the server seemed to be sprinkling some sort of powdered masterpiece on the foamy top of the cappuccino he was preparing for the woman in front. Every now and then, he'd sigh loudly, scrape off his design, reapply the foam and get to work with his chocolate shaker again.

She'd chosen this particular coffee house as the takeaway coffee service was usually pretty rapid. On quieter days, she liked to visit the little tea shop around the corner, tuck herself away at a corner table and scribble in her notebook. Not legal stuff. Poems. She'd been writing in the same battered notebook since she'd been at uni – it was her guilty pleasure and a way of relieving stress.

Toby had found the notebook once. 'What are these?' he'd said. 'Song lyrics or something?'

She'd felt suddenly possessive – as if he was asking to read her diary. 'Nothing. Give it back!' she'd said, sounding about five years old.

I mean, who writes poems? Plus, it was something that was just for her.

'Honestly,' the girl waiting for her coffee told the server now. 'Honestly, it looks fine. I'll take it like that.' She glanced behind her at the growing line of customers apologetically, her immaculate blonde hair fanning out behind her as she moved. 'It's only coffee,' she added.

Her words coincided with a break in the music, meaning that as well as being heard by her individual barista, they were picked up by the older, skinny guy operating the till who glared at her as if she'd been spouting some sort of anti-coffee hate speech. There was an awkward silence before the music kicked back in.

Finally pleased with his design, the barista straightened up and passed the coffee to the girl, who grinned when she saw the intricate rose pattern he'd created. 'Suppose it was worth the wait,' she said, flashing the top of her (probably cold) drink briefly to Clare like some sort of prize.

'Lovely,' Clare said, between gritted teeth.

'Anything for our valued customers,' the barista nodded, doffing his cap like a nineteenth-century chimney sweep.

Clare was normally a fan of a bit of chocolate powder on her cappuccino on the rare occasions she treated herself to anything other than the instant coffee and limescaley water from the work kettle. She glanced at her watch; five minutes to go. She'd have to forgo it today or risk being late.

'Cappuccino, please,' she said, ready to refuse sprinkles – especially ones with an intricate design. 'To go.' She handed him her reusable cup – white, with a pattern of musical notes – a present from Ann last Christmas.

'Right,' came the reply. The barista fiddled about with the stainless steel contraption, dispensed some coffee and duly spooned on some milk foam. Then he plonked the drink unceremoniously in front of her. 'There you go,' he said.

'Excuse me,' Clare said, feeling disproportionately angry, 'but you didn't offer me any sprinkles!'

'Oh. Sorry.'

'Well aren't you going to?'

'Yes, of course. Would you like any sprinkles, madam?' he said, a hint of sarcasm in his tone.

'No, thank you. It's fine like it is.' She picked up her cup in one hand, lid in the other, and went to move towards the till, hearing the collective sigh of the queue behind her.

'So why make a point of it?'

'Excuse me?' she turned back towards the barista, slopping some coffee – which, she noted, was on the cold side – over her hand.

'Why make a point of the sprinkles when you didn't even want them?' The barista, who must have been eighteen years old at most, narrowed his eyes at her as if she was some sort of troublemaker. 'What are you, mystery shopper or something?'

'No, I just saw . . . well, surely it's your job to offer? And,' she felt herself blush but continued anyway, 'you spent all that time on *her* sprinkles; why not give *all* the customers that kind of service?' *Why am I always being ignored?*

'But you didn't want them!'

'Look, can I just get a coffee?' the man at the front of the queue interjected.

'But I *might* have wanted them. In fact, I DID want them. I just don't have time for you to create a Da Vinci masterpiece on the top of my drink!' she replied, feeling her neck getting hot.

'Oh, well, in that case,' he said, his nostrils flaring slightly, 'you ought to have some sprinkles.'

'No!' she held her cup further away from him. 'I don't want them any more.'

'No, I think you should have them! Treat yourself!' He picked up his shaker and launched a load of chocolate powder approximately towards her drink. The lid of the shaker loosened and clattered to the floor as he did so, and she ended up with not only the top of her drink covered in powder, but her hand and a little bit of her sleeve too.

'Thank you,' she said, trying to retain some semblance of dignity.

'There you go,' he said, unabashed. 'Your cup runneth over.'

Before she could retaliate, the man behind her sniggered, pushed past her and ordered. 'Americano please, mate,' he said.

And she was forgotten.

What was it with her? she thought to herself as she walked back to the office, sipping at her overly chocolated drink through the tiny gap in its mouthpiece. Why was she suddenly getting so worked up about everything?

As she pushed open the glass door of the office, she caught her reflection again. She thought of the barista's favourite customer, with her long, glossy hair and shift dress and couldn't help comparing it to her own rather frumpy skirt and messy hair. It wasn't that she'd let her moustache grow, or she'd stopped doing her roots, or she'd even stopped showering. It wasn't as if she was physically repulsive or completely unkempt.

But she wasn't looking great either. Her hair had already lost its hard-won volume, her coat was a relic from three winters ago, and below, her stubbly and now goosebumped legs looked like uncooked chicken thighs. She hated the thought that it mattered. But like it or not, women are always judged on appearances. Even now, after years of feminism, you had to play the game.

It wasn't about people finding her attractive or not; she didn't want a teenage barista to write his phone number on her cup or ask her out on a date. She certainly didn't want Nigel to notice her in *that* way. But maybe her appearance made her look as if she wasn't taking herself seriously. Maybe that was why nobody else seemed to.

Could her evident self-neglect have affected her career too? It wasn't as if she was surrounded by fashionistas in the office, but the same rules didn't apply to men in business. Nigel had bought two suits in the eighties and was clearly hoping they'd see him through to retirement, and even Toby until recently had worn the same shirt and tie to the studio day in and day out. Yet Nigel was a senior partner in his own firm, and Toby had received what he'd described as a 'dream promotion'.

The rules were different for women though. Heaven forbid they let themselves go grey, or forgot to pluck their chin hairs, or shave their armpits. Women were consigned to the garbage pile as soon as they let themselves slip.

Perhaps, she thought, as she reached her office and shook chocolate powder from her hand in the direction of the bin, she ought to do something to make herself feel better. Toby had had a makeover, so why shouldn't she max out the plastic on herself a bit? A bit of retail therapy would make herself feel better, even if it was superficial.

'Ann,' she said, when her PA brought in some folders and plonked them on the desk. 'Do you mind if I head off early today?'

'Aren't you meant to be *my* boss?'

It was true; she was in charge of Ann. But she liked to think of her as a friend foremost. She didn't want to leave her in difficulties by sloping out to go shopping when there was work to do.

'I suppose,' she grinned. 'It's just – well, I'm nipping out for a shopping trip. Bit naughty really.'

'Asda?'

'No, a clothes shop.' The look was brief, but she felt Ann's eyes travel to her legs stretched out below her desk, which as well as being stubbled and goosebumped, were blotched with red as they thawed out from her excursion.

Evidently, she wasn't the only one who thought it was time she had a few new outfits.

'Oh, well, have fun! Don't worry, I'll handle things here,' Ann said. She was, as usual, dressed neatly in a fitted blouse and skinny black jeans. Her hair, tied up in its habitual ponytail, hung elegantly against her neck. Ann was only younger than Clare by a few years, but sometimes she made her feel ancient.

Three hours later, Clare was wandering in the local department store, so overwhelmed with choice and crippled by her fear of changing rooms with their bum-revealing mirrors, she wasn't sure she was going to find anything at all. She picked up a floral top thoughtfully and held it against her torso – could she get away with it? Was it too young, too old? In style or out?

Of course, the sensible thing to do would be to try it on, but with her self-esteem at an all-time low she was loath to venture into the cubicles. For one thing, the white, bright lights always drew her attention to new wrinkles, stray hairs or the fact that her skin was never without at least two pimples. Worse, the mirrors in this particular shop's changing rooms were helpfully arranged with so many different angles that she couldn't avoid a glimpse of her white and wobbly thighs even when she averted her gaze.

Across the store, she could see that she'd been noticed by an assistant who was trying to make eye contact. Clare pretended to be completely preoccupied with sorting through a rail of clothes in the hope that she'd avoid being singled out for help.

Bad luck. 'Can I help you?' asked the woman, sidling up to Clare as she regarded herself in the mirror, yet another blouse held up for inspection.

Usually Clare hated offers of help in department stores. It made her feel so awkward that she'd rather spend hours traipsing around to find the right bra or hunting in piles of jumpers to find a medium than accept any help.

But looking at herself in the mirror holding up a blouse so similar to the one she was already wearing that it almost blended in, she realised that for once she was going to have to swallow her pride.

'Yes, please,' she said, watching the woman's face light up. 'I . . . well, I think I need a new look.'

Actually, it hadn't been too bad, she thought later. None of that standing in your knickers in front of the mirror to analyse your body type and work out what bits you needed to hide, like on the TV shows. Just a few questions about the kind of thing she wanted, and a series of outfits to try on for inspection.

She'd been stuck in a rut, she'd realised, standing in front of the changing room mirror in colourful tops and nipped-in jackets, careful to avoid the rear-view mirror as much as possible. She'd forgotten, somehow, that underneath her clothes was a figure – despite it having been battered and bruised by two pregnancies and the self-neglect that followed. Somewhere, when she'd slipped into the right dress or the neatly cut tailored top, she'd discovered a waist, a bottom that didn't sag as much as she'd feared and even a pair of passable breasts.

I am woman, she thought, inspecting herself in the mirror, wearing an emerald blouse. *Hear me roar, bitches*. She looked a few years younger and several years fresher. Something about the colours brought out her eyes – as the assistant had suggested. And she wasn't too past it to wear clothes bordering on the fashionable.

'You look fab!' the assistant had enthused as she'd tried on outfit after outfit. 'I hope I look as great as you when I'm forty!'

'I'm thirty-six.'

'Oh.'

An hour later, buoyed by her successful shopping, and weighed down by bags full of blouses and trousers and skirts as well as a whole carrier full of silky matching underwear, she'd called local hairdressers until she'd found one that could fit her in and, gliding on a wave of unexpected post-changing room euphoria, had booked herself in for a restyle with a junior stylist called Kevin.

Sitting in front of the hairdresser's mirror, her newly washed hair combed back, exposing every aspect of her less than fresh complexion, she didn't feel quite as confident. What was it with shops and hair salons and ultra-bright lighting? People go to these places to feel better about themselves, not to discover previously unnoticed crinkles, a developing unibrow or that the shadow on their top lip is actually a tash.

She avoided the mirror as best she could by reading one of the women's mags that were scattered around and learned more than she wanted to know about how to completely cut carbs from her diet.

When she'd been completely restyled, she did indeed look like a different woman. It was going to take a while to recognise this stranger in the mirror she thought, as the hairdresser held up yet another mirror so she could inspect the back (did anyone ever say anything negative in these moments? she wondered. All she ever managed was a 'that's lovely'). She looked a little bit like a newsreader – a mixture of glamorous volume and rock-hard hairspray. Perhaps this would finally make Toby listen to her. If all else failed, she could sit at the dining table with a sheaf of papers and read out the highlights of her day in received pronunciation.

Moments later, stepping out of the hairdressers and feeling her hair move slightly in the light breeze, she suddenly felt euphoric – as if she were the star of a rom-com or cheesy musical. She imagined herself breaking into song, while the passers-by who streamed past suddenly stopped and became a backing group.

'Cab for Clare Bailey,' said a voice as a beaten-up Ford drew up, breaking her reverie.

'That's me,' she said, in what she hoped was a glamorous, sexy tone. Flicking what was left of her hair, she eased herself into the back seat like a movie star climbing into the back of a limo. Sure, it was just a haircut, a couple of pairs of shoes and some clothes, but she felt more positive than she had for weeks.

This is it! she thought to herself. This is the day my life is going to change!

Chapter Four

If her life had really been a rom-com, Clare would have woken to the sound of birds cheeping. She'd have stretched, leaped out of bed – in perfectly unrumpled pink PJs – her hair still where she'd left it the night before, teeth sparkling. Her husband would sweep her into his arms and suggest they renewed their marriage vows. At work, they'd lay out the red carpet and recognise her as their star player.

Job done.

Of course, most people's lives don't resemble a rom-com, she thought as she squinted in the morning light, her hair a bird's nest on the pillow. There was no fanfare, no moment of realisation – her life was more blah blah than *La La Land*.

That said, it had been a while since she'd altered her look – and a few smiles and compliments would get the day off to a good start, she thought once dressed and recoiffed, tucking a stray hair behind her ear and grinning at the mirror. Not bad, Mrs Bailey, she said to her reflection. Not bad at all.

She paused outside the kitchen door, gave her hair – which didn't have quite the volume the hairstylist had managed to inject into it last night – one last cautious pat and pushed her way into the kitchen. She'd spent about half an hour trying to style it this morning with the help of a round brush and hairdryer combination, and although she'd achieved a sort of Emma Willis slicked-back-yet-voluminous look, she hadn't quite managed to keep the on-head quiff straight; it leaned slightly to the right like an uncertain politician.

Last night, Toby had come home late from a conference of some sort, and she'd been asleep in the dark by the time he'd come to bed. And as she'd showered when she'd arrived home – still itching from the haircut – any changes had been tucked under a towel when she'd seen the kids in the kitchen yesterday evening. This was the first time any of them would see her new look, and she was both excited and nervous about the reaction she might provoke.

She'd chosen one of the more modest of her new outfits, but it was still a complete change from her usual office garb – black, fitted trousers; a silk blouse and a jacket that cinched in her waist in just the right place. It was harder to breathe than usual, but otherwise she felt if not a million dollars then at least a couple of hundred quid.

She entered and clipped casually over to the kettle. 'Anyone want a tea?' she said, as if nothing was different about her at all, waiting for the flood of amazed and reverent compliments.

'No, just had one,' Toby said, holding up his empty mug as evidence, eyes still fixed on the politics section of the paper.

'Coffee?' she said. 'Croissant?' Surely, if she kept talking he'd have to take his eyes off the paper for a moment and LOOK AT HER?

'Better not.'

'Weetabix?' she said, a little desperately. 'Shredded Wheat? Last night's pizza?'

'No, thanks,' he murmured.

'How about a dead cat's eyeball?' she said, not changing her tone. 'Or, if you like, I could whip you up a dog-shit

27

sandwich?' She felt a small tear well up in the corner of her eye and flicked it away. As usual, he wasn't listening.

'No, thanks, gotta run,' Toby said, getting up from the table and somehow giving her a crumb-laced post-toast kiss on the cheek without making proper eye contact. 'See you later.'

The kids, intent on their phones, hadn't even looked up.

Sod the lot of them, she thought.

She set off in plenty of time for the bus and managed to put her foot firmly inside the vehicle as she waited to board. The same driver looked at her briefly as she paid for her ticket and she gave him what she hoped was a withering look. 'You know you left me at the stop yesterday morning?'

'Pardon, luv?' He pulled one seemingly sticky earpiece from his left ear and leaned closer.

'Yesterday. You left me at the stop. I banged on the glass.'

He shrugged. 'Youz not meant to bang on it, you nah,' he added. 'Regulations, innit?'

'But really, that isn't the point. I was . . .'

'You nah, I should really report ya.'

'What? You, report me?!' She could feel virtual steam ready to billow from her ears. 'You . . .'

But his attention had been taken by the man in the mac who today was at least wearing trousers under his grubby coat, albeit ones that looked to be three inches too short. 'Awight mate,' the driver said to him, and Clare was forgotten.

When she arrived at the office she nipped into the loos to make sure her hair and clothes were arranged just so, then strode into the open-plan area where the PAs and juniors sat together.

'Hello, sir,' she said pointedly to Nigel as she passed him at Will's desk.

He looked at her briefly. 'Good morning, Clare,' he said. 'I mean, Carol.'

Ann, at least, noticed that something was different. 'Ooh, love the new look – very Emma Willis!' she said. 'And your trousers look great!'

'Thanks, you're the first person who's actually noticed.' Clare resisted the urge to give her friend a massive squeeze. It was just a haircut, after all. But she'd begun to think that nobody paid any attention to her at all.

She slipped behind her desk and soon forgot about hairstyles and nipped-in waists (she'd opened the top button on her trousers for breathing purposes). Instead she began to deal with the initial morning admin – the letters and emails and phone calls that came her way each day – and felt herself unwind. Immersing herself in the everyday always relaxed her. Sure it was boring, but it was predictable; it had a shape to it. Subsidence, surveyors' reports, fixtures and fittings lists, rights of way – however big the problem, she could handle it. If only real life was as simple.

Between files, she thought back to her euphoria yesterday, about her new look. Rather than making her feel better it had brought home to her just how little she seemed to matter to everyone else. Nobody *had* to like it. She didn't expect to be scouted by a modelling agency or swept up by a Hollywood film star. But she had thought she might at least get a grunt of acknowledgement from Toby. As it was, he had glanced at her briefly, his eyes glazed, looking through her rather than at her. As if she was a ghost, not a living, breathing wife with pretty frickin' amazing hair!

She thought again of the mythical *Hayley* – the PA with all the answers. I bet he notices her, she thought despondently.

In spite of herself, she felt slightly teary. Leaning back in her chair, she dialled the number of the person she knew would make her feel better.

'So basically you're fed up that you cut your hair and no one noticed, right?' Her sister's voice on the phone was slightly incredulous. In the background, Clare could hear her six-month-old nephew, Wilbur, snuffling against his mum's shoulders.

'No, it's not that, Steph. Not really. I mean, that's part of it . . .' Clare squeezed the point at the top of her nose to hopefully avoid what felt like an impending headache. 'It's everyone. No one seems to *see* me. Toby's so preoccupied with whether he'll get his face on TV he never notices me. He disappears at the crack of dawn – or sometimes before – and the minute he's in bed he's fast asleep. It's not that he doesn't find me attractive, I don't think. It's worse. He doesn't seem to find me interesting. And the kids have their own things going on. I'm basically just a skivvy who rushes around and tidies up after everyone.' Having to let the cleaner go after Toby's last self-indulgent spend had been the icing on the cake.

'OK,' Clare's sister spoke slowly as if trying to rationalise with a mad person. 'But I don't get it – remind me how this relates to sprinkles on a cappuccino again?'

'It doesn't. It's just, well, it would be nice if for once someone noticed I was alive. You know. Even the barista at the coffee house couldn't be bothered to shake a bit of chocolate on my coffee. Until he practically threw the whole lot at me, that is.'

'Oh Clare!'

'And I just secured this really lucrative retainer with some sort of property mogul, but all Nigel can do is spend his time sucking up to Will.'

'Will?'

'Yeah, you know. That kid at work who Nigel seems to worship.'

'Ok . . .' There was a pause while Steph shushed Wilbur who had begun to grizzle. 'I have to say, I still don't get it.'

'You don't?'

'Yeah . . . I mean, I get that you're feeling a bit flat, a bit "meh"; I get that life isn't exactly a laugh a minute at the moment. But I think you're overrating the whole idea of being noticed. All I *do* is get noticed since Wilbur was born. I don't get a moment to myself. John's talking about trying for another one already and I just feel like a human milking machine.'

'Oh, Steph.'

'And the idea of being able to go somewhere and just be . . . well *ignored* for half an hour sounds absolutely blissful!'

'I suppose . . .' Clare looked at herself in the reflection on her computer screen. Her hair did look good – just one compliment wouldn't have hurt, would it?

'And, you know your car didn't break down on purpose – that was completely random?' added Steph.

'Well, yes, obviously.' Although to be honest, Clare wouldn't put it past the old banger. That car had had it in for her for years.

'And – don't take this the wrong way – but don't you think maybe we ought to be beyond all that now?'

'What?'

'Beyond needing validation from others. What is it you used to say? We're strong, independent women – that kind of thing.'

'Yeah, I did say that.' And she was strong, really. But just because you're a feminist, it doesn't mean you don't want someone to throw their cloak down over a puddle for you – or whatever the modern equivalent of that is: saying your bum looks toned in your bikini, or logging off Tinder during a date.

#ModernChivalry.

'So?'

'But it doesn't mean I want to feel completely surplus to requirements. Especially when I'm pretty much holding up the firm when I'm at work and holding the family together when I'm at home. It just wouldn't hurt to hear somebody say thanks, or pay me a bit of attention once in a while.'

'Try looking at it a different way,' Steph said, her voice softer now. 'You've just told me that you've dyed your hair and it looks great, you've bought yourself a couple of new outfits. Your work is going well, and Toby seems to be making a success of things . . .'

'Except for his marriage, of course.'

'Well, yes. But give him a chance. He's a good bloke . . . normally. It's the job, I reckon. Pretty full on.'

'Yeah, I suppose.'

'And you know, fringes can be tricky . . .' Steph quipped, mischievously.

Clare snorted. 'True, it must be very challenging for him!'

'And believe me, most women in your position would be heaving a sigh of relief,' her sister added.

'Relief?'

'Yes, a sex break. Do you know how rare it is to get one of those?'

'Really?'

'Seriously, make the most of it. John's always trying it on, and I feel awful when I reject him. But I just . . . I'm so tired, you know?'

'Oh, Steph, I'm sure he understands.'

'He does, but it still makes me feel shit.'

32

'I'm sorry,' Clare said, as if it was she who was responsible for her brother-in-law's insatiable sex drive.

'Honestly, make the most of it,' her sister continued. 'It probably won't last and you can always buy a vibrator, or a new washing machine.'

'That's true, maybe one with an ultra-fast spinning cycle,' Clare joked. 'Idiot!'

'Seriously though, things are going really well for you! So what if no one's noticed? In fact, if you find the formula for invisibility, please can you let me know. I could do with a break from greedy Wilbur at least once in a while.'

Clare remembered those days only too well. The ache of her nipples. Looking pleadingly into the eyes of a child who saw her, it seemed, as a food source first and a human second (if at all).

'I suppose you're right. I just feel kind of, "meh",' she sighed.

'I think,' Steph said, her voice dropping to a mock whisper, 'we probably have to accept that our thirties are going to be a bit "meh". In fact, if "meh" means we're both in relatively happy relationships, raising healthy kids and have pretty good job prospects, then who needs extra drama?'

'Good point. God, Steph, you always know how to talk me down from a ledge.'

Steph snorted.

'What?'

'Sorry, I was just thinking. Well, I'm good at advising others. But not so hot when it comes to figuring out my own life.'

'What do you mean?'

'Oh, nothing. You know . . .'

'I am here for you, you know,' Clare said. 'I'm more than just a solicitor – I'm your sister.'

'A soli-sister if you will.'

'Exactly.'

'Honestly, ignore me. I'm just tired.'

Had she overreacted to everything? Clare thought, as she hung up. Her younger sister's quiet stoicism made her constant need for reassurance seem ridiculous. Was she just making a fuss about nothing?

But then she thought back to the bus driver, the barista, Nigel, Will; Toby using up all their credit on a car for himself, designer suits, a new briefcase and not considering her feelings at all; Alfie, who had left so many plates on his bedroom floor that she'd trod on at least two mouldy pieces of toast when she'd ventured into his room with a pile of clean pants earlier. Katie, who had actually asked her to drop her off down the road from her dance class last Saturday because – apparently – she was *embarrassing*.

She shook her head. No, she wasn't going to have that kind of life. The kind of life where you're the wind beneath everyone else's wings and don't get to spread your own.

Getting out her battered little notebook, she began to write.

Chapter Five

The following Monday, Clare's wake-up was a little more rom-com and a little less *EastEnders*. For a start, the sun was shining. She'd slept well. Toby had remembered to put his dirty pants into the laundry basket. This was shaping up to be an unusually Good Start to the week.

She'd decided over the weekend, while running errands and taxiing children to football matches and catching up on Corrie – that perhaps she'd gone about it all the wrong way.

In fact, if anything, she felt a bit annoyed at herself for becoming a cliché – or at least she would be if she didn't love her new shoes so much. Like a character in a movie, she'd gone down the 'looks' route when she'd wanted to shake up her life. But actually she didn't want lustful looks on the bus as much as respect in the boardroom (and perhaps a bit of help at home).

As it was, her new look had only served to make her realise just how little attention Toby paid her – which had made her feel even worse.

But maybe Steph was right – maybe she ought not to worry too much about Toby's apparent lack of interest. His personality transplant had happened pretty much as soon as he'd started his new role. It was bound to be stress, rather than any massive problem with their marriage, right? He'd told her Hayley had a boyfriend – she was his PA and that was it. And as he settled down into his new job, perhaps the old Toby would emerge again to replace the frantically busy, distracted new version.

But the moment she walked into the kitchen, her resolve failed her. Not a soul looked up, despite her chirpy 'Good morning!' The kids had been out or in their rooms for most of the weekend, Toby had spent half of Saturday morning at the salon, so this was the first time the whole family had been in the same room at the same time for two days. And nothing.

Toby was silent, sitting behind his paper. The kids were poring over cereal and phones simultaneously.

'Don't suppose you can flick the kettle on for me?' said her husband, who had obviously sensed her come in but hadn't felt the need to glance in her direction.

'Sure,' she said. She walked loudly and deliberately over to the counter and pushed the switch.

She wondered, for a second, whether her life was just a stage set, and she was the only actor without a script. Maybe she should take a leaf out of Bill Murray's book and act outrageously, just because she could? It would certainly sort out the invisibility question once and for all.

'Mmm, what to have, what to have . . .' she said, watching her family carefully. Not one of them looked up. 'Hmm,' she said again. 'Breakfast! The meal of champions! Breaker of the night's fast. Setting oneself up for the day.'

Nothing.

She began to pour herself a bowl of cereal then stopped. Far too ordinary. Instead, she grabbed an enormous glass bowl and her soup ladle, tipped the majority of Alfie's Honey Pops into it and flooded the whole dish with milk. Then she plonked it on the table between her children, slopping a little of its contents dangerously close to Katie's phone and, pulling up a chair, took an enormous ladleful.

'Mmm,' she said. 'Yummy.'

Katie, not looking up, moved her phone protectively away from the splash of milk.

'Got to love Honey Pops!' Clare said, almost desperately, willing someone to look up. Forgoing the spoon, she dipped her face into the bowl and bit into the sticky cereal. 'So tasty!'

'Uh huh.' This was from Toby, still hidden behind his paper.

Clare leaned forward and pushed the page down to reveal her husband with his carefully coiffed mop, new silk tie and lilac shirt. 'Anything interesting?' she said, a honey pop falling from her chin and landing wetly on the market reports.

Toby glanced up at her, then looked again, more intently. Here it was. Here was the moment.

'Clare?' he said.

'Yes, darling one? Light of my life? ITV's answer to Jeremy Vine?'

'Do you think you could pick me up a packet of Y-fronts today if you go to the shops?'

'Sure,' she said, feeling a dribble of milk roll slowly down her chin.

'OK, thanks,' Toby said, flicking the paper back up in front of his face.

What would it take? she wondered. Perhaps she should stage a naked protest outside the studio, glue herself to his laptop, or dress up as Piers Morgan in the bedroom to get his attention. *You seem surprised to see me*, she imagined herself saying. *Come here and let me patronise you.*

At the bus stop, she even wondered for a moment whether she ought to take a leaf out of Mr Flasher's book. Today he was wearing his traditional raincoat, this time with

37

apparently bare legs (despite the fact it was four degrees and windy), white sports socks and a pair of crocs.

While his attire wasn't on trend, it was certainly memorable – and of course left anyone who saw you pondering the slightly fascinating, slightly repulsive possibility that you might be a pervert.

She nodded and smiled as he glanced up. Perhaps nobody noticed him either.

Sitting on the bus, she felt a little teary again. All her life, she'd played by the rules – worried that if she slipped up, if she did something forbidden or wrong, the world would come crashing down around her. Had she got it all wrong? Had blending into the background just made her disappear?

Arriving at the office, she strode in and went immediately to Nigel's room. Foregoing her usual knock (the height of daring), she opened the door to see him sitting at his desk, glasses on the end of his nose, working from the light of a tiny desk lamp, like a character from a Dickens novel.

'If the law supposes that,' she imagined him saying, 'then the law is an ass.'

'Good morning, Nigel!' she gushed, feeling almost high on a surge of adrenaline, anxiety and a weird sense of surrealism. 'Did you get my memo about the retainer?'

He looked up from his computer screen. 'Oh, yes. Yes. Well done, well done,' he said, nodding his head but not entirely convincing her that he knew what she was talking about. 'So . . .' he gestured at the pile of papers as if to suggest she buggered off now and let him get on with it.

Sod this, she was getting his attention no matter what. Ignoring this social cue, she stepped fully in, strode over to his desk and picked up his cup of coffee in his precious 'The Boss' mug. 'Don't mind if I have a quick slug?' she said, 'I'm gasping.' She lifted the cup to her lips and drank deeply. It was cold, and there was a skin of milk on the top which stuck to the roof of her mouth. Yesterday's coffee. She coughed, spraying a cappuccino-like foam onto his paperwork. A small bubble landed on the back of his hand and they both stared at it for a moment.

'Actually,' he said, wiping his hand on his sleeve and looking at her as if nothing unusual had happened, 'I wanted to talk to you.'

'Oh yes?' she said, trying to fight the feeling of post-stale-coffee nausea that was spreading through her body. She sat down on the edge of Nigel's desk, still clutching the mug and feeling a file crumple satisfyingly beneath her bottom. Perhaps this was it, perhaps he was finally going to throw her a crumb of praise for her recent phenomenal turnover.

'We're moving things around a bit in the office,' he said. 'With Will and I spending so much time strategising, it makes sense that he takes the office closest to mine.'

'Right?'

'In fact,' Nigel continued, clearly not finished, 'I think he's rather a rising star – someone to nurture. Full of ideas. And so much energy.'

'Yes, well,' she said, almost drinking another slug from his cup but then thinking better of it.

'Well, anyway. We thought we'd move you to the corner office – you know?' he looked at her, his eyes searching her face for a reaction.

The corner office? she thought. What corner office?

'Sorry,' she said. 'Which corner office?'

'Er, the one . . . well, it needs a lick of paint of course. But next to the . . . um, the loos?'

'There isn't a . . .'

'Well, we'd be repurposing it of course. New chair, et cetera.'

39

'The . . . the coat cupboard?'

Nigel's cheeks flushed. 'Well, I suppose. Well, it is where we hang our coats at present of course. But originally . . . I mean, it's actually quite . . .'

They were moving her office to the coat cupboard.

'There's no window . . .'

'No? Erm. Oh dear. Well, perhaps it won't be a long term . . . er . . . thing?' he trailed off.

'Right.' Trying to retain some sense of dignity, Clare got up, smoothed down her skirt and left.

Later, she wondered why she hadn't taken him to task on his proposition. Refused to budge. Challenged him about the fact that Will was newly qualified and quite capable of walking down the corridor to Nigel's office without the need to boot her out of hers.

It was, she realised, just because it was so awful. So irredeemably surprising and awful. She'd been stunned into silence; acquiescence.

She understood suddenly what made people shoplift, or run naked across football pitches, or send pictures of their private parts to potential partners over the internet. She knew that people loved her, in their way. She knew that she was important, that the balls she kept juggling could not be dropped without seriously impacting her work or family life. But despite the fact she was integral to at least three people's home lives and several people's working lives, she was actually just a cog in the works; an essential part of the engine but not something anyone gave any thought to unless it suddenly stopped whirring.

She didn't want to stop whirring. She liked being a mum, most of the time. It had been more fun when her children actually acknowledged her existence, and needed her, and wanted her to kiss them goodnight once in a while; but she knew deep down that they were evolving, that it was natural for them to grow away from her; that the relationship she had with her children would alter as they grew.

She didn't want to quit her job and do something else – her role was a bit monotonous at times, but she was bloody good at it. And there was satisfaction in seeing how well her department was performing – even if no one else noticed.

She didn't want a red carpet, bunches of flowers or a fanfare each time she went into a room. She didn't expect everyone to bow at her feet or offer to carry her to work in a golden litter.

But it would be nice if, say, once every couple of months, someone acknowledged that she was there; that she was not just a backstage worker in their life, but had an existence of her own.

That she wasn't entirely invisible.

She stopped.

Because in all her failed attempts at self-promotion, all of her nudging of boundaries; in all her self-pitying contemplation she'd overlooked the most important thing of all.

Invisibility wasn't great if you hated not being seen.

But if you embraced it, invisibility could be a superpower.

'I can do,' she whispered to herself, 'whatever the hell I want!'

Chapter Six

'Mum?'

Clare lifted her head wearily from the pillow. 'Yes?'

Outside, it was still dark, but the purr of traffic on the road told her that it must be at least eight o'clock. She sat up, suddenly alert.

'We're off!' Katie's voice.

'OK, have a good day!' she said, trying to sound upbeat and as if she hadn't just been woken from a deathly slumber. The pillow next to her had a dent in it, and the duvet on Toby's side had been flung across; other than that, there was no sign of ITV's rising star.

Was TV work really so interesting that he'd get up and leave her without a word? There had been a time when she'd rarely started her day without the feeling of a semi-erect penis pressing into her back. At the time, she'd found it annoying – she wasn't a morning person when it came to doing the dirty. Now, she looked back on those halcyon days of vertebrae-nudging semis with a fondness usually reserved for precious childhood memories or gifs of cute puppies.

Across the room, her reflection in the mirrored wardrobe caught her eye. Tousled hair, black under-eyes, an empty glass of wine on the bedside table like an accusation.

It wasn't a good look. No wonder Toby had opted to take himself and his unsullied penis to work early.

She thought back to yesterday, when she'd thought being

invisible could actually work in her favour. It seemed ridiculous in the cold light of day.

And now she was late for the only thing in her life that was going well.

She quickly worked on smoothing her hair down, clipped it back and pulled on an old faithful outfit of grey trousers and a blue blouse. Then, grabbing her tote and coat, she rushed out of the door without so much as a sniff of a coffee bean.

It was cold, and she'd forgotten to pull on a jumper in her haste. She walked fast to try to work up some heat, feeling her lips practically crack in the icy air.

At the stop, even Mr Flasher seemed to have upgraded for the cold weather. He was wearing a scarf, although he was still naked from the calf down.

She was getting quite fond of Mr Flasher now. He was reliable; always there. Always nodded a good morning at her these days.

'Hi,' she said. 'I thought I was late!'

He looked at her. 'You probably are,' he replied. 'I'm waiting for a different bus today.'

Shit. She'd have to get the next one.

Ten minutes later, there was still no sign of a bus. But the stop was remarkably busy – a group of girls dressed in strange red outfits huddled together, whispering. A man with an enormous bag on his back looked anxiously at his watch. And a girl with long black hair and a guitar case was leaning against the vodka advert on the bus shelter.

'So, how come you're going somewhere different today?' Clare said at last to Mr Flasher.

'Eh?' he looked at her briefly, his jowly cheeks reddening slightly. 'Well, it's the thing today, isn't it?'

'The?'

'You know,' he said. 'The thing . . . the,' he lowered his voice, '*thing*, thing.' He nodded his head for emphasis and tapped his nose conspiratorially.

'Right.'

Before she could ask anything further, a bus – with 'Auditions' emblazoned across the front – pulled up at the stop.

Of course! She'd read about this in the paper. There was a local 'open call' for a TV talent show. A chance to perform in front of a couple of producers who might put you forward for the Real Thing. The kind of thing she'd have taken part in at university just for the fun of it. She wondered what Mr Flasher's act was. What the others at the stop might be doing. She imagined herself, too, watching. Even walking onto the stage. Would she ever have the guts to do something like that?

She thought about another day at the office. Another day of writing unread memos to Nigel. Another day of Will grandstanding about his latest court date (this time, for a client with – gasp! – unpaid parking tickets). Maybe it was time she did something exciting for once. After all, it wasn't like anyone would notice. She opened her bag to check that her notebook was there. Then followed Mr Flasher onto the bus.

Mr F. sat at the front, briefcase on lap, legs so far akimbo that she hoped for everyone's sake he was wearing *something* under his coat. She chose a seat at the back and sat down, feeling slightly ridiculous. But it wasn't as if she had to *do* anything, she thought to herself. She was just going to see what it was all about. It wasn't as if her own bus had turned up anyway, so she'd definitely have been late in any case. It could be an adventure – something to get her mind off things if nothing else.

Sliding down in her seat as the bus filled up, she felt a shiver of excitement at doing something different for once. And without having had a caffeine hit that morning!

'Do you mind?' the girl with the black hair appeared by her side suddenly, clutching the guitar case.

She did, actually. Especially as there were several other seats available. But Clare found herself saying, 'of course not' anyway. Because she was far too polite.

The girl shuffled onto the seat and rested her guitar case on the floor, supporting it between her unnaturally skinny legs like a giant, misshapen penis.

Looking at her phone as an excuse to avoid conversation, Clare began to think about what she might actually do when she arrived. When she'd read about the open auditions in the local rag a couple of weeks ago she'd imagined herself signing up, dusting off her poems and airing them for the first time.

At the time she'd smiled but turned the page and started reading the property adverts. It had seemed like a funny fantasy, not something she'd actually do. But maybe her subconscious had held on to the idea after all.

As if answering her question, her phone buzzed and her eyes were drawn to a new email notification. The title read: 'Today's Meeting'. It was from Stefan Camberwaddle.

Shit. In all her ridiculous turmoil she'd forgotten that she'd arranged a meeting with her most important client this morning. Her absence would matter after all.

As the bus began to pull away from the stop, Clare felt familiar anxiety bubble up and looked out of the window to calm her thoughts. It was a mistake, but she couldn't do anything about it now. Even if she got off the bus, called a taxi and rushed back to the office she'd be late. Surely Stefan wouldn't mind if she called it off – feigned sickness of some sort?

She tapped her bag, feeling the familiar rectangle of her notebook against her fingers. She'd been carrying this book around for a decade, noting down her thoughts and feelings like a diary; a rhyming diary. But on some level she'd always wondered whether her ditties might actually be a little bit . . . well . . . good, actually. Poems seemed a bit old-fashioned – not something that most people seemed to read or enjoy – and she'd always thought of writing them as a guilty pleasure, the sort of thing she could enjoy for herself but never share.

This was her chance, wasn't it? To read a poem to a room full of strangers and see whether she was actually any good at it. And it wouldn't matter. Nobody would know. She wouldn't have this opportunity again.

An hour later, sitting in a room full of chairs, the idea didn't seem quite as wonderful as it had earlier on. She'd already been waiting for ages; there was clearly at least an hour more to go. Somewhere, back in her office, Camberwaddle had been stood up – she'd texted Ann to say she was sick and asked her to contact him but suspected that he'd be mightily put out at the late cancellation.

The room was alive with excited chatter. Dancers stretched impossibly flexible limbs. Singers carried out vocal exercises. A man dressed as a clown was juggling in the corner. He kept dropping a ball and looked close to tears. Clare was willing to bet none of the acts would be standing there reading poetry like a poor man's version of Pam Ayres. What was she doing?

Then she noticed a familiar coat hanging over the back of a chair. Next to it, a man with grey hair was limbering up. His rotund frame was squeezed into a leotard covered in green sequins. Looking up, Mr Flasher – or perhaps Mr

Flashy – caught her eye and she gave him the thumbs up. A*
for bravery if nothing else! He smiled back.

In the row behind her was a small group of boys – all
dressed in black – together with a man who looked to be in
his early thirties. His hair was curly and cutely unkempt.
The sort of man, she thought, who didn't spend a second
longer than he had to thinking about his fringe. 'Remember
lads,' she heard him saying. 'We've been training for this.
We're ready. Just have fun with it.'

'But we want to win, right?' one of the boys replied.

'Yes, Mark, we want to win,' the man said, leaning forward and ruffling a mop of brown hair. 'But we want to
enjoy it too.' He glanced over at Clare and grinned. 'Pretty
nerve-wracking,' he said. His smile was wide and showed
both sets of teeth. It was impossible for her not to grin back.

'Just a bit,' she said. 'Good luck.'

'Thanks,' he said. Like the boys he was with, he was
dressed in a black T-shirt, but his jeans were blue and covered in fashionable rips. 'I'm just the coach,' he added. 'The
boys are the talent.'

As he lifted his arm to rub his hand across his springy,
curly hair, his T-shirt lifted up to reveal an enviable six-pack.

Oh, I don't know, thought Clare, then felt herself blush as
if she'd said it out loud.

'Anyway, hope it goes well for you,' he said, sitting down
and giving her a wink.

'Me too.' She felt her cheeks flush a little.

She read through her lines again. Well, unlike the boy
dancers she hadn't been training. And she definitely didn't
have a six-pack. But she was here now. What the hell, she
thought. She was damn well going to do it anyway.

Chapter Seven

An hour and a half later, reading her chosen lines for the tenth time, Clare saw Stefan's number flash on her phone. She pressed the red button to bin the call, hoping he would leave a message instead of persisting. Luckily, one flashed up. She nervously lifted the phone to her ear: 'Clare, it's Stefan Camberwaddle. Sorry you're sick. We do need to get this transaction tied up though. I'm afraid nobody else at your office was able to help. Please message me to rearrange things.' She felt a sinking sensation in her stomach. But before she could decide what to do a small, mousy-haired woman appeared at her side like an apparition: 'Would you like to come this way please,' she said. 'Next two rows.'

Too late to back out now, Clare, she told herself. She put the phone back into her bag. She'd call later and sort things out.

The group of boys – all of whom looked to be in their early teens – stood up too, as well as Mr Flasher, who was now modestly covered with his mac again. They walked together, like the strangest and most motley crew imaginable, through the double doors.

Then there was momentum and the low murmur of conversation as they turned a corner. A woman was sitting on an empty box and breathing into a brown paper bag. The passage opened up into a larger area, where a man leaned casually against a wall, sporting a pink tutu and a curly pink wig. 'All right darlin'?' he said as she passed, as if this was just a normal situation.

'I don't . . .' she said to a young lad in a T-shirt marked 'Crew' by her side. 'I just don't . . .'

'Everyone says that,' he reassured her, without making eye contact. 'Don't worry, you'll be fine.'

Mr Flasher was first. Breathing deeply through his nose, he whipped off his mac and sprang through the doors into a room whose door had been labelled 'Audition Room' with the help of a sheet of A4 paper, a biro and some Blu Tack.

Clare peeped in. The room itself was no more than a corporate meeting room. There was a wooden table with metal legs on which someone had put a sign with the word 'Judges' in comic sans typeface. It wasn't exactly a high-budget, live-TV situation. She thought back to the number of times she'd watched *You've Got Talent*, thinking that the auditionees had literally walked in off the street.

'So, who are you and where do you come from?' asked a woman with a clipboard, sitting on the edge of a table.

'I'm Martin, I'm from Hatfield and I'm sixty-nine years old!' said Mr Flasher.

The woman glanced at a man who was seated at the table. They exchanged a look and a nod. Clare thought about talent shows she'd seen on TV, where anyone over sixty got treated as if they were suddenly cute and eccentric, rather than borderline insane and dressed in a ridiculous costume.

Clare's dad was sixty-nine, and if he wanted to go on a talent show dressed in a leotard, she was pretty sure she'd have him sectioned.

Catching her eye, the woman with the clipboard stood up and closed the door gently. 'Sorry,' she said. 'Won't be long.'

Clare blushed – caught out. Now she'd probably never know exactly what Mr Flasher's talent was.

Minutes later he exited the room, beaming.

'How did it go?' Clare asked.

He gave her an excited thumbs up. Then a girl, who looked no older than Katie, clutching a folder of papers, came up and rested her hand on his back. 'Now,' Clare heard her say, 'do you know how you're getting yourself home, sweetheart?'

Clare looked at her crumpled piece of paper again as the man in the pink tutu disappeared into the judges' room, desperately memorising lines before her moment. She wasn't going to get through of course, she told herself. But then she had no desire to get through really. She just wanted to see if she could make a small dent in the consciousness of those around her. And whatever lay in wait for her, at least she didn't have to face it wearing a sequinned leotard.

Minutes later, there was a bang as the door opened abruptly and its handle hit the wall behind. The tutu man, now clutching a saxophone, walked out, red-faced after a stinging dose of reality. Then Clare found herself being shoved in the small of her back.

'You're on!' grinned a girl with a folder.

'I . . .' she said. But it was too late.

'Best of luck!' came a voice. Clare looked. The handsome man with the curly hair was grinning and leaning against the wall, the boys lined up messily behind him. When their eyes met he gave her an elaborate wink.

'Thanks,' she replied, feeling sick but excited at the same time.

'So,' said the woman with a clipboard as Clare entered the room, her knees suddenly jelly-like. 'What's your name and where do you come from?'

'I'm . . .' She thought back to the pseudonym she'd given

when she'd filled in the paperwork. 'Martha. From . . . from Hatfield.'

'Hi Martha. So, when you're ready?'

Clare glanced over towards the slightly open door and saw a couple of the teenagers looking at her, their faces swimming and decapitated in the darkness. One of them gave her a thumbs up, and she returned the gesture on instinct.

Then the door closed. Beyond the silence in her room she could hear the thump of a beat – the boys were clearly having one last rehearsal along the corridor.

'Do you want me to get them to turn it down?' asked the man, leaning forward as if to stand up.

'Oh, no. Honestly, it's OK,' she smiled. The last thing she wanted to do was to spoil someone else's chance.

'OK, well, when you're ready,' prompted the woman.

Then there was nothing to do but to get on with it.

'Why do I feel so down?' she said, her voice sounding small and quivery.

> *'I've got a job, a house in town,*
> *Two kids, a husband,*
> *Everything,*
> *That middle age is meant to bring.*
> *So why is it I feel so "meh"?*
> *I look around me, everywhere,*
> *Are people who look*
> *Just like me*
> *Except they seem content, you see.*
> *I'm not, I'm "meh"*
> *Don't feel like me,*
> *Or not the me*
> *I thought I'd be.*

51

I want to laugh and feel alive
There's more to me than nine to five,
Than being mum, or being wife
Or employee – I need a life.
This might seem dumb
But I want to say
Look around you – every day.
You'll see women, just like me
We look dull, it's true, you see
But peel away the "meh" and look
Not at the cover, but the book!'

She looked up from the notebook, which was shaking slightly in her hand. The man sitting at the table clapped his hands a couple of times. 'Good,' he said. 'Good, but probably not quite right for this.'

He glanced at the woman, who leaned and whispered in his ear. 'But make sure we've got your details Martha,' he added. 'Just in case.'

'OK,' Clare said, wondering what the woman had said. It didn't matter that she wasn't going anywhere. She'd known it was a long shot – but she'd pushed herself to do something different – and it had felt pretty good to put herself out there.

And they might not have roared with approval, but at least she'd had a captive audience for once.

Chapter Eight

Clare splashed out on another taxi to get home – after all, the bus wasn't leaving until all the acts had finished and she needed to resume normal life. It occurred to her that if she kept calling cabs like this, she'd have wasted the price of a small run-around within a few weeks.

Just as she entered the hallway, her mobile rang as if on cue. Nigel.

'Hello, erm, Clare,' he said, getting her name right for once. 'I . . . are you feeling better?'

'Yes, thank you,' she replied, feeling her face get hot.

'Good . . . I mean, obviously can't be helped. But we did have a bit of a to-do with your client in the office today.'

'Oh dear. I'm sorry to hear that.' Clare felt an unusual spike of anxiety. What had happened with Camberwaddle?

Nigel cleared his throat noisily. 'It's just . . . well, perhaps next time you could brief one of the others to take over the meeting? Will, for example, was available. Just to keep continuity, you know?'

'Of course.' Clare had to bite her tongue to avoid pointing out that a) Camberwaddle was *her* client and Nigel had shown no previous interest in him and b) if she really *had* been throwing up all morning, the only thing she'd have been able to share with her colleagues would have been the contents of her stomach.

'Anyway, the good news is your office is almost ready. So

we'll get some of the juniors to start moving filing cabinets and so on soon,' Nigel said, his tone so upbeat that she had to remind herself he was talking about her move into a shoebox rather than upscaling her to a glass-windowed power office.

'Thank you,' she said, through gritted teeth, wondering why she didn't feel able to say how she really felt.

'Well, see you tomorrow.'

'Yep. See you tomorrow.'

She took off her coat and hung it and her straining tote bag over the hallway hook, then dialled Ann's number.

'Hi Clare, feeling better?'

'Yes,' she said, guiltily. 'Yes, much better, thank you.'

'That's good.'

'Yes, look, I'm sorry to call you, but I just wanted to see if everything was OK in the office this morning? Nigel rang and said something about a *to-do*?'

Ann snorted with laughter.

'Oh, no! What happened?!'

'Well, of course, you had that awful Camberwaddle bloke coming in – the one who thinks because he's a billionaire or whatever, people have to roll out the red carpet for him at all times.'

'Yes, about that . . .'

'Well, I tried to ring him, but couldn't get through. So obviously when he came in, I had to tell him you'd called in sick at the last minute, and he was a bit put out.'

'Oh.'

'Yes, which was ridiculous. No one can help being sick. I gave him my best glare on your behalf.'

'Thank you.' Clare tried to suppress her growing sense of guilt.

'Anyway, he looked me up and down and asked me whether

there was anyone "senior" he could speak to – meaning I was obviously not good enough for him.'

'Oh, Ann. I'm sorry,' Clare said. In reality, Ann would have been more than capable of answering any queries that Camberwaddle had – probably more so than anyone else in the office.

'Don't worry. I'm used to it. Nobody expects a secretary to have a brain.'

'Well I certainly know you do!'

'Anyway, I thought I'd better knock on Nigel's door to see if he could come and smooth things out a bit, you know? But when I told Mr Camberwaddle I was going to speak to the senior partner, he sort of tagged along at my heels rather than waiting in your office as I'd thought...'

'Right?'

'And, I got to Nigel's room, and knocked and, well, we went in and...'

'And?'

'Sorry,' Ann snorted. 'I just... well, I opened the door and...' more snorts of laughter.

'Don't keep me in suspense!'

'Oh, Clare, it's not funny really. But Nigel was there with Will. And they were... well they'd both taken their trousers off.'

'What?!'

'But... well, they still had their shirts and ties on, you know? And, well, pants. Bare feet. Sitting on gym mats...'

'What? Seriously?'

'Yes! They were... they had their eyes closed, doing this meditation thing. And humming.'

'Humming?'

'Yes, you know, *hommmm*,' Ann mimicked.

'Oh god, what did Camberwaddle say?' Clare was torn between dissolving into laughter and baulking in horror.

'Well, I'd already . . . well, when I opened the door and saw them, I just said, sorry – but they heard me and both sort of sprang up.'

'Yes?'

'Nigel was in these . . . these floral baggy boxer things, long black socks, hairy legs. Will was in these little tighty whities . . .' Another snort.

'Good grief.'

'So there I was standing with this billionaire client, bringing him to see the senior partner and instead he got greeted by a bald, little man and a tall, young boy sitting around in their pants.' Ann's voice quivered with laughter.

No wonder Nigel had been so put out.

'They said they were doing an inspiration exercise . . . Will's idea, of course. Then Nigel went and sat behind his desk and asked Camberwaddle to take a seat. Will had kind of ducked out of the room by then. I think Nigel did the whole meeting . . . in his pants. You know – like a newsreader: all dressed up on top, but nothing under the table.'

Clare felt laughter bubble up inside. It was bad. Embarrassing. She hated to imagine what Camberwaddle would have made of it. But, well. It was pretty funny. And Ann's laughter was infectious.

'Oh, Ann,' she said. 'I'm really sorry you had to go through that.'

'Oh, it's OK,' Ann replied. 'Nothing that a couple of glasses of wine won't wipe from my memory . . . or at least I hope so.'

'I'll buy you a bottle to make up for it.'

'I'll hold you to that!'

Once Clare had ended the call with Ann, and sent another apologetic email to Camberwaddle, she finally allowed herself to walk through to the kitchen. There to greet her was all the mess from breakfast. In her rush for the bus this morning she hadn't even made it to the kitchen, but evidently everyone had assumed that she'd be there to clear up their post-breakfast debris.

There was a pint of milk on the side, its lid sitting next to it, slowly going off with the warmth of the central heating. A teabag lay on the floor next to the bin where someone had obviously missed their shot but hadn't considered picking it up and trying again. The sink was full of cereal bowls, and as she stepped across the room, there was the unmistakable crunch of cornflakes under her shoe.

Even Toby had left his cup on the table, half-filled with coffee he'd not thought fit to share. His glasses lay on top of the newspaper he'd abandoned on the side and it was all she could do to stop herself dropping them on the floor and crunching them beneath her heel.

Maybe he'd find her more attractive if she was in soft focus anyway.

It was 3 p.m., an hour and a half before the kids would arrive home and at least another two before Toby would appear. But why should she spend her time cleaning up their mess? Seeing it, spread in front of her, was like a slap in the face.

Her phone pinged as the kettle boiled.

TOBY: *Going to be late this evening. They've given me a segment on street lights to do. I couldn't say no. And obviously there needs to be some night-time shots.*

CLARE: *Oh. But I didn't even see you this morning!*

TOBY: *I know. I'm really sorry – Hatty's been trying to get me some extra filming and I couldn't say no.*

CLARE: *Hayley?*

Clare's mind latched on to the idea of Toby staying late with his PA.

TOBY: *No, Hatty. Hatty Bluebottle. She's one of the producers.*

Now Toby mentioned the name, she remembered Hatty from her days as a presenter. A decade or so ago, Hatty had been the person who'd read Clare the news as she'd sipped her morning tea in bed, and the face who'd greeted her when she'd browsed the trashy magazines on the news-stand. A firmly fixed anchor in the news cycle, she'd covered everything from elections to the Golden Globes.

Then she'd fallen from grace – got on the wrong side of the kind of magazines that Clare sometimes picked up – a little guiltily – at the petrol station. The kind that plastered pictures of celebrity couples when they were loved up but even more when they were breaking up, celebrated both weight loss and the 'flaunting of curves' that came with wearing a swimming costume and not being a size zero, and ripped into any well-known woman who dared to venture out for milk without her lippy on.

When Hatty had had her infamous breakdown – she'd burst into tears during a news broadcast and had to rush off the set – memes had started popping up almost instantly online; and the gossip rags and websites had been full of it.

Each mag had chosen a different picture of Hatty looking awful, and chosen headlines like 'Tears for Careers' and 'Batty Hatty'. Now, thinking of Hatty as a real person, Clare felt suddenly guilty as if she'd been part of the character assassination herself.

She knew that Hatty still worked behind the scenes at ITV but hadn't realised Toby was now on first-name terms with her.

To save her aching thumb from further texting, she dialled his number quickly.

'Toby?'

'Yes?'

'I wanted to say—'

'Just a minute,' he said. 'Yeah, of course, Sebastian – won't be a sec. Yeah, just the wife . . .' Then, to her: 'Sorry Clare, I'm a bit busy.'

She'd wanted to share the adventure she'd had that morning – the moment of fun she'd injected into her week. Even though it was a bit embarrassing. Even though she hadn't got through. Maybe it could lead to a bigger conversation – she could talk about how she felt. Really talk. Really get listened to.

But it clearly wasn't the right time.

'Oh, it doesn't matter.'

'Oh, OK. See you later?'

'Sure.'

Taking a deep breath, she poured herself a cup of instant coffee – choosing haste over taste – and pushed open the door to the living room. There, too, plenty of work had been left for her to do. A pile of dirty washing sitting layered like some sort of inedible trifle where Alfie had tipped out his gym bag. Crisp crumbs on the arm of the sofa. Something sticky seeped against her trousers as she sat down.

Bastards.

An hour later, she was still sitting there, ignoring the mess and taking a moment to watch the news. She'd struggled to resist the urge to clear up; sitting with debris scattered everywhere made her feel twitchy. She wasn't Marie Kondo, but she did like a well-hoovered carpet.

A key scraped in the door and suddenly her two children entered the house. 'Mum?' Alfie called almost straightaway.

'In here.'

'Hi,' he looked around the door, his face frowning as he took in the mess still scattered around the room. 'Everything all right, Mum? You're home early.'

'Yes.'

'Didn't you ... didn't you get a chance to clear up before work?' he said, with the innocence of someone who doesn't realise that the lion they are approaching hasn't eaten for several days.

'Funnily enough, no,' she smiled. 'Fancy helping me do it now?' She looked at him, trying to feign an innocent expression.

'Oh.' The question stopped him in his tracks. Did he fancy clearing up? He seemed to ponder for a minute. 'Do you know what,' he said carefully. 'I would, but I've got so much homework ... maybe Katie ...' Already his head had disappeared from view.

'Katie?' called Clare.

'Down in a bit!' called her daughter, from halfway up the stairs – already savvy enough to have read the situation before approaching her mother.

Both of them expected, of course, that by the time they did emerge from their important 'homework' (for which, without doubt, they would need their laptops, phones and use of the internet) she'd probably have cleared up much of the mess and got their dinner on the table.

Because she was the kind of person who couldn't leave things.

And they were the kind of people who'd become used to leaving things for someone else to do.

It was a killer combination.

Chapter Nine

Clare was still sitting up sipping a much-needed glass of red when Toby's car purred into the drive that night. The front door lock clicked and her husband slithered into the hallway, trying to make as little noise as possible. As well he might: it was past midnight.

'It's all right, I'm up,' she said.

'Oh.' He poked a tousled head around the door and grinned sheepishly. 'Sorry. Another late one.'

'Yep.' She looked at her dishevelled husband and wondered how, despite the blob of yellow on his tie, despite the fact he had clearly been chewing a pen and given himself a kind of blue lip liner effect; despite even the fact that his hair was sticking up in the style of a plastic troll, he still managed to look cute and rumpled rather than scruffy and revolting.

Damn that handsome face.

'Come and sit?' she said, patting the crumpled mess next to her on the sofa invitingly.

'It went well,' he said, ignoring her, his eyes wide; face animated. 'Apparently hundreds of residential street lights across London have been broken, and the Government's renewal initiative isn't responding quickly enough – but I'm pretty sure my report will get the mayor's attention,' he added, importantly.

'That's great. Look, Toby ... today—'

'And, well...' her husband sat down beside her heavily, not seeming to realise he was interrupting her. 'I wasn't going to say anything tonight, but... well, Hatty has asked if you and I... could pop over for dinner this Friday?'

'Us?'

'Yes.'

'To Hatty Bluebottle's house?'

'Yes.'

'You and me?'

'Yes.'

She imagined herself sitting at a table with Hatty. It would feel like being interviewed on live TV.

'Maybe.' Another sip of wine. 'I'm just not sure...'

'She's not as fearsome as they say, you know. And her husband, Bill, he's got a normal job – I think she said he's in plastics. Plastic surgeon I think.'

'Right. You don't think... maybe we could go to a restaurant or something? Might be a bit less, well, pressured.'

'Yeah, but Hatty can't really. She gets too much attention.'

'Oh, right.' Of course; even though her breakdown had been years ago, the celeb mags loved to dig out pictures of some of their favourite targets looking ropey. No doubt she couldn't enter a room without everyone getting their phone out. Poor Hatty, Clare thought, resolving never to pick up another of the celeb mags. The opposite of being invisible didn't sound too appealing either.

'And, you know... I think... I think I might be being groomed, Clare.'

'Groomed?' Her mind went to Hayley again.

'Yes!' he said, excitedly. 'I mean I've been trying my damnedest to fit in. The suits? And, you know, going to the bar and stuff after work. And Hatty and I... well, we've – we've kind of become friends.'

'Oh!'

'I know, I know,' he rolled his eyes. 'Rumours and that. The mad lady of ITV. But the breakdown, that bit in the papers. It was all overblown. She's a good advocate to have. And, well, a lot of people avoid her but . . . She . . . well, she has quite a lot of say in how the programmes are run.'

'She does?' Clare thought of the dishevelled woman who graced the cover of gossip mags, underneath headlines such as: 'Has Hatty Had it?' and 'Out of Control: Hatty arrested for D & D'.

'Thank you!' He patted her knee happily. 'Thank you, Clare.'

Had she agreed? She looked at his pleading face. Damn those puppy dog eyes. 'It's OK,' she said. She could hardly say no, after all. Plus, she was all about saying yes these days – embracing difficult situations. It would be terrifying to meet with Hatty and Bill in the flesh, but kind of exciting too.

'So, how was your day?' he said at last, leaning forward and grabbing half a bottle of red and his stained glass from the previous evening.

'Oh, you know. Blew off work. Went on an adventure.'

'Yeah, right,' he said, patting her knee affectionately. 'Sure you did.' He chuckled, shaking his head at her humour.

She looked back; she simply didn't have the energy to tell him now. And he didn't seem to be in the frame of mind to listen.

She tried a different tack: 'I am thinking, though,' she took a breath. 'I am thinking about maybe doing something with my poems?'

'Your poems?'

'You know, ah, my . . . the poems I write. Maybe getting

them bound up or something? Or, I don't know, maybe published.'

'Uh huh,' he replied, eyes on the TV. 'Great. And did the kids leave any shepherd's pie at all?'

'It's in the fridge,' she said, feeling herself tense up. 'So you think it's a good idea?'

'Yeah, always loved shepherd's pie.'

'No, the . . .' but she stopped.

'And how do I heat it?' He looked at her imploringly.

'Useless!' she said, half-joking half-infuriated. She stood up, plonking down her glass of wine and made her way to the kitchen. It was easier to heat up his food herself than witness him fiddling with the microwave, and either burning it to a crisp or undercooking it and spending the rest of the week on the toilet.

In the kitchen, she thought back to that moment in front of the two judges. How they'd nodded and said afterwards they might be in touch. How she knew, really, that it was a rejection. But how she'd stepped out of her comfort zone today – and, like Toby's shepherd's pie on the microwave plate – her world was still turning.

Chapter Ten

Clare had set her alarm for 6 a.m., keen to go in and sort out any backlog from her day off yesterday, but her body had other ideas and instead had woken her up before it at 5 a.m., her heart racing. Still, she thought as she climbed out of bed and crept past the snoring lump of husband next to her, she might as well get a head start.

The bus ride to town was amazingly quick and Clare wondered whether she ought to go in early all the time. According to the last report from the local garage, her car wasn't 'viable' – meaning the repairs would cost more than the cost of replacing her vehicle entirely. So unless she dipped into their ever-decreasing savings or drained their emergency credit card it looked as though she'd be a frequent traveller for the foreseeable.

This early start was a way of making up for her lack of professionalism yesterday, she thought. She'd had her moment of madness, and now it was time to knuckle down and appreciate the fact that she did actually have it pretty good. Well, fairly good. Or not too bad, anyway.

The office was dark when she came in, keying in the alarm code and putting on the lights in all the rooms to make it seem less forbidding. Like many small offices close to the town centre, the Mann Company was based in a Victorian bay windowed building that had once been a house. Once the computers were turned off and the phones went silent, it retreated into itself – there was a different atmosphere, a different smell first thing in the morning. 'Do you think it's haunted?' Ann had asked her once. Clare had laughed, but on the rare times she was alone in the office, she didn't feel quite so amused.

There would be someone else here in a minute, she told herself firmly, and marched up to her office, clutching her latte (a safer bet than cappuccino these days).

Camberwaddle had already replied to her apologetic email.

Dear Clare,

Thank you for your email.

I do understand that yesterday couldn't be helped. My concern is not knowing whether I will have the support I need, going forward.

I can't make a meeting today, but am able to come into the offices tomorrow to discuss what the Mann Company can do for me.

Best,

Stefan

It wasn't particularly warm; it wasn't particularly promising. But he was coming in tomorrow – she'd have the chance for a proper hearing to convince him.

Nigel stuck his head around the door at about 8.30 a.m., making her jump. 'Feeling better, Carol?' he asked.

'It's Clare.'

'Glad to hear it, glad to hear it,' he said. 'Um, any news from Mr Camberwaddle?'

'Yes, he's going to come in tomorrow to discuss every-thing.'

'Good, good. Um . . .' he paused, his cheeks reddening

slightly. 'Er, I don't suppose. I mean, he didn't mention any specifics about yesterday, at all?'

'No, sir,' she said, innocently. 'Like what?'

'Oh, nothing, nothing. I mean . . . well, he may have been privy to a rather . . . an intimate team building exercise between Will and I.'

'No, he didn't mention it,' she replied, truthfully – deciding not to tell him that Ann had filled her in on the details, or ask him what type of boxers he had on today out of interest.

Nigel's shoulders visibly relaxed. 'Right. Well, onwards and upwards, as they say!'

'Indeed.'

'Last day in the old office, eh!' he added.

'Excuse me?'

'You know . . . new carpet today – moving into your corner office tomorrow!' he said, with a gesture that looked as if he'd aimed for a thumbs up but thought better of it.

She felt her stomach sink. 'I—' she said, but he'd already disappeared from view.

She looked around the office that had been her home-from-home for four years. Her certificates on the wall, the blinds she'd chosen herself, her beloved leather chair, purchased after she'd had a brilliant quarter and netted herself a sizeable bonus.

She'd hoped that the whole 'corner office' thing would fizzle out. Nigel had ideas from time to time but didn't always follow them through. And she'd meant to talk to him about it, to tell him it just wasn't acceptable. But Nigel's plans were moving at uncharacteristic speed and it looked as if she'd left it too late.

She'd just thought that when Nigel had seen the office/cupboard properly, when he'd tried to have it renovated, attempted to have her things moved, he would realise that it wasn't fair to do this to her. That there must be another solution.

Should she have pointed it out to him? She worked so, so hard. In spite of herself, she felt the tears come and tried to bury herself in work to get back on an even keel.

Ann was in shortly afterwards. 'Are you all right?' she said, noticing Clare's slightly red eyes.

'Oh, just ignore me.'

'No – seriously, what's up?' Ann put the files down and walked to Clare's side of the desk, slinging a friendly arm around her shoulder.

'Oh, I don't know. I might have lost my best client . . . and I'm being moved into a coat cupboard.' Clare smiled at the ridiculousness of it, despite feeling tears well up again. Perhaps if she tried hard enough, she could make a rainbow.

'What? The cupboard?'

Clare told Ann about Camberwaddle's email. And about the fact she'd soon be moving into her 'corner office' according to Nigel.

'Seriously, you take one day off sick and Camberwaddle's thinking of ditching you? Doesn't sound worth it to me,' Ann said, looking so annoyed on Clare's behalf that it made Clare feel incredibly guilty. She longed to tell Ann that she hadn't been ill, that she'd taken some sort of spontaneous day off. But found that she couldn't.

'And how can Nigel seriously expect you to work in that tiny cupboard? He must be losing his marbles,' Ann fumed. 'His office is big enough for him and Will to work in together I would have thought.'

'Good point – no trousers required.'

'Exactly. Oh Clare – this really sucks. Have you thought about what you're going to do?'

'Do?'

'Have you thought about threatening to walk out? Surely they'd have to sit up and take notice?'

Clare had thought about it, vaguely. 'I think they'd only notice after a couple of months when the bailiffs came around to claim back Will's plush office chair, or whatever,' she said. 'Not when it really mattered.'

Ann rubbed Clare's upper arm and gave her another squeeze. 'Honestly, don't let it get to you. They're not worth it. We'll show them.'

'Thank you.' They smiled at each other. 'Yes, we bloody well will.'

Afterwards, the day moulded into its usual shape. At lunchtime, Clare stayed at her desk, still catching up with yesterday's backlog and wondering what would happen if she actually was sick and out of the office for a week – would the entire conveyancing world grind to a halt?

Just after lunch her phone flashed with an unknown number and she picked it up.

'Hello? Clare Bailey speaking?'

'Hi – can I speak to Martha?'

'Martha?'

'Yes, have I got the right number?'

A sudden realisation. Martha.

'Oh, yes. Well, speaking. Martha is my . . .' she paused, wondering how to explain. 'Well, I suppose it's my stage name.'

'Ah, OK. Understood,' said the voice. 'Look, it's Susan Chalmers – you know, from the talent session?'

'Oh, right?'

'Yes. I've been talking with some of the others and we wondered whether you might consider coming back to see us.'

'Really?' Her stomach churned. 'But I thought...'

'Yes. But...' there was a pause. 'Look, this might sound a little odd – but we're thinking of putting together a group. There weren't as many musical acts as you might expect at the initial audition, and we really want to put Hatfield on the map, you know?'

'Right. But my act was poetry, so...'

'Yes, yes. Sorry, I should have explained. We rather hoped you might join together with one of the groups that came forward.'

'Right?' Perhaps they wanted to use her poem as lyrics. But it wasn't exactly the kind of thing that would lend itself to a song, especially one sung by someone probably much younger than her.

'Yes. Look, there's this troupe of dancers... They auditioned straight after you.'

'Oh, the dance group! Yes, I saw them.'

'Lovely lads, quite deprived backgrounds. Wonderful dancers.'

'OK?'

'Well, and of course you'll have seen the TV talent shows in the past – the groups.'

'Yes?' Clare was struggling to see how this related to her.

'Well, they're good – as I say – but they need a... a USP. You know, something unique.'

'Right?'

'So, what do you think?'

'What do I think about what?'

'Well, we loved your poem. The rhythm... the sentiment. But we wondered – would you think about rapping it?'

'Rapping?' Clare looked down at her work clothes, at her messy desk, at her typically dusty, legal office. She must have misheard. 'You want me to rap? Me?'

'Yes. Well, to try. I just think . . . well, these boys as I say, need something extra . . . The producers are actually quite excited about the idea. The whole generations coming together thing. It's very now. Embraces some of the community-mindedness the channel are championing at the moment.'

'But what about someone their age. A singer? Someone . . . you know?'

'Yes, I do understand. It's just we wondered. Well, it could be fun. It might get people's attention. I didn't say so at the time, but your poem. It really got me thinking. Why do people judge women of a *certain age*?' Susan lowered her voice as if admitting to a terrible secret.

'Well, yes . . .'

'And of course you can't have a twenty-something kid giving out that message.'

'No.'

'And you know, the poem was quite rhythmic. Dan, he's the boys' manager, reckons he could make it work.'

'I just . . . I can't rap. I never . . .'

'I understand. But will you consider it? All we'd want would be for you guys to get together and have a go – see how it works. And if it does work,' Susan paused, 'we might put you forward!'

'Put us forward?'

'Yes, you know. For the next leg of *You've Got Talent*. It's just at the Grand Theatre – not the biggest venue. But it will be filmed so they can use some in the show. Proceeds to charity. The winning acts might get onto the live shows – so fame and fortune may await!' Susan laughed nervously.

'I'm sorry,' Clare said, feeling a little faint with the bizarreness of the conversation. 'I just don't think . . .'

'Look, I realise it's a lot. But give it some thought, please? Don't say no immediately.'

'OK, I'll think about it,' Clare said, before hanging up.

She laughed incredulously as she put her mobile back on her desk. Had that really happened? Someone had literally just asked her to rap.

She wouldn't do it of course. She'd be a laughing stock! But still — it was a compliment to her poems, surely? And something she could regale Steph with over coffee at the weekend.

As a solicitor, she was used to being asked difficult questions. But being asked to become a rapper had to be the strangest one yet.

Chapter Eleven

An hour later, Clare's mobile buzzed with an unknown number and she almost didn't answer. But then, after all, she thought, the day had already reached peak absurdity. She surely had nothing to fear.

'Hello?' she said, expecting sales.

'Clare?'

'Yes?'

'It's Dan.'

'Right?' she wracked her brain for a Dan. Nothing.

'Yeah, look. I'm the coach of Eezee Troupe.'

'Oh . . . the, the dancing group?'

'Yeah.'

'Oh. Hi.' She felt oddly self-conscious, remembering that smile of his.

'I think we spoke yesterday, briefly? Before the audition? I spoke to Susan and she told me about this rap idea.'

'Yes. Look, no offense but it's not really my . . .'

'I know. Look, I get it. I thought you'd probably say no.'

'Oh phew! I was worried you were going to try to force me to . . . well, you know, rap.' Even the idea of it made her cheeks feel hot with embarrassment. Bullet dodged! There was a pause.

'Well, maybe I am a bit,' he replied.

'What?'

'Look, I thought you might not want to. I know you're

73

busy. I get it. But, well, could you at least think about it? Come tonight, just for a few minutes. Watch us rehearse.'

'It's not that I'm busy . . . it's just . . . Well – I'm me!' She gestured to herself sitting at a desk, sensible suit, corporate dress. But of course he couldn't see her. Anyone who did would surely realise that she was almost the opposite of cool. And the idea of her rapping was just ridiculous.

'But think about it. I don't want to pressure you. But this competition. Well, it's the boys' only chance. And you know, rap is just poetry with a bit more rhythm. I could hear you from outside the audition room you know.'

'You could?'

'Yeah, it was brilliant!' he said enthusiastically. 'Well, you know. It could be, with a bit of a beat and more rhythm in the delivery.'

'Brilliant?'

'Yeah, it was lit!'

'Which is good?'

'Which is *definitely* good.'

Clare felt herself smile a bit at the compliment. It was a rare commodity these days. 'Well, thank you,' she said, 'but there's a big difference between reading a poem in front of two people in a meeting room and rapping on stage in front of a crowd of people. Dan, it was just a bit of fun yesterday. I . . . I just don't think I can.'

'But Clare, think about it,' he said, a desperate note creeping into his voice.

'It's the boys' only chance you say. How come?' she asked, more softly.

'Well, you know. It's like, well, they really don't have anything.'

'Right?'

'I've been working with these lads after school for like

74

a year. And they're good Clare, they're really good. But without this... You know. There isn't much of a future for them.'

'But the chances of them getting anything out of this...'

'It's just... Maybe if we got to the TV stage or something. It could be life changing for these guys.'

'But... I mean Dan,' she struggled to keep the frustration out of her voice. 'We won't... I mean they might not even include us in the competition – I can't see how we'd get on TV or win anything. It just isn't going to happen.'

'Little Tyler, he lost his mum last year. Henri, he was running drugs for some nutcase on the estate.'

She felt her heart turn over. The poor boys with their hopeful, happy faces. 'Surely they, I mean can't they just put you through as you are? I mean, those boys are really talented, right?'

He was silent for a moment. 'I did check that,' he said, 'because, you know. I thought you might not want to do it. But they've got lots of dancers, already. In the competition. So no chance. Anyway, Susan said she liked your message.'

'My message?'

'Yeah, it's, highkey as the boys would say.'

'Haiku?'

'No, high key!'

'Oh.'

'It's a good thing,' he clarified.

Clare thought about how invisible she'd felt. And how she now had the power to help someone else get seen. She wasn't sure she could rap. But she ought to at least give them a chance.

'OK,' she said. 'Look, how about I come and see the boys dance. I might have a go at reading the poem. But I'm not promising anything after that.'

'Yes!' Dan said. 'That's all I'm asking . . . for now.'

'Whereabouts do you rehearse?' she said, wondering what on earth she was doing. The man was far too persuasive.

It was six o'clock when her taxi pulled up outside the small church hall on the edge of the estate. Lights were on inside the tiny building and she could hear the sound of music pulsing.

'That'll be eight pounds and fifty pence,' said the driver. She paid and gave him a decent tip.

'Thanks, love,' he said, before driving off and leaving her standing in the cold night air.

Here the streets were narrow and the houses close together. The sound of the main road with its roaring traffic and beeping horns could be heard clearly. Lights were on in many of the windows, illuminating gardens, some well-tended, others filled with rubbish. Cars were parked on kerbs, in front gardens; anywhere they could be squeezed. Over the road, a group of children on bikes stared at her as she turned towards the hall. 'Got a light?' called one. 'Hey, miss? Got a light?'

Nervously, she pushed the door of the hall open and was faced with a further three doors. Two had toilet signs on them – one male, featuring the classic outline of a man that adorns many toilet doors (onto which somebody had drawn a large penis to ensure there were no misunderstandings), one female (whose female stick figure had also been quite generously enhanced) – and the third sign said 'Hall', so at least it was obvious where she needed to go.

As she pushed open the door she felt a thud, and as she entered, a small child skidded across the wooden floor.

'Sorry!' she said, looking at his crumpled form. 'Are you all right?'

'Fine,' he said, climbing to his feet again and grinning.

'Clare!' said a voice, and a familiar man with impossibly broad shoulders and a mop of unkempt brown hair was suddenly by her side, shaking her rather formally by the hand. 'Thanks for coming!'

'Hi Dan,' she said. 'It's nice to see you. But look, I don't think . . .' she trailed off, looking at his chocolate eyes.

'I know,' he said, 'just don't make up your mind yet, right?' He nodded to one of the boys and tapped something on his phone. The music restarted and suddenly they were all moving in synch.

Clare had seen dance troupes on the TV before, but nothing really prepared her for how impressive it all seemed in the flesh. The group moved flawlessly, completely in time. There were flashes of humour when one of the smallest members of the group – Mark – was flung from one side of the room to the other. And a strangely tear-jerking moment where the music slowed and one of the boys, whose frame was tall and whose movements seemed unencumbered by human considerations such as having bones in his limbs, danced slowly around the rest of the group.

When the music finished, they all looked at her expectantly. She felt like one of the judges, as if she was expected to give her verdict. 'Wow,' she said. 'That was amazing.'

And it really had been.

'So you'll do it?' Dan asked. 'You'll work with us?'

All the wide-eyed, expectant faces were just too much for her.

She thought about what might happen if they did get through and their act was featured on the TV show. For her, it could be embarrassing. Did anyone want a solicitor who moonlighted as a rap star? She'd read plenty of articles where people had a side-hustle, but usually people tended to stick to crafty activities such as crochet or embroidering bags. Not stickin' it to the man.

She'd spent ten years getting to where she was, professionally speaking. Working her way up to become the highest biller in the firm. Spending evenings reading legal texts to keep up to date. Putting in the hours. This should be her time to reap the rewards.

Then she thought of Nigel, how he'd had his head turned by a new recruit and how she'd now fallen off his radar. How, despite all her hard work, she'd been relegated to a coat-cupboard office. How no matter what she did, nobody seemed to value or notice her at all. She might as well be invisible.

Without Dan's input, these boys would also be invisible – little numbers vaguely referred to in government reports and crime statistics. But she could change that. Or at least try to help.

She could be the novelty frontman to their act, get them on centre stage and let them make the most of the light of fame shining on them, however briefly. Perhaps it wouldn't damage her career – and it could be life changing for them. And maybe she could do it as 'Martha' – and not get noticed at all.

'Look, you're great. I just . . . Let me think about it,' she said.

It was as if they'd won the lottery. The boys rushed for her en masse and nearly knocked her to the floor. She'd never been the recipient of such a large and enthusiastic hug. Laughing, she looked across at Dan who was watching her, his head nodding slightly, his brown eyes warm.

The taxi home cost another twenty-three pounds, which meant her little excursion to see the troupe had been more expensive than her bus fare for a week. But it had been fun to watch them dance.

She had no doubt that they'd go far, with or without her. She was just their ticket through the stage door.

'Hi!' she called into the quiet hallway when she arrived home.

Silence.

She pushed open the kitchen door and saw that the kitchen she'd tidied up before she left was now strewn with glasses, crumb-covered plates and soggy teabags. 'Alfie?'

'He's gone to football practice,' said Katie, suddenly appearing behind her. 'He's not back for tea, apparently.'

'Great.'

'Dad's home, he's just gone to the shop.'

'Right.'

Her daughter walked past her and put a dirty plate on the kitchen table.

'Couldn't you put that next to the sink? Or even better, wash it up?' Clare asked.

Sighing, Katie picked up the plate and plonked it on the pile next to the sink. She was making a point, but not prepared to go to the length of washing a plate up to prove it.

'Thanks,' Clare responded sarcastically.

'S'OK.'

'Shall I put the pizza in?'

'I've had toast now.'

'Right.'

'Oh, Mum?'

'Yes?'

'Can I FaceTime Tessa?'

Half an hour later, Clare was in the kitchen, picking over a large pizza and feeling thoroughly lonely.

Over on the other side of town were thirteen young men who had been overjoyed to see her.

The boys in that little dance troupe needed her. And, although she hadn't seen it before, perhaps she needed them a little bit too.

The phone rang just once before Dan answered.

'Clare?'

'Hi, Dan.'

There was a pause.

'Everything OK?'

'Yes. I just . . .' She paused – was she really going to do this? 'I just thought I'd ring because, well, I've thought about it and – well, I'm in.'

Chapter Twelve

Clare was surprised the next day to find a hump beside her in bed. Which snored. She glanced at her phone. It was only 6 a.m. She poked the hump.

'Toby?'

'Eh?'

'Tobe – wake up. We need to talk.' Telling Dan a definite yes, taking charge of her life and making decisions yesterday had felt good. And although it was a small thing, it had made her realise just how much she'd given up on herself – how she let life happen to her rather than taking charge. Well, no more, she'd decided. It was time to take back control.

'Eh?' he rolled over and looked at her out of one eye.

'Toby, I'm buying a car today.'

This, it seemed, was the impetus he needed. He sprang up onto an elbow – both eyes open now. 'But . . .' He looked at her open mouthed as if she'd told him she was growing a beard or taking up sumo wrestling.

'But nothing, Toby,' she said firmly. 'If you want to trade in your car and take the train, that's fine. But I can't spend another morning running for the bus.'

'OK,' he nodded. 'Fair enough . . . although . . . ?'

'Although?' she challenged.

'It's just the money . . .' he said, weakly. As well he might, with a wardrobe bursting with designer threads and having recently bought a car worth as much as a two-storey extension.

'Don't worry,' she said. 'I've done some sums, and we can. I don't need much. Just something, you know?'

He reached out and ran his finger softly along the curve of her face. 'I'm sorry. I don't know why I bought that car. It's . . . well, I just wanted to fit in, you know?'

'I know . . . the whole car park thing.'

'Yeah, only I've realised that most of the top-notch execs are taking the train now. Or biking even. All about the green credentials suddenly.'

'Toby,' she said, suddenly. 'Have you thought about what *you* want?'

'What do you mean?'

'I don't know. All these new clothes, this new image. It's great – you look great. But do you . . . is it really you?'

He shrugged. 'It's kind of me. A better me.'

'According to?'

He was silent for a minute. 'You're right,' he said. 'I'm being an idiot.'

'I didn't say that.'

As their eyes met, she felt suddenly warm. He was still Toby, underneath his career-ladder-climbing, overly stressed, image-conscious exterior.

'It's just – well, you don't have to prove yourself to me. Or to Katie or Alfie. We all love you. And I obviously want you to be happy, Toby, but I feel like you're kind of slipping away from me.'

'It'll get better,' he said. 'I . . . I don't know. I'm just finding my feet. Sometimes,' he paused, and glanced at the ceiling, 'I don't even feel like I'm me any more.'

They hugged then, tightly, and she nearly told him about her decision to rap in a local talent show. But somehow, her resolve to be forthright and decisive left her.

*

It was quite fun walking to the bus in the unseasonal early morning sunshine, knowing that it would be the last time she'd have to do it. She'd miss Mr Flasher with his secret under-coat sequins; she'd even developed a soft spot for the hipster driver. Dressed in her best black work suit, she felt smart and professional, and although her files were not yet in a leather satchel as she eventually intended, she'd at least borrowed one of Alfie's old gym bags and ditched the tote.

Yes, she was definitely going up in the world. Although her folders had started to smell of socks.

'Morning!' she breezed to Nigel half an hour later, as she walked through the reception area at 8.05 a.m.

He visibly jumped, like a child caught with his hand in the biscuit tin, she thought. (Then she noticed that he was actually rummaging in Jane, the receptionist's, not-so-secret snack drawer.)

'Morning, Carol,' he said, after a pause. 'Just . . . just getting an envelope or two . . . eh?'

'It's Clare,' she said.

'No, en-vel-opes,' he said, slowly and carefully, as if she was hard of hearing. 'Ah, here they are!' he said loudly, brandishing a couple of manilla A4s and acting as if she couldn't see the bulge of sweets in his pocket.

Despite the fact that her boss seemed incapable of remembering her name, Clare felt uncharacteristically positive. Why had she ever felt so dissatisfied? she wondered. Work was going well, she enjoyed her job most of the time, and while she hadn't made partner yet, she was still young – and well on the way to netting the firm a decent profit as long as Camberwaddle came around. Which of course he would, she reassured herself.

Tonight she was going to find herself a decent second-hand car and get herself back on track . . . or road.

She thought again of last night, when she'd rung Dan. He'd whooped down the phone, almost bursting her eardrum. It was hard to believe that someone really felt she'd make that much difference. Perhaps that was the reason for her good mood this morning, too.

Then: 'Oh, good news,' Nigel said. 'Your new office is furnished and ready to go!'

'It is?' When she'd left work yesterday, she'd passed the door and peeped in. There had been a few carpet tiles scattered on the floor, and an old shoe in the corner. Despite Nigel's assurances, she hadn't really thought things would move so quickly. And, deep down, she'd still convinced herself that he'd see sense.

'Yes! Got some of the boys on it last night. Looking rather swish, I thought.'

'Right. Thank you,' she said, feeling the buzz of anxiety in her chest.

She waited for him to disappear then went up the stairs slowly, like a character in a horror movie convinced they're about to find a body. Reaching the old coat cupboard she saw a printed A4 sheet with the name Carol Bailey on it in comic sans. Feeling sick, she pushed the door open.

In the dim light of the windowless room, she saw her desk, practically filling the whole space. The floor had been hastily carpet tiled and the smell of glue lingered in the air. Her filing cabinet bulged in the corner.

She tried not to cry. Was this dark corner with its tiny electric bulb on a wire really going to be her office from now on? She'd worked hard for this firm, yet was being shoved aside like a coconut eclair in a box of Quality Street. Well, she was no coconut eclair! She was at least an orange creme. Maybe even a strawberry delight. And what was Will? A caramel at best.

But caramels are the kind of sweet that everyone likes, she realised. Orange cremes are opinion splitters. Sure, they're some people's favourite. But some people can't stand them.

'Is he serious?' came a voice over her shoulder.

Clare jumped. It was Ann. She kept her face towards the office, afraid her colleague would see the tears pooling in her eyes.

'I think so.'

'Oh god, Clare.'

'Have you been moved, too?' Ann's desk was currently in the open-plan part of the office, where she sat with several other secretaries.

'Not yet. But I wouldn't put it past them,' her friend replied. 'Oh, Clare. You can't put up with this, you really can't.'

Clare didn't reply. 'Hmm,' she managed at last. Because she knew deep down that she probably *would* put up with it. And it would become normal. And she'd stop thinking about it. Because that, it seemed, is what she tended to do.

At 10.30 a.m., when Ann poked her head around the office door to tell her that Stefan had arrived, Clare didn't notice her at first due to the dim light; meaning that when she did suddenly see what appeared to be a floating head halfway up the wood of the door, she spilled coffee on her leg, screamed and had to dab herself dry with a crumbling tissue.

'Whoops!' Ann's head exclaimed. 'Sorry!'

'Don't worry.'

'Want me to keep hold of Camberwaddle while you get changed?'

'No, think it's sorted,' Clare said, crossing her fingers and holding them up.

'Good luck,' Ann winked.

Stefan Camberwaddle had the confidence and ease that

only comes with having grown up with money and an entourage of people to deliver praise and compliments on tap. 'Mrs Bailey,' he said, holding out his hand.

She took it, standing up, and he shook hers with such a forceful jerk that she felt a muscle tear in her shoulder.

'Good morning, Mr Camberwaddle,' she said, smiling through the pain. 'Do take a seat.'

He sat on the wobbly plastic chair that had replaced the leather seats in her larger office and frowned. Looking up at her, his blue eyes steely sharp, grey hair slicked back in a way she'd only previously seen on white-collar criminals in police dramas, he seemed to take in his surroundings for the first time.

'Your office,' he said. 'Is . . . has it changed?'

'Yes . . . it's just temporary,' she lied, feeling her cheeks go red. But honestly, how was she meant to inspire confidence in this client from a room that still smelled worryingly like feet?

He nodded, his brow furrowed. 'So,' he began. 'You got my message?'

'Yes,' she said, feeling a little as if she'd been summoned to the headmaster's office at school. 'But let me reassure you that this kind of inattention won't happen again.'

He nodded, kindly. 'Yes, I realise you have no intention of it happening again, but I'm not sure you can really guarantee that. After all, your firm is rather on the small side. I was quite distressed yesterday when the meeting had to be cancelled due to your illness.'

'Yes, I'm sorry.'

He waved her comment away with one of his large hands. 'Yes, yes, not your fault, of course. Just made me realise that perhaps the Mann Company aren't up to the job.'

'I understand,' she said. 'But honestly, it's not really a case of . . . well, we do have other conveyancing solicitors. It was more . . . well, the absence was so unexpected and so early on in our relationship, I hadn't briefed any of my colleagues . . .'

'I see . . .' he frowned and clasped his hands together, with the tips of his fingers touching his lips. 'I see . . . So you're saying that you're going to bring other people up to speed on this? Experienced people.'

'Of course! Believe me, sir, once you've had the full Mann Company experience, you'll never look back!'

'OK. Look.' He dropped his hands and looked at her with such a penetrating gaze that she felt almost violated. 'I like to be upfront with my business interests – I'm sure you understand. I'll give it some thought, speak to my team, and let you know by the end of the day. I can't risk making a mistake.'

'Of course,' she said.

'Bailey,' he said, almost to himself. 'You mentioned your husband was in television when we last met.'

'Yes, that's right.'

'I saw a Bailey the other day, on the news,' he continued. 'Something about street lights, or some such. Was that him?'

'Oh yes,' she said. 'That's Toby.'

'Interesting,' he said. 'Interesting. Well, it certainly wouldn't hurt to have an influential TV star's wife on the payroll.'

Clare was tempted to say that actually she wouldn't be on *his* payroll, and that having the ear of her husband meant very little these days.

But she didn't. She kept silent. She figured, while doing so, that if she had to be married to Toby; had to watch the man she loved morph into some sort of male mannequin, to wait with her legs crossed each morning as he preened himself in front of the bathroom mirror; to rush home every time he was late to keep their family life going, there ought to be some benefit for her.

Maybe one of them would be retaining her multi-million-pound client.

When Camberwaddle finally rang her later that afternoon to confirm that he would be remaining with the firm, she felt her stomach flip over with relief. After a day of angst, the news even made her forget briefly that she was sitting in a cupboard, like an old broom, or a forgotten tin of beans.

She stuck her head into Nigel's office before leaving to give him a quick thumbs up. 'Meeting went well with Stefan Camberwaddle,' she said, as he looked up from a pile of papers.

'Excellent news,' he smiled, listening to her for once.

She turned to leave – a quick taxi ride to the garage and hopefully a new car by the next day. Her credit card was nearly burning a hole in her handbag.

'Oh, and Clare?' Nigel said, just as the door was closing. She was so used to being called Carol that she nearly didn't answer.

'Yes?'

'Could you tell Will his prototypes are in?'

'Prototypes?' she said, wondering what on earth Will was trying now. The last thing he'd ordered on behalf of the firm had been car stickers displaying the proud words: 'Trip or fall? Mann up!'

'Rather innovative I thought.' Nigel held up a couple of translucent labels which read 'Accident? Who cares?!' alongside the firm's logo.

'Wow,' she said.

'Yes. All part of this rather modern business strategy of

Will's,' he continued, settling back contentedly in his chair. 'All about embracing positive thought and whatnot.'

'Yes.'

'And, you know, visualisation and body language.'

'Right. And these are going where?'

'Oh, on the paddle thingies in the hospital.'

'The defibrillators?'

'That's it! Just think.' Nigel shook his head in awe at the genius of Will's idea.

She could imagine it now. A patient, blearily coming around from cardiac arrest suddenly leaping from the bed and jotting down the number so that he could make a negligence claim.

'Great,' she said, not quite wanting to burst the bubble of delusion Nigel was clearly happily living in. 'I'll let him know.'

Chapter Thirteen

When Clare woke the next day and looked out of the window at her new car she experienced a strange sinking sensation, not unlike the feeling she used to have at university when she'd woken up with a hangover to discover a stolen traffic cone in the corner, or realised she'd nabbed an ashtray from the student bar. Something that had seemed like a good idea at the time, but was a bit embarrassing in the cold light of day.

Last night, in the garage, the car had seemed the obvious choice. As soon as she'd leaned in and smelled the leather seats, seen the automatic top fold back into a neat slot in front of the boot, she'd been seduced.

Sure, she'd gone in with a budget of six thousand pounds, but with nought per cent finance over ten years, she'd barely notice the monthly payment. At least, that's what she'd told herself.

'It's a limited edition,' the garage owner had told her proudly. 'Safety features, and even a built-in on-board virtual assistant, we call Claudia.'

'Wow.'

'Quite.'

She'd driven it around the block and been told how the assistant could dial numbers for her, would remind her to fasten her seat belt and even warn her if she was going too fast.

'A bit like a nagging wife!' he quipped, completely mis-judging his audience.

When she'd roared into the driveway last night, almost totalling two of their solar garden lights, Toby had told her it was lovely, although the expression that briefly flickered across his face was more one of panic.

Today, looking at her new purchase, she saw it for what it probably was. A classic 'look at me' midlife crisis car.

No. She refused to believe it.

Perhaps she was overthinking? Why shouldn't she have a glamorous car? And why was she suddenly feeling self-conscious in any case? She'd agreed to perform as a rap artist – if she could do that, she could do anything. Perhaps she should have gone for tinted windows and a bangin' sound system as well as the latest in AI technology.

She felt better, too, when a little later Katie asked her to take her to her gymnastics lesson in the new wheels and actually let Clare drop her off at the gate rather than around the corner as usual. 'Bye, Mum!' her suddenly communicative daughter said loudly, making sure as many people saw her as possible.

On the way home, Clare's mobile began to ring. She answered hands-free on the dashboard.

'Hi, Clare.'

'Hi, Dan.'

'Look, we need to start rehearsing obviously and I thought maybe later . . .' Clare felt a prickle of panic. She'd forgotten somehow that they'd need to rehearse.

'I can't later, sorry. Busy weekend!' she said.

'Oh. Maybe tomorrow?'

'I just can't, Dan. Monday maybe?'

'But we really need you. This sort of thing, we can't just put it together overnight.'

'I know, but I'm busy. I have a job, a family – weekends are busy. I want to help, but . . .'

Dan was silent.

'Are you still there?'

'Yeah, I just . . . Clare you seem like a great person – you want to support the boys I can see that. But if we're going to do anything worthwhile, we're going to have to start rehearsin' as soon as we can.'

'Of course. It's just . . .'

There was a silence. 'Look, Clare, I don't know what your life is like. Probably pretty good if you're a lawyer, right?'

'I wouldn't say . . .'

'What I mean is – you've got enough money, security, right?'

'Well, yes.'

'Qualifications, right?'

'Well, I worked pretty hard for those.'

'I know, I'm not saying . . . Look, Clare. These boys, they're not like you. This is their thing. Their chance.'

'But . . .' She could feel herself wavering.

'And if we're gonna do it. We need to *do it*. I don't want to blow it, you know?'

'Look,' she said, feeling a little cross. 'I'm not really sure why I said yes, Dan. I mean, I'm no rapper. And I've got a reputation – a serious job.'

'Look,' he said, gently. 'If that's what you're worried about, don't. You don't have to be Clare on stage, you can have a persona.'

'What, like Beyoncé?'

'A bit more like Ali G!'

'Thanks a lot!'

'No, I mean, unrecognisable from your normal self. You've

92

already got a fake name. We can make you look like a different person.'

'Well, maybe, but . . .'

'My sister, Nadia; she does make-up and that. She could make you up so you look like a totally different person.'

'I suppose I could.'

'Then what would it matter? It's just a couple of rehearsals. And a night out at the theatre. Nobody's gonna see you. Unless we win . . . but you know . . .'

He was right; that possibility was a long way down the road.

'OK,' she said with a sigh, her guilt getting the better of her as usual. 'I can't do tonight – I really can't. But I'll try to meet you tomorrow after lunch if you're free?'

'Thank you,' his voice was pityingly grateful. 'Seriously, thanks Clare.'

She pulled up in front of her house and looked at it for a moment. Was she privileged? Their home wasn't impressive, particularly. But their 1930s semi, with its big bay windows, was roomy and had cost a fortune.

'Toby,' she said later, trying to decide which pair of earrings to wear for their evening with Hatty and Bill. 'Do you think we're privileged?'

'Where has that come from?' he asked, his eyes widening. 'Has someone written something about me? Not that bitch from the *Daily Mole*?'

'No . . . No, I'm just thinking, you know. We're pretty lucky, right?'

'Well, yes.'

'And OK we didn't come from wealthy backgrounds, but our families were OK. And we got chances – the chance to work hard.'

'Sure . . .' he said, peering closely at himself in the mirror and smoothing down his eyebrows with his index finger.

'And now, tonight, we're going around to a TV star's house for dinner.'

'True.'

Their eyes met silently. It sounded pretty privileged when you put it like that.

Before she could think any further, she brought up Dan's number on her phone. Wondering what she was getting herself into, she typed 'Sorry for the wobble. Will definitely see you tomorrow.'

When she looked up again her eyes locked with Toby's in the mirror. 'Who's that?' he asked.

'Oh, no one.'

'But Mum! Why do I need a babysitter? Alfie'll be here!' Katie whined when Clare told her that Angela from two doors down was going to pop round while they were out.

'Because you're only twelve. And because not only is Alfie only fourteen, he's . . . well, he's *Alfie*,' Clare said, nodding at her son who was sitting slumped on the sofa, headphones on, laughing at something on his phone. 'He wouldn't notice if the house burned down.'

'But *I* would! I'd notice!'

It wasn't the most reassuring of reassurances.

Once Angela had arrived and already started on the plate of biscuits they put out for her, Clare and Toby climbed into his car and pulled out onto the dark road.

It had been ages since they'd gone out together like this. All those late evenings, all those meetings. It wasn't just Toby, she realised. She'd started to bring work home – had let it bleed into the evenings and the weekends.

Both of their jobs were the kind that could expand and

keep on expanding until you weren't sure where the job ended and life began. The email you just had to answer; a call from a client in the evening. Bags full of folders.

It wasn't just Toby not seeing her, she realised. They'd stopped seeing each other.

'Nice to be going out,' she said into the silence.

'You sure?' he said, his hand briefly leaving the wheel and hovering near to his mouth for a moment. 'Even to Batty Hatty's?'

'Don't,' she said, feeling guilty that she'd laughed at the label once. 'It's . . . well, you know. She's OK, isn't she? You said she'd helped you.'

'You're right. Just joking. But, yeah . . .'

They drove on, listening to a radio discussion on the pros and cons of recycled loo roll. Sitting in the – ridiculously comfortable – leather seats, Clare began to relax. Darkness had fallen and the street lamps glowed orange in the gloom. Watching them, leaning her head on the window, she remembered sitting in the back of her parents' car, aged about five, watching the lights on the motorway flash past on the way back from somewhere or other. It was oddly soothing.

Hatty Bluebottle's London residence was more modest than Clare might have expected. She'd only seen Hatty on TV in the past and she'd struck her as someone who'd been born with a silver spoon in her mouth.

Clare had imagined some sort of four-storey white townhouse – the kind you see in TV dramas; so impossibly expensive and immaculate that the most an ordinary person could do was drool and dream.

Instead, Toby pulled up in front of a tiny terrace of yellow bricked Victorian houses in Farringdon. Still probably easily into the millions, but somehow homely and modest at the same time.

After about half an hour of back and forthing, Toby managed to squeeze his car into the tiny space outside. 'Residents' parking,' he said. 'Hatty said she'd give us a pass.'

'Great,' she said, climbing out of the car.

The Hatty who opened the door looked a world away from the intimidating figure Clare remembered from her TV heyday. In place of the suit and blouse combo she'd sported on screen, she wore some floral leggings, a mis-matched blouse and had grey hair that stuck up like a bird's nest. In fact, she looked like an actual, real human being.

'Well hello!' Hatty said, with more enthusiasm than she'd ever had on *Morning Briefing*, or *99 Questions*. 'Lovely to meet you. You must be Clare – Toby's always talking about you!' She grabbed Clare's head between her man-sized hands and planted a large kiss on each of her cheeks.

'Hi, Hatty,' Toby said, before he, too, was swooped and engulfed in a perfume-clouded welcome.

'Bill is in the dining room,' said their host. 'The kids are both out this evening, thank god. Not that you can call them kids these days of course – they both think they're far more grown up than they really are. Thirteen is the new thirty, or so it would seem.'

'Know the feeling,' Clare said, smiling in spite of herself.

Perhaps the evening wasn't going to be too bad after all.

Chapter Fourteen

It was almost fifteen years since Clare had last had a hangover.

She knew that, because it was the day she'd taken a pregnancy test and discovered Alfie was on his way, after which she'd duly given up her two-glasses-a-night-but-make-it-three habit. And she had never really developed a taste for alcohol afterwards. These days she was like a teenager. A couple of sips, a grimace, and she was on to the Diet Coke.

It was good, really. Great for the waistline. But she did miss the gentle oblivion she used to feel after a couple of drinks.

Toby, however, had had no such enforced abstinence.

Which meant that after one of their rare nights out, she was usually up and about with no qualms, while he lay in bed in a wretched state of his own making.

This morning, the first sound that pierced her consciousness as she lay half-comatose in bed, was a deep, pitiful groan.

'Toby? Everything all right?'

She turned over to see her husband sitting up, head in hands, face a little on the grey side.

'Are you going to be sick?' she asked, suddenly filled with adrenaline. The last thing she wanted to do was scrub alcohol-scented vomit from the duvet this morning. 'Do you want me to get a bucket?'

'No. It's not that.' Toby allowed one slightly reddened eye

to peek out from between his fingers. 'I mean . . . I've felt better. It's just . . . last night. Did I really?'

'Yes, Toby. You did.'

'Oh, fucking hell.'

'Which bit?'

'What do you mean, which bit?' he said, his hands falling from his face in horror and his voice jumping up an octave in panic. 'There was more than one bit?'

The first thing they'd been offered at Hatty's was an 'aperitif' – basically a shot of something sticky, sweet and alcoholic. Toby – more of a beer drinker ordinarily – had clearly underestimated the kind of power this sort of snifter had and had gone back for seconds, and thirds.

By the time they'd sat down to dinner, his face had been flushed and his eyes alight with a kind of excited abandon.

'So Hatty, tell me,' he'd slurred over the lamb shank, 'who do I have to sleep with to get a slot on prime time.'

Thankfully, Hatty had laughed it off. 'Well, certainly not *me*,' she'd said. 'The only reason they promoted me, I think, is to get me off the screen. Nobody wants to look at a middle-aged has-been.'

Clare had seen a flicker of something behind Hatty's smile.

'You don't really think that, though?' she'd said. 'I mean, you were great. I used to love your bulletins.'

'Ah, but you're not the target demographic, you see,' Hatty had replied, making little quotation marks with her fingers. 'They told me they'd recognised my talent and thought it would be better used off-screen. But I knew what they really meant.'

'Oh. Didn't you say anything?'

'No, I suppose I quite fancied the chance of producing. Thought *I'll show them!* And I do like it. It's going well.

Just – well, unfortunately no matter how good the ratings are, they're always quick to praise someone else for them.'

Toby had shifted uncomfortably.

'You'll have noticed?' Hatty had said, turning to him. 'It's always "Good job, Piers" or "The figures are great, we must feature more animals!" They don't seem to take into account the mug who chooses the segments or selects the topic.'

'Oh,' Toby had said, looking at Hatty as if for the first time. 'I didn't realise you felt . . .'

Hatty had sipped her wine. 'Sorry,' she'd said. 'Had too much of this. You'll have heard, though. They call me Batty Hatty at work – like I'm some mad lady who ought to be confined to the attic.'

'Yes, but you know, I don't think you *are* batty at all. In fact, I've always admired you for being so ordinary,' Toby had declared clumsily.

'Really?' Hatty had raised an eyebrow at Clare over the table, and she'd shrugged embarrassedly and poked Toby firmly in the ribs.

'Sorry, sorry,' he'd said, looking at his wife and entirely missing the point. 'You're *both* ordinary. *Both* of you.'

Later, after yet another little 'palette cleanser', he'd begun to talk to Bill, and Clare had relaxed a little. Hatty had started to regale her with stories of the old days when she'd read the news. 'The guy I read with's still on screen, of course,' she'd said.

'That's so unfair,' Clare had said. 'You know, I know how it feels to be overlooked . . .'

She'd been about to confide in Hatty in a way she hadn't even with Toby, when she'd overheard a snippet of Toby and Bill's conversation.

'Do you think,' Toby had been saying, 'I should get my bags done?'

'Your bags?'

'Yes, you know. I'm trying to get more . . . screen time. And just wondering . . .' Toby had shifted his head around to give Bill a better view of his face, helpfully pulling the skin under his eyes taut.

'Oh dear,' Bill had said, his intelligent, sober eyes alighting on Clare for an amused moment before turning his attention back to Toby. 'Well, I'm probably not the best person to advise . . .'

'Have some wine, Clare?' Hatty had asked, a bottle teetering over Clare's empty glass.

'No, no. I'm fine,' she'd said. 'Definitely the designated driver tonight.'

The two women had exchanged a look of mutual sympathy. 'Yes, sorry. I didn't realise that cherry liqueur was so strong,' Hatty had said.

'And I've heard that more and more men are getting their lips done,' Toby had continued, pursing his into an exaggerated kiss shape and looking quizzically at Bill. 'What do you think? Is less more? Or is more more? Too sexy? Or just sexy enough?'

There had been a silence, before Bill coughed into his hand and said, rather quietly. 'I'm sure, it might be . . . only it's not quite my specialism you see.'

'Oh, sorry,' Toby had blushed. 'Sorry, I thought Hatty said you worked in plastics.'

'Ah, well . . . not quite.'

'What . . . what *is* your medical specialism out of interest?'

'Classics,' Bill had replied, chuckling slightly. 'My qualification isn't so much medical as literary. I've got a doctorate in classical literature.'

'Oh, classics . . . I thought . . .'

*

100

'Which bit do you remember?' Clare asked now, carefully watching Toby's face.

'The . . . did I . . . I mean, I didn't mention, you know, procedures?' he asked, lowering his voice as if by saying the word quietly he could make it go away. 'I've been thinking about . . .'

'Well, yes. But I'm sure Bill . . .' she trailed off. There was no way she could make this sound any better.

'But did I say something about getting my lips done? About . . . being sexy?' he asked. 'I was reading about the procedure yesterday . . . but maybe . . . did I dream that bit?' he said, hopefully.

Clare toyed with the idea of telling him a lie. Who would it hurt, after all? But then, he had to be prepared for whatever comments or humorous anecdotes Hatty was going to regale everyone with in the Monday meeting.

'It's probably best not to think about it,' she said at last, watching him bury his head in his hands again.

It was kinder not to mention the things he didn't remember about the night, she decided, sipping her hot black beverage. The fact that he'd shared his idea for doing a piece about alien abductions; the moment he'd lifted his shirt and asked them whether they thought he had a paunch, and when he'd tried to show off his non-existent limbo skills by attempting to slither under the breakfast bar, putting his back out in the process.

This morning, Katie was already in the kitchen, plugged into her phone and lost in a world where YouTubers with enormous eyebrows shared their 'style secrets'. Clare looked at Katie, so unaware of her own natural beauty and completely taken in by these women with faces so full of poison they were probably toxic.

'Hey,' she said, tapping her daughter on the shoulder. 'You know you don't need any of that stuff, right?'

Before Katie had time to answer, or even scowl, Toby burst into the kitchen in his boxer shorts. 'Seriously Clare, though,' he said. 'What am I going to *do*?'

'Dad!' cried Katie, horrified. 'You're in your pants!'

'Just call her. Apologise.'

'Put some trousers on!'

'What? Speak to her?'

'Or a dressing gown, at least!'

'Yes! Give her a call.'

'Oh, I give up!' Katie flounced out of the kitchen in disgust.

'On . . . on the *phone*?'

'Yes! Tell her you're sorry, that you drank too much, that you're embarrassed and that you'd like her to come to ours at some point to make up for it.'

'Hatty? Come *here*?'

'Why not?'

'It's just . . . you know . . . I was hoping . . .' he sank into a chair. 'What if this was my chance to impress someone on the decision-making team? I mean, I know it was only Hatty. What if I've completely blown it?'

She felt sorry for him then. And for Hatty, too. 'You haven't. Just call her.'

An hour later when they were absolutely sure that the majority of ordinary people would be out of bed and able to cope with a phone call, she stood beside Toby as he nervously dialled Hatty's number.

'Hello. Yes. Hello,' he said. 'Yes, Toby. Yes, yes, I know. Thank you. Thank you for the lovely, eh, meal and . . .' He paused, listening. 'Well, yes a little worse for wear . . .

Really? Well that's nice of him. Look, I'm sorry if I was a bit over the top, you know. Rude. Last night. Hello? Hello?'

Toby turned to her then. *I think she's hung up*, he mouthed, his eyes wide with terror. Then. 'Oh! Thank goodness. I thought . . . Yes, I was saying sorry. Sorry I messed up. Oh! Thank you. Very nice of . . . Thank you. OK. Goodbye.'

Coming off the line, he gave his wife a thumbs up. 'Think we're OK,' he said.

'Yes?'

'Yes. She said it's the first time a man has thought to apologise to her in about a decade. I think she was joking.'

Clare wasn't so sure. 'Well, that's great! See, you're back in the game!' she said.

'Well, not quite,' he said, his face suddenly changing as he turned and charged into the downstairs loo.

Chapter Fifteen

As she pulled up outside the church hall later that afternoon, Clare realised she had butterflies.

She'd told Toby she had to pop into the office to pick up some forgotten files after lunch; he'd offered to come with her for the drive, and she'd had to turn him down. 'I won't be long,' she'd said. 'But I might pop into Steph on the way back.'

'Oh. But ... I ...'

'She wants to talk about women's stuff,' she'd added darkly, to put to bed any idea he might have about coming with her.

Now, standing on the gravel outside the little hall, she wondered whether she should have just told the truth. He might be wrapped up in his work at the moment, but as far as she knew he hadn't started lying to her.

She hadn't meant to lie, really. He'd have probably had a bit of a laugh when he'd found out what she'd got herself into. But he would have been supportive. Either that or completely oblivious. He wasn't the kind of man who'd have asked her not to go, or anything like that.

It was part of a bad habit, she realised. Her ridiculous self-consciousness about her writing, her poetry. She'd never felt comfortable with Toby, or anyone, reading it. Somehow it would be easier to read it (or rap it) in front of strangers than her own husband. Less personal, sort of.

She felt a flutter of nerves as she looked at the hall and thought about going in. It was odd, because she didn't feel at all worried these days when she was meeting clients. Going to meetings. She'd switch on her professional persona and breeze through them. So why the butterflies now? Could it be that this was the first time she'd stepped outside her comfort zone in a while? Or was it that, somewhere deep down, this actually mattered to her?

She got out of the car, locking it and making sure the alarm was on. The road was busy, but the group of kids who'd been hanging about last time were nowhere to be seen.

Music was already pumping and she felt a bit like a parent coming to pick her kid up from a school disco. Here's mum to spoil the fun, she thought – noticing that the trainers she was sporting were grubby and scuffed.

The minute she walked into the room, Dan rushed over and gave her an enormous hug. 'Oh thank god,' he said. 'I didn't think you'd come.'

He squeezed her to him, and she inhaled his scent – a clean, freshly showered, soapy smell. Hopefully she didn't smell too strongly of the chicken she'd cooked for lunch – cooking smells had a habit of clinging to her clothes. His arms felt strong around her back and as he released her, she stumbled slightly.

'But I said I'd come!' she said.

'People say stuff,' he said darkly, 'but they don't always do it.'

The rest of the troupe gathered round her like eager puppies. Dan introduced them and she desperately tried to remember their names: Eric, the nine-year-old with glasses who'd joined the dance club after he was bullied at school. Gav, who at thirteen was the oldest of the group. James who lived next door to Gav's aunt. The names swirled around her head. She'd do her best.

'All right?' they said, one by one. And ''sup?'

'Great thanks,' she said, feeling more like a teacher than a potential rapper. She'd definitely need to change her image if she was going to perform with this little gang.

'So you've brought the . . . rap?' Dan asked.

'Yes.' She pulled the paper out of her pocket, torn from her notebook.

His eyes scanned the page. 'This is actually really sick!'

'Thanks.' She felt weirdly proud as if she'd been endorsed by one of the cool kids at school.

'Well we've got a track laid down that will probably fit this. If we run through things you can find your rhythm,' he said.

Her stomach turned over. Rhythm. Did she have any rhythm left in her to find? Or had she shed it with motherhood, together with the ability to bounce on a trampoline or read a book uninterrupted or have a normal-looking belly button. 'I'll try,' she said.

The beat started and the boys' heads began to move in time.

'Right gang,' Dan said. 'As we rehearsed. One . . . two . . . three.'

Clare turned her back on the troupe – who after all would be dancing behind her at their audition – and began to mouth the words from the paper. She began to see how she could shape them and gradually raised her voice, so she could be heard, just slightly, above the backing track.

'Right,' Dan said, when they'd run through a couple of times like that. 'Do you want to go for it, for real?' He handed her a wireless mic. 'The kids need to be able to hear you properly.'

It was now or never.

Part of her would have preferred never. But then she thought back to how she'd been feeling recently. Feeling as if nothing in her life was ever going to change and that things were going to be miserably predictable and disappointing for ever.

And here she was. She wasn't sure exactly what she was doing, but at least it was an adventure.

'OK,' she said, hearing her voice amplified alarmingly in the little space. 'Let's do this.'

Chapter Sixteen

'Hello,' Steph said, three hours later, standing on the door-step with Wilbur under one arm and an enormous playseat under the other. 'Is the lady of the house in?'

'No, she's bloody not. It's me or no one,' giggled Clare.

'What a disappointment. I suppose you'll have to do.'

'Do you want some help? That looks enormous.'

'Thanks.' Steph shoved Wilbur into Clare's arms and he clung to her, his breath hot and quick against her neck.

'I actually meant the playseat, but I suppose I'll have to carry the kid instead,' joked Clare.

'Honestly, it's just nice to have something in my arms that will survive if I drop it – I am so knackered.'

'Oh, Steph, I should have come to yours.'

'No, honestly, I had to get out of the house. I'd forget how to drive if I didn't get out sometimes. Plus you have the fancier coffee maker.'

'Well, that's true.'

'Anyway,' Steph said, once Wilbur had been placed safely in his seat and was playing with what looked like an enormous walrus on a string. 'You wanted my advice on something. What's Toby done now?'

Clare had called Steph on her way back from the church hall and asked if she could pop in. Steph had suggested she came over instead. 'I'll bring cake,' she said. 'And I promise to change Wilbur's nappy first.'

'You're on.'

Now, with crumb-covered plates between them, and nursing their half-drunk coffees, it was time to get the advice of one of the people she trusted most in the world. Alfie was out playing football; Toby was cleaning his shoes in the utility room; Katie was in her room.

'I . . . well, I don't know how to start really,' Clare said, realising she was blushing. She shifted in her chair slightly, feeling her legs ache from yesterday's unaccustomed dancing.

'Toby? Don't tell me, he's run off with his secretary,' Steph laughed.

Clare smiled, but found it hard to join in. Once that would have seemed like a ridiculous joke. These days, she wasn't sure exactly where she and Toby were. She'd noticed how often he'd drop Hayley's name into conversations. 'Hayley says orange is the new magenta.' Or 'Hayley says these are bang on trend.' She pushed the thoughts away.

'Actually, it's me,' she said.

'You?'

'Yeah. I've got myself in a bit of a weird situation, let's say.'

'Why doesn't that surprise me?'

The sisters smiled at each other. Then Clare took a deep breath.

'The other day,' she said, 'I took a day off work . . .'

'Wow. Wonders will never cease. Did you cope OK away from the daily grind?'

'Ha, ha. Look, I know it sounds weird, but I auditioned for "You've Got Talent"!'

'What?' Steph put her coffee down on the table, slopping a little onto the wood.

'Hey, don't be so surprised. I've got some talent you know.'

'Yes, but yours is more of the . . . well, paperwork variety.'

'Thanks a lot.'

'No, no, it's a good thing. Much more lucrative than my rusty tap-dancing skills.' Steph had been mad on tap dancing when they were kids, taking exams – even performing in a show or two. Clare, who had two left feet, had taken piano lessons for a while, then simply dropped out and concentrated on her homework.

'Maybe,' Clare continued.

'Anyway, seriously – this happened?'

'Yes.'

'You're going to have to take me back a step.'

Clare explained about Mr Flasher. About her overwhelming desire to make a difference to her day, to her life. 'I was just so fed up,' she said. 'I wanted to do something different. Then suddenly I thought, why not? I had my little book of scribbles with me. I just wanted to make myself feel alive, shake things up a bit.'

'You realise that most people would have bought themselves a new pair of shoes or got a haircut?' Steph said, incredulously. 'Usually when I want to perk myself up, I buy a new lipstick. Or, I don't know, stuff some chocolate in my face. Most people don't relieve the boredom of everyday life by auditioning for a national talent show.'

'No, I realise it's a bit . . . well, unusual. I can't really explain it – I just, it just sort of happened,' Clare said, looking at her sister over the top of her mug and shrugging as if it was no big deal. 'Anyway, I think I could dye my hair blue and no one would notice.'

Steph looked incredulous. 'Really?'

'Yeah, really. I know it sounds odd. Even odder, I actually enjoyed it!'

'Well you're a braver woman than me. Anyway, how did it go?'

'Well, pretty much as you'd imagine. I think they felt sorry for me actually.'

'Oh, sis. So you didn't get through to the grand final, or whatever?'

'Actually . . .'

Clare explained that she'd been asked to go back as a rapper. And how her automatic 'no' had faltered when she'd realised how much it had meant to the group of dancing boys. 'I've been rehearsing with them this afternoon,' she admitted. 'I told Toby I needed to pick something up from work.'

'Oh my god!' Steph giggled. 'This would only happen to you, wouldn't it? How do you get yourself into these situations?'

'These situations?'

'Oh, you know. When we were kids. You were always the one who ended up pushing yourself forward, volunteering for things. Remember when you decided to be mascot for the school football team? Dressing up as that giant bird?'

Yes. She'd forgotten about that.

'And that time when you auditioned for a background role in the school play and ended up getting one of the main parts.'

It was true, she'd only joined to fit in with her friends.

Perhaps she had form after all. Where had that version of herself gone in the intervening years, she wondered – the part of her who was unpredictable, spontaneous and even occasionally fun?

'Anyway,' Clare continued, changing the subject a bit, 'I'm just not sure what I should do!'

'What you should do?'

'Yeah, do I go through with it – they're talking about a possible TV appearance if we're chosen. It could get really embarrassing.'

111

'Possibly . . .'

'And, can you imagine? I'm not sure it would go down very well at work, if I make myself a laughing stock.'

'But would you be one? Lots of people have hidden talents. Yours is, well, unexpected. But pretty cool. And they'd probably do a back-story on you. You know, about your poems and how it all came about. I don't think anyone would be laughing.'

'Maybe. But is it worth the risk? I just don't know.'

'God, you're full of surprises,' Steph said, shaking her head. 'I thought you were going to ask me something about the kids, or Toby, or – you know – something *normal*.'

'It's a ridiculous problem to have,' Clare agreed. 'But it is a problem. I don't feel like I can back out. But what if I'm making a huge mistake?'

'What was the rap about, anyway?'

'The rap?'

'Yeah, you and your mates hitting the clubs? Your take on the youf culture of today? The fact that you like big butts?'

Clare laughed. 'No, it was about . . . well, how I feel. You know, being a bit "meh" – invisible. Like we spoke about the other day.'

'A rap about being middle aged?!'

'I wish people would stop describing me as middle aged!'

'Sorry. Anyway, what does Toby think?'

'Toby? He doesn't know anything about it.'

'You haven't told him?' Steph raised a surprised eyebrow.

'Well, I sort of tried, but he wasn't really listening,' Clare said, shrugging her shoulders.

Steph was silent for a minute, stirring her coffee and absent-mindedly adding another sugar to the already over-sweet brew. 'But surely you should tell him now?'

Clare shrugged. 'I might,' she said. 'But I just feel a bit embarrassed about it all. I don't know why. And Toby's so busy . . .'

Steph nodded. 'Still, he'd want to know,' she said.

Clare wasn't so sure. 'I suppose . . . But you know, Toby aside. Do you think I should do it?'

'Seriously, you reckon these boys deserve a chance?'

'Yep.'

'And they think – you can do it in some sort of disguise, right?'

'I hope so.'

'Then I think,' Steph said, looking directly at her with her intense, blue eyes. 'I think you're kind of stuck with it, aren't you?'

'That's what I thought.'

Toby walked into the kitchen at that point, and they fell into a sudden silence. 'Oops,' he said, grinning at them from under his uncharacteristically messy fringe. 'Hope I haven't interrupted anything.'

'No, don't worry.'

'Talking about me, by any chance?' he grinned, half-serious.

'Nah,' Clare said, winking at Steph. 'We're just talking about whether I should enter a talent show with a rap about what it's like to be a neglected wife.'

Toby snorted. 'You two, when you get together,' he said, fondly. 'Completely and utterly mad.'

'How's life in the TV fast lane, anyway?' Steph asked. 'I hear you're quite the dinner party hit?'

Toby blushed. 'I wouldn't say that.'

'Don't worry, Toby, I haven't told her everything about the other night,' Clare said.

'Thank god for that.'

'Although I'd love it if you could show me your limbo moves later!' Steph quipped.

Toby blushed and Clare felt suddenly sorry for him. 'Honestly, don't worry,' she said. 'It wasn't that bad.'

He leaned down and kissed her cheek, for the first time in ages. 'Thanks, love.' Then, straightened. 'Well, I'll leave you ladies to it,' he said. 'See you soon, Steph. Bye little nephew!' he added, tickling Wilbur under the chin.

Wilbur laughed, a river of drool running stickily from his mouth, as he bounced enthusiastically.

'Poor Toby,' Clare said. 'I've been a bit hard on him. He's really stressed with the new job.'

'Actually he looks a bit ... well, thin – "peaky", as mum used to say,' Steph said, nodding.

Does he? 'I hadn't noticed,' Clare said. 'I mean, I know he's stressed, but ... I think he's OK.'

'Don't worry,' Steph replied with a grin. 'You're a rap star now – you can't get too hung up worrying about the little people.'

'Ha! Yes. Check me out!'

'So, let's see this rap,' Steph said, genuinely interested.

'Really? What about you? You've hardly told me anything about what you've been up to recently.'

'You forget, I spend all my time with a six-month-old. I have to live vicariously through your life, or I wouldn't be living at all.' There was a catch in Steph's voice as she said it.

'You all right Steph?'

'Yeah, never better.'

Clare reached over the table and squeezed her sister's hand. 'OK, if you're sure.'

'Course I am. Come on, let's see you perform. I need cheering up!'

Chapter Seventeen

'Seat belt,' said 'Claudia's' automated voice, rather impatiently, when Clare got in the car on Monday morning. 'Seat belt, seat belt, seat belt.'

'OK, OK, Claudia!' she snapped, clicking the belt into place. 'Stop nagging.'

Great, now she was talking to the car.

'Seat belt engaged,' Claudia replied. 'Seat belt engaged, seat belt engaged.' Clare didn't remember this happening before. Had Claudia gone into some sort of hyper-vigilance mode?

'Thank you,' she said, 'you can shut up now.'

'Searching for shut up online,' the car replied.

'No, no. Don't search for it,' she said. 'Um. Stop search.'

Claudia silenced, Clare began to drive, admiring the smooth steering and easy acceleration. Perhaps the car hadn't been such a bad choice after all.

'YOU ARE EXCEEDING THE SPEED LIMIT!' Claudia suddenly barked at her, when she rounded the corner and headed towards the town centre. 'YOU ARE EXCEEDING THE SPEED LIMIT!'

Clare looked at the dial. She was doing twenty-four in a twenty miles per hour zone. The car couldn't really do twenty without stalling. She tried lifting her foot even further from the pedal and was rewarded by a series of bucks and starts. A light flashed on the dashboard – a little car with an 'x' through it. That couldn't be good.

Instead, she accelerated again, wound her windows up and tried to cover the sound of her on-board computer having a near-breakdown with the radio. By the time she parked the car, she had a headache and had treated half of Hatfield to the delights of a nineties pop compilation.

'Meeting in twenty minutes!' Ann said as she entered Clare's office with a big bunch of files an hour later, her nose wrinkling slightly as she took in the 'old shoe' smell that refused to leave. 'Nigel and Will to lead it, apparently.'

The two women exchanged a look.

'Fabulous.'

'Thought you'd be pleased!' Ann smiled. 'It's more of a training session, apparently.'

'Yes?'

'Yes. Goal setting and motivation.'

'Right.'

Ann's face creased again. 'What's that smell?'

'Nothing, I don't think. Ancient shoes?'

'Yeah, it smells like a locker room in here. Can't you open the—' Ann stopped, remembering that for an office that was meant to have all the mod cons, Clare's new 'work cupboard' had rather a shortage of windows. 'God, I'm sorry Clare.'

'All these years, waiting to be promoted to the corner office, eh,' Clare smiled, blinking away the tears which threatened to come once again.

'You have to say something.'

'I know.'

Half an hour later Clare was sitting in the meeting room, with a steaming mug of coffee. She'd actually arrived first, taking advantage of the large table and wall of windows to make a call and top up her no-doubt rapidly declining vitamin D levels. Others had arrived in dribs and drabs and there were now eighteen of them there in total: two other conveyancers who worked solely on residential properties; Ann and three other secretaries, and an assortment of people from litigation and criminal law whom she rarely saw. They nodded hellos and exchanged basic news about family. 'Do wish your husband well done for me, won't you,' said Brian, the semi-retired head of criminal. 'Bloody good show, the other night. Who knew street lights were such complex machines?'

'Thank you,' she said.

Then the door opened, hitting the wall opposite with a bang. In the doorway stood Nigel and Will, side by side, both clutching clipboards. There was an awkward moment when they both tried to get through the door at the same time, collided, then spent longer than was absolutely necessary trying to wave each other through. 'After you!', 'No, no, after *you!*'

In the end, Nigel walked in, and stood with his legs so widely spread apart that Clare wondered whether Will was going to skid through the gap and strike a pose. But instead, Will stood by his side, legs also in a bizarrely wide stance.

'Good morning,' Nigel said, looking round his staff with a benign smile. 'Lovely to see you all here.'

'Yes,' Will said, graciously, as if he was also employing and paying all of them, 'thank you so much for coming.'

Ann caught Clare's eye for a brief second and they glanced away to avoid giggling. They'd made that mistake in a training session before when asked to act out a 'difficult client' scene during some customer relations training. 'I don't think people usually find this sort of thing funny,' Nigel had remarked crossly, as the two of them had clutched each other, shaking with laughter.

'You may wonder,' Nigel continued, 'why we've called this meeting. Well, as some of you know, Will and I have been working closely together for the past few weeks and we'd finally like to roll out our plans to the rest of the firm.'

'Yes,' Will said, stepping forward. 'Nigel and I have been exploring the philosophy of Hans Hankerton, the world-renowned motivational coach.' He held up an enormous book with the picture of a smiling, moustachioed man on the front. The man was standing in a prayer position, looking up at money which appeared to be falling from the heavens. 'His philosophy is that we should all look to ourselves before we look to our business – look at what motivates us, what makes us feel good, powerful at work . . . Basically make ourselves more corporately sexy.' The last two words were emphasised by finger quotes.

Corporately sexy?

Nigel, to whom the word 'sexy' had never been applied before, stepped forward. 'Being corporately sexy,' he said, with no flicker of a smile, 'is being self-assured, attractive in business – and just as confidence might attract a new partner in a discotheque, so corporate sexiness should lead to new business connections.'

Ann was staring at her pad, face fixed, cheeks flushed. She looked up, caught Clare's eye and mouthed the word *discotheque*, her shoulders shaking.

Clare looked at her boss with a mixture of amusement and despair. 'But how?' she said. 'Why?'

'Of course,' Will stepped in, 'Nigel and I are much further along the path to corporate sexiness than the rest of you – we've been working together on this for some time now. So please don't feel bad if you don't reach our level for a while. But we'd like to introduce you to some of the basic principles this morning.'

'Lesson one,' Nigel said, stepping forward again. 'Power stance.' The stepping forward was proving difficult in the small space they had at the front of the room. Evidently, wherever they'd rehearsed had been more spacious. Nigel's crotch was now only inches from Brian's face.

The two widened their legs even further, until Clare worried that they might drop into the splits.

'Power stance is one of the core pillars of corporate sexiness,' explained Will. 'At the Mann Company, we stand erect, we stand proud; others see us as powerful, masterful, dominant. Standing this way send a message to your subconscious that you're strong and ready for action!'

'Could you all stand up, please,' Nigel continued.

Reluctantly, the staff got to their feet, glancing at each other.

'Now the distance recommended between feet is one metre thirty,' Nigel said. 'As you can see,' he continued, proudly, 'I've recently achieved this, and Will here has even clocked up one metre forty-five.' He began a small round of applause and a few joined in, dutifully.

'Feel free,' Will added, to take off your trousers or hitch up your skirts to release your legs for the exercise. Really, Nigel and I didn't get where we are today without shedding our inhibitions and allowing free movement.'

'Indeed we didn't,' nodded Nigel.

'In fact, while we may remain outwardly clothed on this occasion, I'm sure Nigel won't mind me sharing with you that we've both elected to go pant-free today to limit restriction.'

Will turned and picked up a series of long rulers. 'If you could take one of these and lay it on the floor in front of you, then place your feet at either end. That's it, that's it . . . and if any of you are feeling particularly corporately sexy, do feel free to stretch a little further.'

Gradually, as if humouring a madman, the staff acquiesced. Some making it to a metre, some further. Mike, the IT guy from the fourth floor, ripped off his trousers with the ease of a hen night stripper, revealing a pair of Batman boxer shorts.

'That's it! That's it!' cried Nigel enthusiastically, as if cheering on a school football team. 'Look at you all, I couldn't be prouder.'

'Now for the mantra,' Will said, opening the book for reference. 'I have power, I AM power . . . I have power, I AM power,' he looked up and nodded at them.

'I have power,' they chanted obediently, 'I AM power.'

'And as you're chanting,' Will said, dropping out of the chant and letting them continue, 'try to push your legs just a little bit further. Imagine the muscles stretching – feel your own strength!'

Clare glanced at her watch. Half an hour until the Jones's would expect the keys to their newbuild. She'd give it another five. She stood, her feet neatly at each end of the ruler, and waited for the meeting to end.

'*Aaannnddd relaxxx*,' finished Will finally, stepping into a more normal pose. 'Well done everyone! Give yourself a round of applause!' He tucked the book under his arm and led the clapping.

After a brief self-congratulatory clap, they all sank gratefully back into their seats; Mike, rather reluctantly, pulled his trousers back on.

Nigel remained standing at the front of the room, his face a little flushed. Will looked at him for a second. 'No, no,' he said. 'I think I'll stay in the stance.'

'That's dedication, sir.'

'Thank you. Anyway, we're looking to hold these sessions every Thursday morning, with a couple of after-work events for those who are interested. Details to follow.'

'We really think,' added Will, 'that this could be good for the firm. Great for our image, great for our clients.'

'Quite right,' Nigel added. 'Let's draw this to a close now, shall we?' His voice sounded slightly strained. Perhaps, Clare thought, he'd finally seen that Will had stepped over the line – acting as if he was their boss; telling Nigel what to do.

'Meeting concluded,' Will said. 'Go out and be sexy! Corporately sexy, I mean,' he added hastily, just in case any of them had been about to throw themselves onto the next warm body that walked through the door.

Nigel remained *in situ*, nodding to them as they went past. 'Thank you,' he said, still in the strange, rather hoarse voice. 'Thank you. Have a good day.'

Clare was the last one out of the room, and as she went to close the door she heard Will say, 'Well I think that went well, don't you?'

To which Nigel gasped, his voice an urgent whisper, 'For God's sake, Will. Help me. Something's gone horribly wrong.'

Chapter Eighteen

Clare stayed half an hour later than planned at work, before leaving and grabbing a sandwich from the small garage en route to the church hall Dan now referred to as 'the dance studio.' She ate it while driving, feeling almost rebellious and expecting to be ticked off by Claudia at any moment.

Once parked, she got out of the car and brushed the crumbs of cheese and pickle from her lap. She'd changed into tracksuit bottoms and a hoody in the staff toilets before she left, feigning a trip to the gym. The joggers were old and now had pickle stains on the thighs. But they would do.

Walking up to the small building, Clare felt more than a little bit nervous. She was holding the crumpled piece of paper with her original poem written on it and felt incredibly self-conscious about what she was about to do. Glancing about her furtively, she pulled open the door and stepped inside.

The crew – all thirteen of them – were mid-rehearsal and there was some pretty mind-blowing back-flipping going on. Music pounded out of a tiny Bluetooth speaker on one of the windowsills and all the boys seemed completely lost in the moment. As the music ended in a pounding crescendo, the boys dropped into the splits, except for little Henri, who did some sort of elaborate flip from the back of the troupe to the front, landing on his knees with his arms outstretched.

In the silence that followed, Clare clapped eagerly, feeling a bit like a parent at a school play or an over-enthusiastic teacher. 'Well done,' she said. 'That was great.'

'Brilliant - thanks!' Dan said, striding from the back of the group and, for some reason, shaking her hand.

'I can't believe you think you need me,' she said, trying to picture herself through their eyes. The oldest member of the group was thirteen – she was nearly three times his age. She must seem geriatric to them.

'I'm so glad you made it,' Dan said.

'Me too,' Clare said. And for once, she was telling the truth. Sure she was nervous, but she also had a feeling that it was going to be fun.

Dan's sister Nadia had sent over a wig and sunglasses as part of her disguise and Clare tried them on for the rehearsal. The wig was itchy and the glasses made it hard to see at times – but she had to admit when she looked in the mirror she didn't look like herself.

'She'll come and help you with it all properly before we do it for real,' Dan said. 'It's just to give an idea, you know?'

As she tried to learn the simple side-stepping dance routine that the troupe had worked out for her, Clare felt less confident about their readiness. The boys would be devastated if they didn't get in; but although she had rhythm in her words, her legs were refusing to cooperate. Next to the lithe, fit boys she felt old and clunky.

'It's great,' Dan said enthusiastically, as she stepped slightly out of time. 'Now let's go from the top. Put the whole thing together.'

'OK!' she said, feeling anything but.

'And you know it now, right? You can manage without the paper?'

'I think so.' She put the crumpled poem in her pocket,

feeling more nervous than she should by rights. 'Dan, are you sure this is going to work?'

'I know it is,' he said, with such confidence she was taken aback.

'But won't having a . . . gimmick – a humorous sort of rapper – make the whole thing look a bit . . . well, silly?'

'Humorous?'

'Yeah, you know – Martha B., the middle-aged rapper. Livin' it large,' she said, striking a pose. 'Doesn't it make it all a bit, well, novelty?'

'I think you're better than you think you are,' he said, walking over and putting a reassuring hand on her shoulder. She felt a shiver of electricity as his eyes looked deeply into hers.

'Really?'

'Yeah. Do you think I'd ask you to be part of this if I thought it would be a joke? That the boys would get laughed at? That *you* would?'

'Well, I thought . . .'

'Clare, I don't think the judges want us to be a novelty act at all. I think they saw something. And I've watched you now; heard you. I think you've got something.'

'You do?' She enjoyed performing more than she thought, sure. But being told she was good at it by someone who seemed almost impossibly cool? She hadn't expected that. 'But it's not even a rap really,' she said. 'It's a poem.'

'Look, I'll record it on my phone. So you can watch back. See what you're really like.' He brandished his phone, thumb hovering over 'record'.

'I'm not sure . . .' She would probably die of embarrassment. But his smile was so wide, so somehow hopeful and innocent that she nodded. 'OK.'

After an hour or so of missteps and rhythmic lines she told

them she had to go. The kids would be wondering where she was. Plus, she had to admit, although she was getting a feel for the dance moves, her leg muscles were screaming in protest. Despite all this, she also felt a new determination. If she was intended to be genuine talent rather than a gimmick, she knew she could do better.

'I'll get something new written,' she said before walking out. 'Something that will appeal to people more.'

'You think?'

'Yeah,' she said. After all, if she was going to do this, she was going to do the best she could.

The blazing lights at Clare's house practically illuminated the whole street as she arrived home. And as she stepped inside, Toby bounced up to her like an excited puppy.

'You'll never guess!' he said with no acknowledgement that she was home two hours later than usual and was wearing what appeared to be a pair of dance shoes. 'Something amazing has happened!'

'What?' she said, a little impatiently, as she hung her coat up. 'Your friend Matt's been abducted by aliens again?'

That brought him up short; a look of horror flashed briefly over his features. 'Oh ... I didn't – did I mention that at Hatty's?'

'Forget it, forget it.' It was too cruel. 'Go on, what happened?'

'Rumour has it,' he said, soon shedding his horror at the kind of madness he might have revealed at the dinner party, 'that the studio is looking to mix things up a bit. Move a couple of people around, commission some new shows. Tap into new talent.'

'Yeah?'

'And someone let me know, you know, on the quiet, that my name might be on a list somewhere!'

'Wow,' she said, hearing the uncertainty in her own voice. 'That's great!' Because it was great, wasn't it? It was just, since he had started to work at the TV centre, spent more time away, got preoccupied with work, they'd grown apart a bit. She felt it – did he?

'Don't you see?' – he clutched one of Clare's hands in both of his – 'This could be it! This could be my chance!'

Clare looked at the excited man-child on the end of her arm and couldn't help smiling a bit. His enthusiasm was infectious. When had she last felt that way about work? she wondered, thinking of her tiny new office. Maybe it wasn't Toby's enthusiasm or career goals creating her feeling of being disconnected – maybe it was just that his success had made her reflect on her own situation and see how side-lined she was.

Then she thought about the thirteen boys. Her rap. The competition. Giving them a chance to maybe hit the big time. She felt the corners of her lips turn up a little in spite of herself. She'd watched the performance back on Dan's phone and had actually felt quite proud. It wasn't bad at all. 'Actually, I've got my own news,' she said.

'Oh yes?' he said. 'That Camberwaddle fellow gave you some more business?' He turned and began to walk to the kitchen.

'No,' she said, feeling suddenly enraged at his apparent indifference. 'I'm part of a rapping dance troupe destined for national fame.'

'What?' he said, turning back as he went into the kitchen. 'A rapping what?'

'Dance troupe.'

'Right!' he said, nodding and grinning as if she'd told him

a joke he didn't quite understand, or he was patronising someone who'd lost more than a few of their marbles. 'Yeah, me too! Heh.'

'Seriously . . .'

'What?' he turned, only half hearing.

'Oh, never mind,' she snapped, suddenly angry.

Of course he'd thought it was a joke. That's what she'd felt, hadn't she? At first. But she'd started to see it differently. Watching herself on video had been like watching someone else. Someone who needed to rehearse a lot more – but a person with natural talent. An engaging voice. Maybe it was actually a chance to show off a skill that she'd never shared with anyone. Nobody read poems much did they? But raps were another thing altogether.

Could she actually get herself heard?

Later, sipping her final pre-bed cup of tea, she drew the scrap of paper from her pocket, with the beginnings of her next rap scribbled on it.

> *Yo, I'm Martha, Martha B.,*
> *Part of the Eezee Family,*
> *I'm the mother, the one in charge,*
> *Lovin' life and livin' it large!*

What a load of rubbish.

Dan had convinced her about the 'Eezee Family' bit – and she hadn't minded that.

But the last thing she was doing was 'livin' it large'. If anything, she was living life under the radar.

And if she was going to be brave enough to rap in front of an audience, she might as well do it from the heart.

> Yo, I'm Martha, Martha B.,
> Yeah, I see how you look at me.
> Not your normal rapping star,
> More like your sister, or your ma.
> But just 'cos I don't look street and cool,
> It don't mean I am a fool.
> I'm older right, but wiser too,
> I've got some things I could teach you . . .

She crossed out the lines and turned to a clean page.
This was going to be hard work.

Chapter Nineteen

Clare's legs were still aching the following morning as she went downstairs. Katie was already up and dressed, and Toby had been whisked away an hour before. Alfie was nowhere to be seen. Sighing, she made him a cup of tea with two sugars. The boy who had once woken her every day at 5 a.m. had suddenly become nocturnal and never seemed to want to leave his bed in the mornings.

'Alfie?' Clare took a deep breath of clean air before pushing open her son's bedroom door. As she'd suspected, he was still in bed – a tousled head just visible above the mound of tangled duvet. 'Alfie?' she repeated. 'You're late.'

He sighed with such force that she was surprised the duvet didn't levitate. 'OK, OK,' he groaned resentfully, as if she was responsible for inventing concepts such as time, and sleep, and the necessity to function like a human being and get up in the morning.

'I've made you a cuppa,' she said, stepping into the room and feeling a strange prickling sensation beneath her stockinged foot.

'Ouch!' She placed the cup of tea on the tiny space she managed to find on his messy desk and inspected the bottom of her foot. It was peppered with half-yellow nail clippings. 'For God's sake, Alfie! I've told you before, don't cut your nails onto the carpet! Use a bin.'

Her son grunted indistinctly.

She stepped back, her foot touching something mushy – a half-eaten sandwich on a plate. She picked up the plate, involuntarily, to take to the kitchen, then looked around the rest of the room.

There was barely a patch of carpet visible amongst the scattered debris of teenage boy. Crumpled T-shirts and pants surrounded his empty washing basket. His desk was covered in wrappers and plates and cups with fungus growing in them. His school bag lay on the floor, spewing forth his books into the mess. She breathed in – the room smelled of socks and mould and stale farts. 'For God's sake, Alfie. You're fourteen!' she said. 'Don't you think it's time you cleared up after yourself?'

Another grunt.

Katie was fully dressed and eating Weetabix on the couch, balancing the over-full bowl dangerously on her knees, when Clare arrived downstairs with half a dinner service worth of dirty plates.

'Dad left a note saying bye,' Katie said.

'Right, thanks,' Clare replied, eyeing the mess that her husband had left in his wake.

She didn't mind doing a bit of cleaning; it was the fact that, it seemed, her family assumed it was her job to do it and no one else seemed to consider the idea of pitching in. This was what had prompted her to hire a cleaner a couple of mornings a week for a bit– but Toby's excess spending (and now hers, admittedly) meant they couldn't afford any help these days. Somehow, everyone else seemed to be carrying on as normal, leaving her to pick up the slack: to remove crusted bowls of cereal and scrape the leftover contents into the bin; or pick up tissues and teacups and toenail clippings from whatever floor they saw fit to scatter them on.

'You all right, Mum?' Katie asked. 'You look all weird.'

'Yes,' she said, smiling. 'Yes, I'm fine.'

Because, she'd had an idea. The only way to show them exactly how disgusting they were was to leave everything they abandoned in their wake exactly as she found it. The question was, who would notice first? Would she be able to cope? And would her family all die some horrible bacteria-infested death before they realised they had to take responsibility for themselves?

She self-righteously piled Alfie's plates next to the sink, before pointedly rinsing out her own coffee mug and setting it on the side. Then she called, 'Bye kids – school bus in twenty minutes!' before leaving the house and settling into her car.

'Seat belt,' Claudia reminded her.

'Thanks Claudia,' she replied. At least someone seemed to care about her wellbeing. Even if it was a borderline psychotic on-board computer.

'Searching for thanks,' said Claudia.

'Cancel, thanks.'

'Cancelling.'

'You know, Claudia,' she said, as she turned out of the drive. 'I think you and I are going to become good friends.'

Clare had barely arrived in the office before Nigel poked his head around the door of her coat-cupboard. 'Morning, Carol,' he said. 'Bit soggy today.'

'It's Clare, actually', she replied automatically, resisting the urge to tell him that she wouldn't know what the weather was like seeing as she DIDN'T HAVE A WINDOW.

'Oh, really? Well, um. Good news!' he replied, in an offhand way. 'Anyway, I noticed you hadn't signed up for the after-work class and I wanted to see whether you might consider coming along – it'll be a fascinating experience.'

'Yes, I'm sure,' she said. 'I, well . . . I've got a lot on as you can see.' She gestured at the pile of files she had just started working on.

'Ah, yes, but you see . . .' Nigel said, stepping fully into the room, then checking himself and spreading his feet a little wider apart, filling the entire sum of her empty floorspace. 'One of the principles of Hans's philosophy is working smarter, not harder,' he said, treating her to air quotes to emphasise that this was a saying worth committing to memory.

'Yes, but, you know, I think I've got . . .'

'Will's been preparing for weeks,' Nigel continued, trying to shuffle his feet further, then clearly thinking better of it and bringing them back together. 'He's . . . I think it would be a good show if some of our more senior colleagues demonstrated that they had something to learn too . . .'

'It's just . . .' She lay down her pen and looked at Nigel. 'Nigel, it's not really my thing, and you know I do have rather a lot of clients.'

'Ah,' Nigel said, 'but are you corporately sexy?'

'Am I what?'

Her boss's cheeks flushed. 'You know,' he said, slightly less confidently, 'corporate sexiness, the ah . . . the method of appearing attractive, in a business sense.'

'Right.'

'I mean . . . ah, well, Will understands it more than I do, of course. It's a young man's game these days, eh! But the formula really does work, apparently.'

'I see.' A small part of her began to feel sorry for Nigel.

'So you'll come?' he continued, having established that her corporate sexiness was clearly in need of further instruction.

'I'll pop in,' she said, at last.

'Excellent, excellent.' He finally left the room, limping slightly, and she was left with the files which proved, if evidence were needed, that whatever corporate sexiness was, she already had it in buckets.

Her phone pinged around lunchtime and she had a quick look.

STEPH: *Feeling a bit shit, actually.*

CLARE: *What's up?*

STEPH: *Just my entire life.*

CLARE: *What?*

STEPH: *Yeah, my life sucks. Basically.*

The phone rang twice before Steph answered.

'Hi.'

'Seriously, Steph. Are you OK?'

'I'm OK,' Steph's voice sounded teary. 'Just you know, having a moment I suppose. About my joke of a life.'

'Oh, Steph. Don't be silly.'

'Is it silly though? All I do is sit at home with Wilbur – who I love, by the way.'

'I know you do, of course you do.'

'And clean up the house, wash the nappies, change the nappies, clear the house again, make the dinner, forget to eat my own, go to bed and it all starts again.'

'Oh, Steph . . .' Clare remembered those days of early mother-hood so vividly. Where the rest of the world cooed over your baby but forgot about the struggle that comes hand in hand with tiny fingers and toes. 'Do you want me to come over?'

'Oh no, no . . . it's not that bad. I just needed to . . . well, tell someone.'

'Steph, you know, it's totally normal to feel like this.'

'I know, but . . .'

'It sucks sometimes. It's wonderful other times. Then they grow up a bit, and it gets a bit easier. Things sort of . . . well, open up a bit more.'

'They do?' Steph sounded just a tiny bit hopeful.

'Yeah. And you don't have to wait till they're as old as my two. A couple more months and he won't want to be in your arms all the time. And he'll be sleeping better.'

'God, I hope so.'

'Honestly, I felt completely exhausted with Alfie for about eight months, then things sort of . . . you begin to see gaps in the clouds.'

'Right.'

'And you know, there's always lovely Aunt Clare to come and babysit if you need a proper break.'

'But you're so busy.'

'Never too busy.'

'And it gets better? You promise?' Steph sounded like a hopeful child, asking for reassurance.

'I promise. Mind you, then they become teenagers and start cutting their nails and leaving the clippings on the bedroom carpet.'

'They what?'

Clare told Steph about her morning, about Alfie and Katie and the disgusting mess her house was in. 'I've decided, no more,' she concluded.

'You're not leaving?'

'Oh, no, not that drastic. I'm just going to stop. Stop cleaning up after them all and see how long it takes for them to notice.'

'Oh, Clare,' Steph laughed briefly, 'you always manage to make me giggle.'

'Maybe,' Clare grinned, 'but this is deadly serious.'

Clare hung up the phone. Poor Steph. It was easy to get wrapped up in her own gripes and forget there were other people struggling. She made a note in her diary to ring her sister tomorrow to see if she felt any better. Then felt bad for having to diarise what should be such a natural thing to do.

Five hours later, she was standing outside the conference room reading the words 'Corporate Sexiness Seminar'. With a deep breath, she entered to find a smattering of reluctant-looking colleagues who'd also been coerced into taking part. The group included a clearly motivated Mike from IT, who'd already donned a pair of shorts in readiness, and judging by the collection of paper cups and Mars Bar wrappers around him, had been waiting in the room for quite some time. She slipped into the seat next to Ann. 'This should be fun,' she said quietly.

Five minutes later when they were all glancing at their watches and hoping that the meeting had been cancelled, Will entered the room.

The murmur of conversation that had built up fell away as they collectively stopped to look. Because Will was not wearing his characteristic suit, with its fashionably tiny collar and pencil-thin tie. He was not even wearing a dress-down version of his usual look – perhaps a pair of coloured jeans and a short-sleeved shirt.

In fact, Will was – to all intents and purposes – naked. He'd shed his suit and instead had pulled on some sort of shiny, gold-coloured Lycra body stocking. Every lump, every contour and even every hair of his naked form was accentuated – each one shone out in the harsh light of the meeting room. It was the last place she wanted to look, but Clare couldn't seem to take her eyes from the very graphic bulge between his legs. It was like going to the Royal Ballet all over again.

Nigel followed, nodding at staff members as if nothing was out of the ordinary. Clare was just going to offer a prayer of thanks that her boss had decided to stay in his usual attire when he turned to face them all, and she saw the shimmer of shiny red material under his suit jacket.

'Good afternoon!' Will said, as if everything was completely normal and he wasn't standing, legs akimbo, giving them all much more information about his anatomy than was completely necessary. 'Glad you could all make it.'

'Good afternoon,' they murmured, like schoolkids in assembly and with the same level of enthusiasm.

'So, you might ask, Will, why are you wearing gym gear?' he continued.

Gym gear?

Admittedly, Clare hadn't been to the gym for a while. But she was pretty sure that what Will was wearing wouldn't be acceptable in any of the sports centres she'd graced in the past.

'Well, today's seminar is all about trust. And what better way to trust than to be honestly and authentically ourselves. Nigel?' Will looked pointedly at his boss who at least had the good grace to blush a little before dropping his trousers, removing his jacket and revealing a red body stocking that accentuated every curve and fold of his flesh. Thankfully, his belly hung pretty low, shielding his Lycra-clad crotch area.

'Good grief,' Ann whispered to Clare. 'He looks like a cherry on a cocktail stick.'

'Stop it!' Clare hissed, holding back the giggles.

The two men at the front of the room continued, as if there was nothing unusual about any of this. They turned and faced each other.

'I am Will,' Will said to Nigel. 'I live with my mum in Stevenage. I'm twenty-five years old. I worry that my eyes are too close together. I hope one day to run my own successful law firm.'

'I am Nigel,' replied Nigel. 'I am fixty-six years old and

136

I live on my own. I'm divorced. I have a son who lives in Edinburgh. I already run a successful law firm, but I hope to make it even more successful. When I was twelve I wanted to be a dancer. I worry that women no longer find me attractive.'

Clare felt a sound bubble up in her throat – a mixture between a laugh and a hysterical scream. She forced it back down and avoided eye contact with anyone else in the room. Bill, in the corner, was barely supressing his laughter – his shoulders trembled with the effort.

'OK, so in the bag under your chair you'll each find a similar suit – Hans calls them "honesty suits" as when we wear them, we have nothing to hide,' continued Will. 'I want you to change into the suit. Then, with a partner, admit your deepest fears and desires. The idea is that this total honesty opens up the lines of communication.'

Yep, so would a glass or two of wine, thought Clare, looking into the bag under her chair to find that her outfit was flesh-coloured, meaning, if it were possible, she'd look even more naked than the rest of her colleagues.

I'm Clare, she imagined saying. *I'm married with kids, but nobody in my life seems to notice me. I have an alter ego called Martha B. I hope to get through the rest of my life without ever having to wear a Lycra all-in-one.*

Panicking slightly, she glanced at Ann, who looked equally horrified. Thinking on her feet, Clare grabbed her mobile phone. 'Hello?' she said to no one. 'This is Clare Bailey.'

A couple of people glanced at her.

'Oh, Mr Camberwaddle!' she said loudly, making sure she caught Nigel's eye. 'Of course. Yes, right away.'

She held the phone against her chest as if to muffle the

sound and spoke to Nigel. 'Really sorry, but some sort of conveyancing emergency with Mr . . .'

'Of course, of course . . .' her boss nodded. 'You can always take the costume with you.'

'And,' Clare added, catching Ann's pleading gaze, 'I'm going to have to ask Ann to come with me.'

'Right . . . OK, well don't forget.'

The pair of them scrambled to their feet and virtually raced out of the room.

'So, what's the emergency?' Ann asked, looking at her sideways as they walked along the corridor.

'The emergency,' Clare said, holding open the door to the stairs, 'is that I can think of better ways to spend my time than parading my flaws in front of half the office.'

'Oh my god,' her friend said almost slumping against the wall with relief, 'I was hoping that was it. I completely and utterly owe you one. Thanks for rescuing me.'

'No problem,' Clare smiled. 'What are friends for if not to rescue each other from parading around the room in Lycra onesies in front of the senior legal team.'

'You know, you should put that out on Twitter as an inspirational quote,' giggled Ann.

'I might just do that.'

Chapter Twenty

Dan was delighted when Clare called a few minutes after leaving the meeting to say she could make the teatime rehearsal after all. When she'd phoned to tell him that she'd be staying late for a work thing and wouldn't make their arranged time, he'd been quite down. 'We'll still be practicing when you're done,' he'd told her. 'Maybe come by after?'

At the time, she'd doubted she'd manage to squeeze it in on the way home. After all, Nigel's training meetings were renowned for going on at least an hour longer than they needed to.

But high on the euphoria of playing hooky, she and Ann had raced to the car park and driven off at top speed. And as soon as she'd put some distance between herself and a Lycra-clad staffroom, she'd dialled to tell him the good news.

Driving to the hall, she realised she was smiling. Had it been Dan's enthusiasm that had made her feel good? His almost ridiculous gratefulness? Or was it actually that she was looking forward to seeing him? It was hard to know.

Clare pulled up outside the hall, hearing the now familiar beat bursting forth from the tiny building. Stepping inside, she watched the troupe flip and jump the final bars of the track and then clapped, her notebook tucked under her arm.

'Hey, Clare!' they said, almost in unison.

'Hey, yourselves,' she replied, grinning.

'Is that a new rap you've got under your arm?' Dan said.

'Well,' she said, 'kind of. You know, for the audition.'

'Brilliant,' he said as she gave it to him. There was an awkward silence as he read the lines, his lips moving unconsciously as his eyes scanned the words.

After a moment's pause, she could hardly bear it. 'Is it OK?' she asked.

'You're . . . well, I'm blown away,' he said at last.

'Seriously?'

'Of course, seriously! Look, you've got to get over this.'

'What?'

'You know, this feeling you're not good enough. You obviously *are* good enough,' he said, looking at the paper again. 'Wow!'

'I don't know . . .'

'But you do though,' he said, pulling out his mobile and putting up the footage again. 'Or at least, Martha does.'

'Oh.'

'That woman,' he said, gesturing to the flickering figure on his phone. 'She knows she's got what it takes.'

Clare watched again as the stranger that was really her danced and rapped on the tiny screen. Martha looked confident, full of something she never felt she had these days.

'Yeah,' she said. 'I guess she does. I guess I do.'

'And you're good. You're like really good.'

'Seriously?'

'If you don't believe me, let me post it online. No one will recognise you,' he said, his thumb already poised for action.

'I dunno.' She made a face.

'There you go again. Look, they talk about the X factor, right? Star quality or whatever.'

'Yeah?'

'Yeah. And you've got it. When you perform, you change. Something comes out – it's like you're free, you know? Like something's being released.'

'Oh.'

'So, I'll put it up?'

'OK,' she said, only half sure. 'As long as you don't think . . .'

'No, no one's gonna know it's you.' Dan rolled his eyes.

'What was that for?'

'What?'

'The face?' She rolled her eyes back at him and he grinned.

'Sorry, didn't know it was that obvious. I suppose it's that if it was me, I'd want people to see it. I'd want them to know it was me.'

Clare nodded. She understood. But it was going to take a lot more for her to come out of the rap star closet.

Dan pressed upload before she was absolutely sure she'd agreed, and then it was gone. Lost in cyberspace to be judged by the masses.

The rehearsal was a bit shaky at times – she'd barely memorised the new lyrics, so her performance was a little off base. Once or twice she'd had to stop and pull the paper from her pocket to check something. Otherwise, though, she had to admit they were getting pretty good. It had felt good, too.

Maybe Dan was right. Maybe Martha B. had been there all along.

'Already one hundred and twenty likes,' Dan said, waving his phone at her when they were packing up to leave.

'You're kidding?'
'And mostly good comments.'
'Wow.'
'See, Martha B. You're gonna hit the big time in no time.'

Chapter Twenty-One

Clare woke up, feeling the flickers of white winter sunshine on her skin, and opened her eyes. 'What's up with you?' said a voice. Toby.

She squinted at him. 'What do you mean?'

'You're smiling!'

She was, she realised. 'And that's OK, I presume?' she said, in a mock-haughty voice.

'Of course, m'lady,' he said, grinning and doffing an imaginary cap. 'It's just nice to see you happy.'

'Oh.'

'Not saying you're usually miserable or anything,' he added hastily. 'But ... well, you know.'

She nodded. She knew.

Their eyes locked for a second. He was standing by the chest of drawers, trousers on but not buttoned, holding a T-shirt he was in the process of slipping on. His stomach was flatter than it had been for years. He was no Dan, she found herself thinking, but he was looking pretty hot. Catching her gaze, Toby dropped the T-shirt suddenly and walked over to her.

'Don't suppose you'd like me to help keep that smile there,' he said, leaning towards her.

'Oh, and how do you intend to do that?' she grinned, holding her arms up to receive his embrace.

'I have my little ways,' he smiled, bringing his lips closer to hers for a kiss. He tasted of toothpaste and she was aware that having only just woken up she probably tasted slightly less than minty fresh.

'Let me just . . .' she said, trying to wriggle out of his embrace.

'What's the matter?'

'Pretty sure I stink.'

'You smell just fine to me,' he said, kissing her again.

'If you insist . . .'

Later, when she was filling in new client forms and logging phone calls on her time sheet, Clare found she was still smiling. She hadn't realised how long it had been and had all but forgotten how nice sex with Toby actually could be. They'd lain there afterwards for a while, like a cliché in a romance film, her leaning up on his chest, his arm around her back.

She was thinking about it again when her phone pinged into life: *Good news!* said the text from Dan. *We're trending!*

Trending?

What do you mean? she replied.

Take a look! It's all over Twitter!

She'd got an account on Twitter but was more of an Instagram person really. As a result, she only had about ten followers – at least two of whom were bots. She logged into her account anyway and clicked the list of hashtag trends for mentions of Eezee Troupe or Martha B. There was nothing.

Perhaps Dan hadn't meant genuinely trending – after all that would mean thousands of people were retweeting the video. Perhaps he just meant they had a few likes.

Can't see it? she texted Dan.

Look on my profile @Dan_The_Man, he replied.

And her blood ran cold. There was a little video playing,

with her face, luckily too out-of-focus to be properly recognised, but her rap was loud and clear.

And the reason she hadn't noticed a hashtag trending was because it wasn't Eezee Troupe or even Martha B., or You've Got Talent that had been picked up, but a word from her rap.

This is brilliant! You're right girl — I feel #Meh a lot of the time.

I agree with her — fed up with being judged for my looks #Meh!

Me too. #MehToo

Too right I feel #MehToo

About time someone spoke up for women like me #MehToo

Martha B. is the nuts! #MehToo

Looking at the hashtag as it gathered pace, Clare put her hands to her face. What on earth was happening?

Chapter Twenty-Two

Driving to the office, the following morning, Clare felt herself relax. Although people would probably think she was weird if she admitted it, she found work – the sheer routine of it – soothing. She was at the top of her game and things rarely floored her once she was in her element. She didn't have to think about dirty plates, dinner times, distracted husbands or the fact she'd become something of an internet sensation.

She felt less positive when she thought about how her lovely office with its muted green walls and solid wooden bookshelves was no longer hers. Entering her new room, she could still smell the ghost of trainers past. She could hardly fit herself around the corner to get to her seat and, as she sank into the tattered office chair and felt its habitual wobble, she was reminded again that down the hall in her old office Will was enjoying the delights of her specially purchased, leather swivel chair.

'It goes with the desk, though?' he'd said when she'd asked whether she could swap it back. 'The other one's too small.'

'So, swap the desks too?' she said. 'I've been using that one for years.'

'Ah, Nige reckons it wouldn't fit in the cupbo... your office.' He'd smiled, apologetically and she'd had to retreat to her office sharpish before she'd given in to the urge to grab the chair from under him and roll it off down the corridor.

Martha B. would never put up with this shit, she thought darkly.

Other than having to take regular breaks to remind herself that she didn't live underground, the rest of her day at work went OK. She stopped briefly on the way home to run through a couple of new moves in the now familiar church hall and promised faithfully to practice them herself at home.

As she got home and unlocked the front door her phone began to ring. She put it to her ear and, kicking an empty crisp packet out of the way, began to speak. 'Hello?'

'Hello, Martha B.' The voice was husky, unrecognisable.

'Who is this?'

'Pfft, it's Steph, you idiot!' replied her sister, this time using her normal voice.

'God's sake, Steph – you scared the life out of me then!' she said, placing her keys gently on the hall table before slipping off her coat and carefully hanging it on the empty hooks. Everyone else's coats, she noticed – even Toby's – had been flung towards the hooks, missed, and were left on the floor for her to pick up.

Feigning obliviousness, she walked across them towards the kitchen.

'Sorry. Viral star!'

'Oh, don't. You saw it?' Clare could feel herself getting hot.

'You bet I saw it! I even tweeted about it!'

'You didn't!'

'Why not? I loved it – that whole "meh" thing. You may have started a whole new feminist movement!'

'You're not going to tell anyone, though, are you?' Clare said, wondering if she might have to bribe her sister to avoid being outed on social media.

'Why not? You were actually great!'

'Yeah, but work . . .'

147

'Come on, those old fuddy duddies at work need shaking up – you could teach them some proper moves instead of that . . . what was it – corporately slutty stuff?'

'Corporately sexy. And you'd better be joking.'

'Don't worry, Martha. Your secret is safe with me. Although to be honest, I doubt anyone would believe me anyway. I showed John the footage and he said he thought he'd seen you on TV before sometime, but that was it.'

'Seriously?'

'Yeah, he said something like "Hasn't she been on *EastEnders* or something?" ' Steph said in a remarkably accurate impression of her husband.

'Probably thought I was Dot Cotton.'

'More like Phil Mitchell.'

'Thanks a lot! So, you're feeling better?'

'Same as usual, I guess.' Steph's voice wavered slightly. 'You know. Knackered, wondering what the point of it all is.'

'Really?'

'Oh, ignore me. I'm OK. Hormones.'

'Are you sure? I can come over, you know.'

'I know. Thanks sis. I just . . . I'll be fine.'

'Seriously? You're not feeling, well, too low?'

'Don't be daft,' Steph replied, sounding more normal. 'I'm just moaning. It's therapeutic to let it all out, so they say.'

The idea of letting it all hang out brought a vivid picture of Nigel into Clare's mind and she shuddered slightly. 'It'll get easier you know,' she said softly. 'I can't explain it, but it just does.'

'So you say.'

'It's true.'

'Anyway, don't go changing the subject, rap star!'

'Oh, stop it.'

'Have you thought what you're going to do when your

148

family see it properly?' Steph said then. 'I mean, are they seriously not going to recognise you?'

'I'm trying not to think about it.'

'Just tell them.'

'I tried,' Clare explained. 'Toby thought I was joking.'

'Well, it's understandable.'

'And I was going to sit him down and really explain. But then I thought, well, maybe this can just be something for me, for now. The boys, Dan, they really love me, you know? It's like I'm in this little secret club and for once I'm the most important member.'

'Dan, eh? The one with those come-to-bed eyes?'

'Oh, it's nothing like that,' Clare said, perhaps a little too quickly. 'I can't explain it. It's like I can be a whole different me when I'm there. A me who maybe hasn't been able to take the reins much in my life so far.' She may have mentioned to Steph that Dan was attractive, and seemed to *see* her. But she didn't feel anything for him, not like that. Not really.

'Crazy you?'

'Fun me.'

'I'll take your word for it.'

'Ha.'

'Actually,' her sister said, sounding more serious. 'I do get it, you know. Sometimes having a bit of an escape, it just — well, it's stress relieving isn't it?'

'That's it. And, don't say anything to anyone, but Dan reckons I'm actually good at it. And I sort of don't want that bubble to burst. I don't want people to laugh at me or say I'm ridiculous or whatever.'

'You're waiting until you're on TV for that?'

'That probably won't happen,' Clare swallowed. 'I'm ... I don't know ... If it does, I ... Maybe people will like it.'

'Course they will. You're a Twitter sensation! Already a hashtag.'

'Thanks, sis.'

Steph sighed. 'I'd better go anyway, Wilbur's grizzling. Guess he wants to drain my poor boobs again.'

'Ouch, poor you.'

'Yep. Still, keeps John off them I suppose!'

'Steph!'

'Yes, Martha?'

'See you soon?'

'Definitely.'

After the usual chaos of dinner time, Clare walked through to the living room with her coffee, half amazed and half aghast at how much debris had accumulated there over the last couple of days. Had she really been clearing up after her family to this extent all the time? And, if so, why hadn't anyone mentioned the change, or thought to clear a bit of the mess themselves?

Rather than sit looking at it, or getting into an argument with Toby, who seemed intent on watching the news to see if his segment on remote controlled Zimmer frames had made it, she decided to go upstairs. 'I'll do a bit of reading in the bedroom,' she said to Toby. 'See you in a bit?'

'Night love.'

'Bloody family,' she said to the cat, who was sitting on her duvet licking its arse. 'At least you clean up after yourself, puss. Even if it does involve doing that.'

The cat jumped off the bed before regarding her haughtily and snaking around the half-open door onto the landing.

Settling onto her bed, Clare allowed herself a bit of social media time to unwind. She'd have a little scroll, read a bit of news – nothing political – then go to bed. It was either that, commit murder, or give in and do the washing-up – and she was determined not to fall for either temptation, at least for now.

Her news feed had helpfully provided her with a selection of random articles from different publications chosen through an algorithm based on her Google history. 'Anti-ageing secrets of the over 40s!', 'Five diet tricks for losing weight!', 'Celeb Fashion Fails!' and 'People living in Hatfield are going wild for this new pizza recipe!'

Scrolling down, she stopped on an article towards the bottom of the page. 'Why Britain's Women Need Martha B.' It had been written by Felicity Bradshaw, who penned a column for one of the broadsheets once a week.

Feeling sick, Clare clicked on the link and there in high resolution was a photo of her leering into the camera, brows furrowed, mouth in a snarl, shades thankfully obscuring any identifying features.

'A new sensation leapt to our attention this week in the form of Martha B. – a middle-aged rapper on a mission to change the view of women of a certain age,' the article began.

Backed by a dance troupe, Martha, forty-seven, bewitched the YouTube audience with her rap about the plight of the older woman.

But what is it about this slightly ordinary-looking woman that has captured viewers' hearts? Is it her dance moves? (Probably not.) Her rapping? (Possibly.) Or is it simply that women up and down the land can see a little of themselves in Martha?

Who says that rappers have to be current and cool? Or that women have to quietly blend into the background at a certain age?

With her rap, which encourages listeners to see the 'book'

151

rather than its 'cover', Martha has set down a challenge to the people of the UK – don't write others off because of their age. And never, ever, underestimate a middle-aged woman.

As a campaigner for women's rights, I myself have come in for criticism over my appearance – have found myself seen but not heard. And I for one applaud Martha B. for bringing this important issue into the public conscience.

Read more of Stephanie's Hard Truths in tomorrow's *Chronicle*.

Clare sat, stunned, for a moment. Could it really be that through a little YouTube rehearsal clip she was touching a nerve with women all over the country? She'd felt so alone a couple of weeks ago, but now it seemed as if everyone was in her corner – even if they didn't actually know who she was. Although she was a little disgruntled that they'd marked up her age by a decade.

The bedroom door opened and Clare quickly flicked back to the homepage, as if somehow by hiding a story that had already been shared over three thousand times she could avoid her husband seeing it.

'Hi, love,' he said, dropping his trousers without ceremony, stepping out of them and kicking them into the corner, before beginning to unknot his tie. 'Finishing up a bit of work?'

'Something like that.'

The tie also hit the carpet and was kicked in the direction of the laundry basket. 'Good dinner tonight,' Toby said, unbuttoning his shirt to reveal a slightly grey vest. *When had he started to wear vests?* 'Kids ate well.'

'Yeah,' she said, watching as item after item hit the carpet without even an attempt to pile them together or put them in the right place. Then her eye was drawn to his stomach – if

152

she wasn't mistaken, he seemed to be developing if not a six-pack then definitely a two.

He was annoying, sure. But he was pretty sexy, all things considered. She thought of the way she'd been enjoying Dan's attention and felt suddenly guilty.

'Um, Toby?'

'Yes?'

'Do you think we should try to get our date night up and running again?' she said, tucking a loose strand of hair behind her ear and feeling suddenly almost teenage with self-consciousness.

He looked at her then, and for a moment it was as if time had slipped back six months and they were once more on the same wavelength. 'It's been too long, hasn't it?'

'Just a bit.'

They smiled. 'I'm a bit crap, aren't I?' he said.

'We both are, I think. But yes. Yes, you are,' she said, half smiling. 'Look, Toby, is ... is anything going on at work, anything I need to know about?'

'Like what?'

'I don't know. You're stressed ... or, I don't know, there's someone else or something.'

'Don't be silly,' he said, sitting down next to her and touching her hand. 'I've just ... I don't know. All I seem to be able to think about is work. And I know I seem distant and ... I know I haven't been here much. I keep thinking to myself that I've got to sort it out. But, it's kind of – that environment. I get lost, you know?' He looked at her and she felt a wave of sympathy.

'There ... there isn't, you know. Someone else?' she asked tentatively, searching his face.

His cheeks flushed. 'Someone else?' he exclaimed.

'Yeah, I don't know. The wonderful Hayley perhaps.'

'She's twenty-five.'

'And?'

'Don't you trust me?'

'I do, of course I do. I'm not saying you're sleeping with her or anything, just . . . well. Maybe you like her.' A vision of Dan came into her mind and she pushed it away guiltily.

'There's nothing like that. Honestly. I mean, I value her opinion about stuff. But it's only because I'm so clueless. She makes me feel about a hundred years old if I'm honest.'

'OK,' she said. 'Sorry, I just feel, well, things aren't great at the moment, are they?'

'Sorry.'

'You don't have to be. It's not you, it's . . . well, it's us isn't it?'

'Guess so,' he said. Then looked at her as if for the first time. 'Hang on, have you done something different with your hair?'

Chapter Twenty-Three

Clare woke up with a start at six o'clock, half an hour before her alarm. She'd been dreaming of having toothache; dialling the number of the dentist again and again but getting it wrong each time. Her stomach fluttered a little when she remembered their callback was tonight – they'd be performing again for the judges to see if their combined acts would work for the competition. What would happen if they didn't get through? And what would happen if they did?

The bed next to her was empty – a small dent in the pillow the only evidence that Toby had been there at all. Even though a lot of his footage was now filmed in more social hours, the need for him to be in London and his desire to make a good impression meant he was slipping out at some ungodly hour at least three times a week. 'I've got to demonstrate my commitment!' he'd told her when she'd called him on it. 'It won't be for ever.'

She silenced the voice of doubt inside her. If they were ever going to get back on track they had to trust each other. He hadn't said much about her own irregular hours – she could hardly start quizzing him on his.

She yawned. Despite having almost eight hours of kip, she felt exhausted. Too frequently she was up in the night with racing thoughts, worrying about the kids, work, stressing over whether she was trending on Twitter – everyday stuff. Picking up her phone, she idly read her updates, and noticed a text from Dan. It had been sent about 10 minutes earlier. WATCH THE NEWS, it said. Feeling slightly unnerved, she reached for the remote and switched on the small TV that sat on top of a chest of drawers in their bedroom. The news was just starting, so she propped herself up against a pillow and blearily watched the credits.

'PM confirms that reshuffle will be announced tomorrow,' said the official-sounding newsreader over the top of the dramatic opening music. 'Supermarkets warn that the price of turnips is set to rise.' Clare yawned indulgently and shuffled into a more comfortable position.

'But first, the unlikely talent act that's taken the internet by storm,' the newsreader smiled, as the camera zoomed in. 'Rap star Martha B., with her backing dancers Eezee Troupe, has sparked an internet craze, with women taking to their keyboards to complain about being hashtag MehToo. Gilbert Humbuckle reports.'

Clare felt a strange, sinking sensation in her stomach. Surely, she had imagined that?

'Millions of people post videos on YouTube each day, in the hope of getting likes and clicks,' said the voice-over, completely oblivious to the fact that Clare was frozen in horror. 'But few have taken off so quickly as a novelty rap act, known only as Martha B.'

A clip of Clare, conveniently shielded by her enormous dark glasses, played on the screen. 'Not the cover, but the book!' her televised self said, striking a pose she couldn't even remember.

'In the viral clip, Martha is accompanied by an innovative street dance troupe made up of thirteen boys, each at least half her age. But the main reaction seems to have been in response to this unlikely rap star – and the message she's sharing with the world.'

A scrolling Twitter page showed on the screen.

'You may have heard of the word "meh",' continued Gilbert Humbuckle's voice. 'Often used in texts and tweets, it means to feel a little ordinary or dull. But this word is used in Martha B.'s rap to describe how she feels as a woman in her forties.'

Forties. Clare straightened up, offended. 'Thirties, actually', she hissed at the screen.

'Women have complained for years about feeling invisible as they get older, and Martha B.'s clever summation of this feeling clearly resonated with her audience, who created the hashtag MehToo as a way to connect with others feeling the same way.

'Women from across the country, and even further afield, have gone online to complain of the bitter blow life deals women of a certain age – the fact that they feel stretched beyond belief, but invisible at the same time. The feeling that life hasn't quite worked out the way they'd hoped.

'We spoke to Professor Agnus Alder, Director of Women's Studies at the University of Oxford, for her opinion.'

The camera cut to a white haired, female professor. 'This idea of women feeling dull or taken for granted at a certain age is nothing new. But Martha B.'s rap seems to have provided a platform for an outpouring of suppressed rage that has been building up across the country,' the woman said to her nodding interviewer. 'Bringing attention to what is quite a significant problem for this demographic can only be a good thing.'

The camera now panned onto Gilbert's face, zooming in on his clear skin, designer stubble and piercing blue eyes. 'By midnight on the evening it was posted, the hashtag had been used almost four million times. At one point, the site crashed from overuse.'

Tweets started appearing on the screen. *I'm fed up! #MehToo*, *Time we got noticed #MehToo* and *Women power! #MehToo*.

'One thing's for sure,' concluded Gilbert, half hidden behind the messages. 'The mysterious Martha B. has captured the imagination of millions of women and given them a collective voice with which to call for change.'

Clare stood in the shower moments later, feeling surreal. When she'd boarded that bus, agreed to some rehearsals – even when she'd agreed to let Dan post the footage on YouTube – she'd never expected things to gather pace the way they had.

Like it or not, Martha B. had taken on a life of her own. After this coverage, surely tonight's run-through would just be a formality – there was no way the judges were going to say no. People would be watching the competition to see them. They'd expect them to make it to the next stage of the contest at least. She felt a flicker of something a bit like fear.

At the same time, she thought, as she scrubbed her hair with something that promised not only to wash the grease from the roots but transform her into some sort of natural goddess, it was a strange situation but it was something she'd created. Something that in some odd way she'd maybe needed.

That battered book of poems she'd carted around for all those years, feeling slightly embarrassed, didn't seem so daft now. Sure, she loved her job in the law – but there was something great about putting your feelings out there to the world and have the world embrace you. All that time thinking she was the only one who felt the way she did – when there were millions of women feeling the same.

She thought back to the times when Toby had begged to have a peek at her writing; when Katie had found her book in the bottom of a bag and Clare had snatched it from her hands. All the competitions she'd thought about entering. The social media posts she'd been tempted to write. You can't exactly complain of invisibility, she thought, if you're hiding.

Chapter Twenty-Four

There was no sign of Eezee Troupe when Clare drew up outside the audition venue after work. The car park was almost empty – there were a couple of motorbikes in the corner and three battered-looking silver cars parked randomly in the other spaces. She parked her red, overpriced, car of the future in the corner – feeling conspicuous – and turned on the radio to pass the time before the boys arrived.

A few minutes later, a rattling minibus pulled up next to her. The doors opened and the boys came tumbling out of the back like a spilt load on a motorway.

'Do you like it?' Dan said, walking over to her open car window with a grin. 'My mate coaches a footie team and he let us borrow it.'

'Very nice,' she smiled.

He was dressed in light blue jeans, a white T-shirt and a black jacket that had 'Crew' stitched across the top pocket. 'You look nice,' she said.

'Reckon?'

'Yeah.'

She snapped off the radio and got out of the car, locking it before Claudia had time to start nagging, and they walked into the building together. A woman dressed in jeans and a T-shirt that said 'Mellow Grooves 1984' was waiting in the small reception area with a clipboard and a worried expression. 'Are you Martha?' she said to Clare.

'Well ... yes.'

'Great. You're the last act on the callback, if you'd like to come and wait here?'

She gestured to a room on their left where a few blue cushioned chairs had been placed in rows. A sign on the wall, wonkily applied with Blu Tack, said 'Wait Here'.

They filed in, the boys sitting and wriggling like infants in assembly. The room smelled of sweat, and the window was steamed up. Mark went over and drew a face, which began to drip and run as soon as his finger left the glass.

'Pack it in, Mark. This isn't your mum's sitting room, mate,' Dan said, standing at the front like an impossibly young, cool teacher.

'Sorry, Dan.'

'So, remember,' Dan said to the boys, who were all dressed in black tracksuit bottoms and green T-shirts, 'this is your chance. We ain't gonna mess it up are we?'

'No,' replied the boys in unison.

'I can't hear ya?' Dan said, reminding Clare of the panto-mime she'd watched with the kids last Christmas. 'What did you say?'

'No, Dan!' the boys chorused.

'God, no pressure,' she whispered as he sat down next to her. 'What if *I* mess it up?'

'You won't,' he said, so confidently that she began to feel even more anxious.

'You really care about these boys, don't you?' she said.

He shrugged. 'Remind me of me, I suppose.'

'You?'

'Yeah. You know, I was pretty good at dancing back in the day.'

'Back in the day – what are you, twenty-eight or something?'

161

'Thirty-two. But you know, if you haven't made it as a dancer by twenty or so, you can forget it.'

'Really? That sucks.'

'Yeah, plus I went and put my back out before the biggest audition of my life. Which pretty much scuppered any chance I had.'

'Ouch. Poor you.'

'But these boys,' he said, rubbing a hand over his face, 'these boys, they've got so much talent, but nobody to support them. Half of them would be hanging round outside the corner shop or at the park smoking if they weren't doing this.'

'I know,' she said. 'They're lucky to have you.' She covered his hand with hers and gave it a squeeze, without really thinking about what she was doing and what it might mean.

They grinned at each other, and she had to look away.

Before either of them could speak, the door opened and Susan appeared, wearing a powder-blue jumper and a long floral skirt. 'Welcome, welcome!' she said, almost too enthusiastically. 'Thank you for taking the time to come and see us again!'

'No problem,' Clare said, as she and the rest of the troupe stood up. Dan put his hand gently on her back as they walked to the room. 'You'll do great,' he told her, and she felt herself smile.

The room looked much as it had before: the same table in the corner, the same sign. The blinds had been pulled down halfway and the table was in shadow. A silhouette was visible and as her eyes focused in the gloom, Clare could make out a man in his fifties with a moustache and bald head.

'This is Jack Higham, manager of the Grand Theatre,' Susan said. 'I invited him along to see you, I hope that's OK?'

'Of course.'

'Pleasure,' Jack said, in a surprisingly high voice. 'I've seen your show already of course, your act should I say. Rather a fan.'

'Oh . . . thanks!'

Susan took her seat next to Jack behind the table they'd set in the corner. The rest of the room was free for Clare and the troupe to strut their stuff.

'We wanted to say,' Susan added, looking at Jack as if for permission, 'that we're ever so thrilled you decided to come back. Especially after . . . well, fame and fortune have found you!'

'Thanks,' Dan said.

'Yes,' Susan said, 'I mean, when I made the suggestion, well . . . about the rap, I wasn't sure how it was going to go. I'll be honest, I thought it might be more of a novelty act . . . but – well, seeing you all over the news. I've been stunned.'

'Yes,' added Jack. 'I must say that by this stage, having seen the video and the . . . the *reaction* this is more or less a formality. A treat if you will.'

'Right. Thank you.'

They took their places and Dan set up his speaker in the corner. Then they were ready.

Chapter Twenty-Five

Yet again Toby disappeared in the early hours the next morning. This time into a sleek black people carrier which pulled to a stop outside the house at about 5 a.m. He vanished into its shaded depths as Clare looked from the window and gave a little wave. She'd been told he was interviewing a major celebrity today. 'All very hush-hush,' he'd said, tapping the side of his nose.

'I see.'

He was using his car less and less, she realised.

In fact, seeing it glistening in the drive when she left the house just after eight, Clare was tempted to borrow it for a day, just to avoid the constant chatter of her convertible. Claudia had seemed a great feature at first, but she had to admit the cow had been driving her just a little bit mad.

'Can it be disabled?' she'd asked the garage owner when she'd phoned him yesterday after a particularly taxing journey.

''Fraid not, love,' he'd said. 'No one's ever asked that before! Besides,' he'd added, a little affronted, 'Claudia is a *she*, not an *it*.'

'Seat belt, seat belt,' Claudia said to Clare in greeting when she inserted the key in the ignition.

'No problem.' She clipped it into place. 'All right now,

Mum?' she said, then realised that she was both insulting mums and conversing with a car.

'Claudia, find me the latest news,' she said, as she turned out of the drive onto the main road.

'Headlines: Two injured in motorway pile-up on the A34; Amendment 45 returns to Parliament for the seventh time; Parliament braced for another reshuffle; social media hails the sudden rise of a middle-aged rapper known only as Martha B.'

'Claudia please play . . . Take That,' she said, hastily. And with that, she disappeared into her teenage years, at least mentally, for a while.

Ten minutes later, she drew into the office car park – still early. As she entered through the heavy door, she switched her mind into solicitor mode and let the documents and deadlines push all other worries from her brain.

Later she had a meeting with Camberwaddle to give him some pre-auction advice, and otherwise her day was filled with last-minute jobs and paperwork. The pace of her work was what kept her going in every day. 'It's like a rollercoaster ride,' she'd told a friend once, 'just the cars are folders and the rails are legal procedure.'

You probably have to be of a particular personality type to understand.

She'd just settled down in front of a clean legal pad, relishing the moment when she'd raise a pen and make the first mark on the fresh paper, when the phone rang.

'Hello?' a man's voice said. 'The other day, I caught my toe in the hoover pipe. Caused quite a nasty bruise. Have I got a claim, do you think?'

'Pardon?'

'You know, compensation. That Dyson fella's loaded, right?'

'Um? Who is this, please?'

'Ah, right, me name's Philip, but you can call me Pip. Pip Trotter.'

'OK,' she scribbled the name down – sometimes these cold calls led to real bona fide clients, even when they sounded a bit odd. 'And, do you have a house to sell or purchase?'

'D'ye think I might be able to buy a house?' he asked, incredulous. 'I thought it'd be a couple o' grand at best. Mind you, it didn't half smart.'

'Smart?'

'Yes, the toe. Look is this the Mann Company?'

'Yes?'

'Great. I saw an ad – any injury deserves a reward. So how do I go about it?'

Clare jotted down the man's details and promised to pass them on.

She groaned when, as she finally set herself up to work once again, her mobile phone rang. But at least this time she could see who was calling.

Dan said the screen.

'Hi Dan,' she said. 'Everything OK?' Despite the interruption, she found herself smiling.

'Yeah, great. Look sorry to call you at work. I know you'll be over later or whatever.'

'Right?'

'But . . . Anyway, I just wanted to let you know . . . Clare, we've had a call from the BBC!'

'We've what?'

'Yeah, the producer saw us on the news and they want us to do a performance on the *One Show*. They're doing an "online star of the week" segment and we've come to the producer's attention.'

'Oh god.'

'Yeah, I mean, it's great news! Right?'

'When . . . ? Where . . . ?'

'Monday, they said. Get there for four, London. You know?'

'But Monday . . . I mean, I work. Do you not think you can . . .' she began. Then stopped herself. She'd made a commitment to the boys and she couldn't just let them down without good reason. Besides, she was owed about four weeks' holiday and hadn't yet taken a day. 'OK, I'll sort it,' she said. 'Can Nadia help?'

'She's got some pink spray for your hair,' he said, 'and some glasses 'n' that.'

'Right, thank you.'

Oh god. But at least it wasn't yet ITV. She wasn't going to bump into Toby strolling through the corridors.

Ann stepped in and placed a pile of post on her desk. 'Nothing urgent,' she smiled. 'I'm off to grab a coffee, fancy one?'

'Think I'm going to need one.'

'Don't forget there's a lunchtime training session!'

'How could I?'

'Do you want sprinkles?'

'Um, no. Actually I'll just have black coffee I think.'

'No problem.'

The last thing Clare needed was any more complication in her life.

As she turned her attention back to her mobile, a text message flashed on the screen. *Great news!* Toby had written. *Call me!*

She turned the phone over to face the desk and finally made her first mark on the legal pad. Everything else could just wait for a bit.

Chapter Twenty-Six

'Sure, that's fine.' Nigel nodded, making an indecipherable scribble in his diary.

'Thank you,' Clare said. Why was it that she had to clear any holiday with Nigel, when in reality she was the one who managed her workload? Was it a power thing with him, she wondered?

'So,' he added, sitting back slightly, the back of his chair leaning dangerously as he did so. 'Doing anything nice?' The chair slipped slightly too far and he shot out a hand and grabbed the desk to stop himself from falling. 'Bloody chair,' he muttered.

'I'm sorry?'

'Doing anything nice on your afternoon off? I assume it might be some sort of celebration?' He looked at her over his glasses and, although it was hard to tell, he might have even winked.

'Celebration?' she replied, feeling a familiar gurgle in her stomach. Was Nigel telling her that he knew she was Martha B.? That she was off to perform on national TV?

Or maybe it was good news. Maybe he was finally acknowledging how her career was going from strength to strength, how impressed Camberwaddle was; how he intended to introduce more clients to the firm.

'Yes, you know. Your husband's success?' Nigel tapped

his finger against his nose. 'I heard a rumour that he might be in line for a bigger role at ITV – Will saw it on Twitter.'

'Oh yes! That,' she said.

'Wish him luck from me, won't you!'

'Will do.'

'Oh, and Clare?'

'Yes.'

'You must be very proud of him. What a success!'

'Yes.' Clare smiled thinly, then turned to go.

'And you, of course.'

She stopped. Was this the recognition of her recent achievement she'd been waiting for?

'Me?' she replied, modestly. 'Success?'

'Yes, you're there in the background supporting him – the wind beneath his wings, as they say. You, too, on some level, bask in his glory.'

It took a great deal of self-restraint to stop herself saying that the report sitting unread on his desk detailing the amount of billing her department had done for the month, together with the retainer from Camberwaddle that she'd fought for, made her pretty successful herself. Before she went back to sit in the cupboard she'd been relegated to.

But success, it seemed, was only in the eyes of the beholder. And if it was played out on the grand stage, it was more meaningful than her endeavours to keep the money rolling in for their little firm.

'Anyway, I'm around today so if you want to discuss the report . . .' she said, eyeing it again on his desk.

'Oh, yes. Yes, of course . . . I . . .'

But at that moment, Will entered. Clare expected her junior colleague to be told to wait, just as she had been, when interrupting a meeting between him and Nigel.

Instead, Nigel's cheeks flushed and a beam spread across his face. 'Here he is!' he said. 'The man of the moment!'

'Hello, sir,' Will said, and strode past Clare, shaking his boss's hand like a royal greeting a peasant in the crowd. 'You wanted to see me?'

'Yes, I wanted to congratulate you for your latest advertising push. We've already had two client enquiries.'

'That's marvellous!'

'Yes.' Nigel paused and looked over his glasses at Clare. 'Sorry, was there anything else?'

'No, that's it.'

'Good, good. Well tell that husband of yours to keep up the good work!'

Walking back to her office, Clare realised that suddenly for the first time in a long while she didn't actually feel like working. Her office was dark, even with the lamp she'd brought in from home. Sitting there reminded her of how little recognition she'd had. How little she seemed to matter. And at home, too, she was feeling sidelined. Ludicrously, it was only when she was dancing in front of a group of teenage boys that she really felt alive.

But once she'd settled into her uncomfortable chair, she smiled. Next to her keyboard was a muffin with a Post-it note on which Ann had scribbled a smiley face and thumbs up. That woman definitely didn't get paid enough.

Maybe she wasn't being fair on Toby, she thought moments later, feeling more at one with the world after a mouthful of crumbs and chocolate. After all, they'd both been preoccupied with work. To make herself feel better, she picked up her mobile and flicked Toby's number onto the screen. It rang just once before he answered it, breathless.

'Clare!' he gasped. 'I've just come out of a meeting. They've given me the top job! Well, not the top job. But a good job!

I'm not going to be on the morning programme. They're . . . well, I can hardly believe it. They're giving me a chance to host my own show!'

'Wow, Toby, that's amazing!' she said. And she meant it, genuinely. 'What programme?'

'Well, you'll never guess. Actually,' he said, 'it was down to Hatty – she'd had a word with the top dog. He'd noticed me, of course, but it was her who suggested me for this particular post. After our dinner party, you know?'

'Hatty?'

'Yes. She has the director's ear, you know. They go back a long way.'

'Uh huh.'

'Anyway, he'd marked me out as having potential, obviously.'

'Obviously.'

'But it was Hatty's idea that I should be thrust into the limelight now, so to speak.'

'OK?'

'Yeah, I mean I mentioned how I encouraged you to go back to work after the kids, you know?'

'Yes?' If she remembered rightly, they'd come to the decision together after a particularly horrendous electricity bill landed on their doormat. Less about empowering her, and more about powering their central heating.

'Yeah, and how we're always supporting each other with career stuff. You support me, I support you. We understand each other.'

Funnily enough, half a year ago she'd have agreed with that statement, she realised.

'Uh huh?'

'Yes, you know. We often chat after work. You were telling me the other night about your . . . work problem. I gave you advice, that kind of thing. I suppose it helps me to understand what women go through in the workplace. Their insecurities, their struggles.'

'Right. Anyway . . .'

'Anyway, sorry. That's why she recommended me for this show.'

'Yes, Toby. What show?'

'*Woman's World*! Exploring the topics of the day, speaking to influential women. Gaining insight, you know?'

'What?' Clare had watched *Woman's World* once or twice when she'd worked from home last year. The host, a tall, rather intimidating-looking blonde had recently chucked in the role to run for local government. There'd been a series of – female – hosts in the interim. But . . . Toby?

'*Woman's World*!' he repeated. 'Just picture it!'

'*Woman's World*?' she said again.

'Yes, yes. They said that it was a little unusual to give the position to a man, obviously. But someone like me, you know, proud husband, father to a girl, that sort of thing. Someone who puts the women in his life first . . . they thought I'd be in an ideal position to break down the barriers in society.'

'Well . . . congratulations!' Clare said, feeling almost as odd as she had when she'd watched herself on the news, dressed as Martha B.

'Thank you.'

'Actually,' she said after a pause. 'I could do with your advice on something with Nigel.'

'Right, well, I suppose I'd better get on . . .' he said, seemingly oblivious to her second sentence.

'It's just, do you think I should talk to Nigel about Will and the fact that I feel overlooked? I've been wondering whether I ought to leave and start my own . . .'

But Toby was talking to someone in the background. 'Yes, thank you, Tom!' he said. 'Yes, looking forward to it.'

'OK, love, better go!' he said to her before the line went dead.

Woman's World, thought Clare. He has absolutely no idea.

Chapter Twenty-Seven

'This is the bit where we all do the splits,' Dan explained when Clare finally made it to rehearsal that evening. He'd got the boys to show her the new routine so she could see how her performance fit the dance moves.

Clare gave him a look.

'No worries, no worries. I know you can't do the splits, I just thought maybe you could like do the half-splits, or whatever.'

'What like this?' Clare said, pushing her legs as far as they were willing to go. Her hamstrings were roaring in protest, but admittedly her pose was less than impressive.

'Oh, right.' He looked a little alarmed at her lack of flexibility – which surely should be the least of their problems.

She'd arrived late – as always – and already out of breath after having to wait for some purchase money to hit the client account. She'd forgotten her tracksuit bottoms so was trying her best to be flexible in trousers that refused to give and threatened to split if she went too far.

Her mind wasn't completely on the dance either, if she was honest. Work had ramped up and tomorrow she had three completions. It was hard to concentrate.

The rest of the troupe bent themselves effortlessly out of their final pose and began chatting and stretching as Dan took Clare to one side.

'You seem tense, Clare,' he said, which was officially the

understatement of the year. He put an arm across her shoulders and gave her a quick squeeze. His body smelled of soap and aftershave and was damp with fresh sweat.

'I know. I guess I didn't expect to have to get ready so soon,' she said. 'Why are they booking us on the back of a ropey YouTube rehearsal video? It's . . . I mean, it wasn't *that* good!'

'Yeah, but you've kind of captured something,' he said. 'You know, the mood – lots of women, they feel like you do. I think it's more important than you realise.'

'I know, but . . .'

'And isn't your whole rap – poem – about wanting people to see that women like you are worth noticing and shouldn't be ignored? This is kind of what you wanted,' he said. 'And maybe it's what other women, you know, the ones you're speaking to, maybe they need this too?'

He was right, she realised. She had wanted to be noticed, appreciated. She hadn't really thought that anyone else, any other women, might feel exactly the same. Perhaps she didn't see them either.

'I mean, I know you didn't want to rap,' he added, 'but the poem thing, that was you, wasn't it? That was how you feel? What you wanted to say?'

'Yeah, I suppose.'

He stepped back, hand still on her shoulder and focused his dark brown eyes on her face. 'It didn't come from nowhere, Clare,' he said, more gently. 'It was . . . I mean, like a cry for help, or whatever. Like you needed someone to hear you.'

Had it been? 'Maybe, I mean, I was just really fed up that day so . . .'

'Yeah, and it was great. I know you don't think so, but your poem spoke to people. That's why all those women

175

like you. You've kind of told the world what they want to say. That they feel invisible, that no one really sees them for who they are.'

'Is that . . . did you . . . ?' She was lost for words. How was it that Dan seemed to really *see* her when her own husband didn't seem to have a clue about how she was feeling? Could he read between the lines of her rushed, half-written poem and understand how she felt?

'So, it'd be nice, wouldn't it, if something you did helped people to understand a bit more what it's like?'

'What it's like?'

'You know, to be a bit older. A bit more boring. To be in a boring job, with a boring life. Just a normal, boring, middle-aged woman. How you want to break free, that kind of thing.'

'Lot of borings there, Dan.'

'I don't have the words, you're the one with the words,' he grinned. 'That's why we need you. Come on, Clare – if you're in this, you've got to be really *in* it.'

He was right. This wasn't some little audition in a back-room in Hatfield. Eezee Troupe had the chance to be on national TV. And she ought to put everything she had into making it work. For them, and for herself too. And seemingly – and she gulped at the idea – for her fans.

Moments later, the door opened again and a small woman with skinny jeans and a checked shirt walked in. Everyone seemed to know her – the boys bounced up to her like excited puppies.

'Hey, guys!' she said. 'Hey, Dan, Clare.'

'Hey?' Clare said, uncertainly. 'Nadia?'

'That's right,' the woman said, with a grin.

'Oh, thank god,' Clare replied, dramatically wiping her

forehead with the back of her hand. 'Dan wasn't sure if you'd make it tonight.'

'Bit last minute,' Nadia nodded. 'But can't have you going on *The One Show* without a bit of bling.'

'And a disguise?'

Nadia glanced at Dan briefly and a look passed between them. 'Sure,' she said. 'I've got some pretty good ideas about wigs and make-up and that.'

'Thank you.'

Clare could feel Dan's eyes on her as she disappeared into the women's loos with Nadia for a try-on.

'You know, you're doing a good thing,' Nadia said to her softly as Clare tried on a pair of shiny black trousers and grimaced at the result in the mirror. 'Those boys, they really need this.'

'I know,' Clare said. 'I suppose . . . that's why I'm doing it.'

'That can't be the only reason though,' Nadia said, holding out a blonde wig for her to try. 'I mean, you're pretty good you know?'

'You think?'

'I'd buy your track, and I don't even like rap normally.'

'Thank you.' Clare felt her cheeks go red at the unexpected praise.

'And you know, your dancing's not so bad, whatever Dan says.'

'Oh, I don't know about that!'

Nadia looked her up and down and nodded. 'That looks cool,' she said.

Clare turned and looked in the small mirror – she could just about see the top of the trousers. The silver top she'd put on was brighter than she'd usually choose – but the colour suited her. 'Thanks,' she said. 'And the hair?'

'Well, that wig looks OK. I've got other ones though. And

colour spray . . . But maybe we should wait till the day itself before experimenting? The stuff doesn't wear off quickly!' Nadia said. 'But don't worry. No one will know it's you, once I've finished.'

'Thank you.'

'No problem, Martha B.!'

Clare changed back into her office clothes before exiting the bathroom to find Dan standing outside expectantly. 'Oh,' he said. 'I was hoping to see . . .'

'Oh, sorry,' she said.

'Don't worry,' Nadia told him. 'You'll love it.'

Clare felt herself blush.

Twenty minutes later, after one more run through, Clare left the hall, clutching a bundle of clothes and with a promise to fine-tune her new lyrics. She dumped everything on the passenger seat, before climbing into her car and putting on her seat belt.

Before she could turn the key, Dan appeared, jogging effortlessly towards the car.

'Everything OK?' she said, winding down the window.

'Yeah,' he said. 'I just . . .'

'Yes?'

'I just thought you should know, I think you should ditch the disguise.'

'Oh, but I can't.'

'Look, I get it. But think about it. It's not for the boys. I guess it makes no real difference to them. I'm just a bit gutted that you seem to think being who you are is going to stop people liking you, or wanting to work with you.'

'Oh.'

'Gutted for you, I mean. That you feel that way about

yourself. I reckon it'll just make people realise that you're brilliant in a whole other way.'

'Thanks.'

'I just wish,' he said, his face close to hers. 'I just wish you could see yourself through my eyes.'

'Really?'

'Yeah, really. I just think you're brilliant. Really brilliant.' He shrugged, as if it was obvious.

'Oh.' She looked at him for a minute – was he saying he liked her? It was impossible to imagine.

He leaned in slightly and she thought for a moment he might kiss her. But then he seemed to check himself. 'Well, see you, Clare,' he said, straightening up.

'See you, Dan.'

Her hands on the wheel felt slightly sweaty. Why? she wondered. Nerves? Excitement? Would she, she wondered . . . If he had kissed her would she have kissed him back?

She started the car as Dan walked slowly back to the hall. 'Seat belt, seat belt, seat belt,' said Claudia.

'Thanks, car,' Clare said. Then, 'Claudia, radio.'

'Radio on.'

The radio blared out an advert for solid-wood furniture.

'News,' Clare said.

And suddenly, when the channel changed, Clare heard a voice she recognised. 'Claudia, turn up the volume.'

'Turning up volume.'

' . . . that giving women a voice is crucial in this day and age,' the man's voice was saying. It was Toby! 'But it's about finding the right sort of voice. All this hashtag stuff – all the protests – there must be a better way – and that's where I come in.'

'So, you feel you can represent women, despite being

179

male?' the newscaster asked, her voice incredulous. 'What insight do you think you can bring to the role?'

'Well, as a husband and a father to a young girl, I'm more than aware of the difficulties women still face in society,' he said.

'Really?'

'My wife, for example, she finds herself incredibly frustrated at work at times.'

Clare turned up the volume a little more; perhaps Toby was listening to her occasionally after all.

'Of course, we frequently talk about her concerns, and I like to flatter myself that I understand what it's like to be a working mother.'

'Right,' the interviewer sounded yet to be convinced. 'What about your daughter? What's that dynamic like?'

'We talk – I mean, she's almost a teenager, so she doesn't tell me everything, I'm sure! But she does confide in me.'

'About what?'

'Now that would be telling,' he said, with a chuckle.

'That all sounds wonderful, Toby,' the interviewer interjected. 'But do you really think you can provide the insight that the viewers have come to expect? For example, what's your take on the chronic dissatisfaction that women seem to be feeling – highlighted by the rise of the MehToo movement?'

'Ah yes,' Toby replied. 'Well, MehToo, while an interesting concept, is really a protest about nothing. A bit of fun online, if you like. Women wanting to be noticed by the men in their lives, that kind of thing.'

'Really?' The newscaster's tone became a little more clipped.

'Absolutely,' Toby replied confidently. 'That's what women want more than anything.'

In the driver's seat, Clare grimaced. It was like watching her husband walking into a lions' den with absolutely no understanding of the danger he was in.

'But saying that, I would welcome a dialogue – a consultation if you will – with this Maggie character so that we can discuss more positive ways forward.'

'That was Toby Bailey, newly appointed presenter for *Woman's World*, speaking earlier about his role,' a voice-over cut in. 'Now to the weather . . .'

It wasn't entirely a disaster, Clare thought to herself as she parked the car. 'Handbrake, handbrake, handbrake,' Claudia said as she put the gear into neutral.

'Calm down,' Clare said, clicking up on the brake.

'You are now parked. You are now parked. You are now parked.'

She unlocked the door to exit the car.

'Press one for alarm. Press one for alarm. Press one for alarm . . .'

'Oh, shut up,' she snapped, pressing the button as she was told. Honestly, was there anything more paranoid than modern technology?

Chapter Twenty-Eight

'So,' Clare said, walking into the living room after dinner and sweeping a pile of crisp packets, abandoned jumpers and dirty plates to one side so she could sit down. 'You must be on top of the world!'

Because even though it was probably the most ridiculous appointment in the history of TV, it was still impressive that her husband had suddenly risen to prominence, even if partly on a misapprehension about his feminist credentials.

'Yeah,' he said, his brow furrowed.

She pushed another pile of rubbish to the side to make room for him. 'What's wrong? Come and sit down.'

'Oh, thanks,' he said. 'I couldn't find a space.'

'You know, you could, maybe, move some things?' she said, trying to keep the edge out of her voice. Because telling him to tidy up wasn't part of the plan. He had to realise it for himself. Hopefully before they all contracted salmonella.

'Yeah, right,' he said, thoughtfully. 'You know, maybe the house is getting too small for us now, though. I never noticed it before. But the last couple of weeks, things have seemed a bit well . . . cramped.'

'Right.'

'I can't put my finger on why, but suddenly it's as if everything's sort of closing in. Maybe we need to move?'

'Possibly.' Clare tried to remain calm. If she let the stress get the better of her she'd end up pointing out the obvious,

182

or clearing everything up before he realised that perhaps he ought to start taking his share of the housework. Then it would just lead to an argument, rather than the life lesson she was aiming for.

It was just . . . when she started leaving everyone in charge of their own mess, she hadn't realised it would take more than a week for them to get the message. What would it take, she wondered? Being buried alive under crockery? Some sort of cockroach infestation? Stray dogs wandering around and shitting on the floor?

'Anyway, I mean, I'm stoked about the job, but some of the lads, you know, Tim and Derek, they've been laughing at me a bit, you know, on Facebook,' he said, moving the topic back to himself.

'Laughing?'

'Yeah, about *Woman's World*. Like, it's no job for a man, or whatever.'

'Oh, don't worry about it.'

'Is it a bit weird though,' he said, looking at her. 'Being a man in a woman's world? I mean, imagine what it feels like to have lots of people questioning whether I can cope with my job simply because of my sex.'

'Do you know what? I think you'll survive,' she said, giving him a nudge. 'Come on, those two were going to laugh no matter what role you got. It's just what they do.'

'I suppose,' he said, looking a little more heartened and chewing distractedly on a shred of fingernail. 'It's just . . . it's when you work *so hard* and have no one take you seriously or say, I dunno, well done or whatever. I feel invisible, Clare.'

'I can only imagine . . .'

'You know, even Hatty was a bit weird today,' Toby continued, still completely wrapped up in his own crisis.

'As opposed to every other day, you mean?'

183

'Yeah, I mean, she said something a bit odd.'

'Did she?'

'Yeah,' he said, twiddling a well-oiled strand of hair around his finger. 'You know she put a good word in for me, right? About this job thing.

'Well, she was talking about my appointment and she told me that she'd had a word with the head honcho about the role.'

'Yes?'

'And she kind of looked like she might have been crying or something.'

'Oh, poor Hatty.'

'Yeah, I mean I know she was happy for me, but...'

'Maybe you should talk to her. Maybe something's up,' suggested Clare.

'You think she'd want me to?'

'I know she would.'

He put his arm around her and gave her a squeeze. 'Thank you,' he said.

'Anyway, well done!' she said, again. 'It's kind of a dream job, isn't it!'

'I never thought,' he said, 'when I was stuck on regional news... well, I kind of thought maybe that was as good as it would get for me.'

'Oh, Toby. You were always better than that.' She caught his eye and as they studied each other's faces she was relieved to feel a flicker of attraction. The Dan thing was a distraction, she told herself. But this man – despite his obsession with coiffing his hair and donning overpriced designer threads – was still her Toby underneath. The person she'd shared so much with. She couldn't give up on him just yet.

'So,' he said. 'How shall we celebrate?' He made a slight

shift towards her on the sofa and put a suggestive hand on her knee. She jumped at the unexpected contact.

But just as she was about to lean in for a kiss, debris fell off one of the cushions onto the floor, setting off a chain reaction which resulted in a cup of festering tea being tipped on its side.

At this moment, Alfie lolloped into the room, slinging his kit bag onto the carpet and what was left of the moment was finally broken.

'Good footie practice?' Clare asked.

'Yeah, OK. But my kit was dirty,' he said, accusingly.

'Dirty?'

'Yeah. Muddy.'

'Oh dear. Well, I wonder why that was?' she said, feigning incredulity.

'Not washed,' he said, glowering at her from under his fringe.

'Well, never mind!' she said, hoping that it wasn't too late to save her son from a life of complete dependence on others to get his shit together. Had he put his kit in the laundry basket, she'd have gladly washed it. Hopefully he'd work that out for himself by next week or he was going to start losing friends.

'Right,' he said, looking confused, 'anyway, what's for tea?'

'Alfie!' she said. 'For goodness sake!'

'Yeah,' Toby said. 'Have some consideration, Alfie!'

Clare looked at Toby. Had he actually realised how she felt?

'We don't just ask mum what's for tea,' Toby said, sternly, 'we say, what's for tea, *please*?' He looked at Clare expectantly.

Once she'd put the chicken in the oven, Clare went up to

her daughter's room. Knocking, she went in, to find Katie at her desk doing some science homework.

'Hi, love,' she said. 'Going OK?'

'Yeah, thanks.'

'Dinner won't be long.'

'Great.'

'Katie?' she said.

'Yes?' her daughter replied, with an edge of impatience.

'Do you talk to Dad?'

'What do you mean? Of course I do!'

'No, I mean ... *talk* to him. Tell him stuff ... Maybe stuff that you can't tell me?'

Katie was silent for a moment. 'Maybe sometimes,' she said. 'Recently, you know, when you've been out.'

'Is ... what's going on?'

'Oh, it's nothing. I just had a bit of a problem with someone at school, that's all.'

'What, bullying?'

'Sort of.'

'Do you want me to ...'

'Don't worry Mum,' said Katie. 'Dad gave me some advice and I think it's going to be OK.'

'But you know you can always talk to me, right?'

Her daughter shrugged again. 'It's no big deal, Mum. Anyway, it's hard to talk to you in your car, what with Claudia and that. It's like ... I dunno, you listen to her more than you listen to *me*.'

As she closed the door, Clare wondered whether Toby was actually the only bad listener in the family. Perhaps she had some lessons to learn, too.

Before she had time to think, her phone flashed with Dan's number.

'Hello?'

'All OK?' He sounded worried.

'Yeah, don't worry. I've sorted out that final lyric. I'll send you a copy later so you can have a look.'

There was a moment of silence. 'Look, what I said . . . I mean, it's true. I like you, Clare. But I know . . . I get that you have a whole life and that, well, nothing can happen.' Dan said at last.

'Uh huh,' she said, feeling her face get hot. So he *had* been telling her something?

'I just wanted to say it, you know?'

'Thank you. And, you know, you too,' she found herself saying. 'I mean, if things were different . . .'

He was silent again for a moment and she felt her heart thundering against her ribs.

'Dan?' she said.

'Right. I've just had the producer on and they said the car will be with us by 2 p.m. – is that going to work out?'

'Yeah, that's fine. Just . . . you know. Around the corner from my office if possible.'

'OK – like a secret agent.'

'Ha!'

'You'll have to get changed in a phone box.'

'What?'

'You know, like Clark Kent.'

She snorted. 'Think I'll find somewhere a bit less . . . well, covered in windows.'

'Good point. And Clare? Sorry if I've been pressuring you about this. I realise you're doing the best you can.'

Chapter Twenty-Nine

Clare felt a bit of a fraud when she left the office at one thirty and Ann had wished her a good afternoon. 'Have fun,' she'd said, 'whatever you're up to!'

'Thanks.'

She hated lying to her friend. Although she wasn't lying as such, but simply neglecting to tell her the truth. There was a difference, right?

The car arrived dead on time outside the corner shop and she dived into it gratefully. The ride was quiet – Dan and the boys had been picked up separately, so she was able to sit and collect her thoughts.

She was surprised at the enormity of the TV studio, but was eventually shown to the changing room where Nadia met her to help her with her outfit. Now, sitting with the troupe of fidgeting boys, plus Nadia and Dan, in some sort of green room she felt as if she might be sick at any minute.

She tugged at her silver top. 'I look ridiculous,' she said. 'Are you sure this suits me?'

'You look great,' Dan said, catching her eye. She'd never noticed how intense his gaze could be and found herself going red.

'Thank you. It's . . . it's a bit different from my usual style.'

'Seriously, take it from me,' he said, 'you're a MILF.'

'A MILF?'

'Dan!' Nadia said, sharply.

'You know,' he continued, 'mother I'd like to . . . Oh, well, you know. I just mean you're going to drive the watching dads wild.'

'Good save,' she said, giving him a nudge.

'Thanks,' he said, grinning and wiping the back of his hand across his forehead in a 'phew' motion.

'And you don't think anyone will recognise me?' Clare pulled at the ends of the very realistic wig which Nadia had found for her.

'Not once you get your shades on. Remember, nobody's going to expect it, are they? Clare the solicitor rapping on TV,' Nadia smiled.

'No, that's true.'

There was still ten minutes before they'd be going through. And the rehearsal had gone well. She'd even noticed Pete – the show's brand-new presenter – nodding his head to the beat.

The dancing had got easier, too. She'd become fitter over the course of the rehearsals, felt her body move more easily. She'd never really been a natural dancer, but she reckoned she could just about pull it off.

For a moment, she wondered whether she ought to just come out – to admit who she was, rather than the mysterious character she'd invented for herself. Be proud of it.

But then she thought about her day job. The serious office atmosphere. Corporate sexiness, whatever that was.

It was better to remain under the radar for now, at least.

'Are you sure?' Dan said, suddenly, as if reading her thoughts.

'Sure?'

'Yeah, about the wig. I mean it looks good, but I just thought, well, Eezee Troupe, we're about keepin' it real . . .'

This again?

'Look, Dan. I get it,' she said. 'I get that you want to give the act the best chance. That you want to *keep things real*,' – in retrospect, it probably wasn't a good idea to use her fingers for air quotes at this point – 'but I have a job. A boss. A new client who's pretty high profile.'

'I know but . . .'

'This isn't my life. This isn't going to be my life. I get that it's your chance. I get that we've kind of been stuck together in this weird situation, but after the show, the competition, Martha B. is probably going to disappear.'

'Really?' he seemed surprised. Surely he had known this wasn't for ever?

'Yeah. Look as soon as Eezee Troupe have an audience, a following, they won't need me any more. I'm just . . . well, something that makes the act more noticeable I suppose. I'm not the talent. Not really. I know you said I'm good . . . and I know I can hold a beat a bit, but when it comes down to it, I'm a gimmick. People get bored of gimmicks.'

'But . . .'

'And I wouldn't be able to show my face at work after rapping on live TV. Nobody would take me seriously again.'

'What about the women?' he said. 'They don't think you're a gimmick.'

'Women?'

'Yeah. All the women who started the hashtag stuff. Women are starting to challenge their bosses, ask for pay rises. There was an article in the news about a woman who's divorcing her husband because of you.'

'Divorcing?'

'No, no, it's a good thing. He was a right bastard by the sound of it.'

'Right.' She still wasn't sure if she wanted to be responsible for breaking up a marriage. 'I don't see what this has got to do with my wearing a wig though.'

'The whole rap thing – your poem, whatever – you've encouraged them to be honest. You've got women talking about how they feel. My mum thinks you're amazing!'

'That's nice, but . . .'

'We *all* think you're amazing. And it kind of seems wrong if you don't have the courage to be yourself; to stand up on that stage and own it, you know?'

'Dan, I just can't. I get it, but I just can't.'

'OK,' he nodded. 'But just know I'm not going to let you quit without a fight!'

Clare smiled weakly. She was risking a lot by being involved in this. Toby was already suspicious about her afternoon out 'shopping with the girls'. And although he didn't say anything, Nigel had seemed a little edgy about her referring any queries from Camberwaddle to Will this afternoon. 'I'll think about it,' she said at last.

'Thanks,' Dan said. 'Thanks, Clare.'

'Hey, don't reveal my secret identity,' she laughed, poking him in the ribs.

'I won't if you don't.'

When the runner came and led them to their positions on a small stage area across from the main presenters, she felt for a moment as if this was something that was happening to someone else, not her. It was weird seeing the set of a show she watched every now and then in the flesh – it looked messy and rudimentary compared to the way it appeared on camera.

'But first,' Pete said, turning towards the camera and flashing a short smile. 'An unlikely act has taken the internet by storm. Martha B. with dance troupe Eezee Troupe have captured the imagination of the masses with their raps about women's rights.'

'And they're here now to perform in the studio,' continued his co-host, Melissa. 'So give it up for Martha B. and her boys!'

With her heart hammering and her lips stretched into a smile, Clare listened to the beat and came in on cue:

'It's Martha B., here to disrupt your life,
I'm speakin' to your sister, your mother, your wife.
Got my boys Eezee Troupe and they're keepin' it real,
Got a message about your women and just how they feel.
We're tired of being sidelined, tired of being ignored,
Being judged on how we look, that's not what we stand for.
We are liberated, educated, ready to go,
We're fit, legit and loving it, enjoyin' the flow.
Yeah, we keep things goin', do the tidying up,
We like things smooth, get in the groove, like fillin' your cup.
But it's hard to keep things goin' when you're being ignored,
When we tell you what our day's been like and you just look
     bored.
Yeah, hashtag MehToo! I hear ya all the women out there,
It's time we started stepping out and makin' things clear.
Just because we're getting older doesn't mean we are less,
Like wine the years improve us – but, dress to impress?
Why should we think about you when we're getting dressed?
It's our minds you should be seeing, look and you'll be
     impressed!
We're invisible? Yeah right, we blend right into the crowd,
Well no longer, Martha's women gonna shout it aloud.
The world is run by men, well just look where that got us,
It's time for a new movement, just in case you forgot us.

No matter if we're older, or not part of your game,
It's gonna change, I'm Martha B.,
Remember my name.'

The camera zoomed in and, as instructed, Clare dropped into a half-split. For the first time, she made it, although her hamstrings screamied in protest.

The presenters and crew clapped. 'Well, that told us!' said Pete, shaking his head and smiling. 'Well done, guys.'

'Yes, brilliant,' smiled Melissa. 'And now, to a story of a tortoise who trekked twenty miles to find his owner after a house move . . .'

In what felt like a complete anti-climax, Clare and the boys were ushered from the stage and back into the changing room. 'Great job,' the runner said, giving them the thumbs up.

'Was that OK?' she asked Dan when they were sitting in the foyer afterwards. 'Do you think people will like it?'

'I don't think,' he said, flashing his phone, which he seemed to be able to carry with him invisibly whatever he was wearing, 'I know.'

'Already?'

'Yeah. Twitter's gone crazy!'

It was what she'd hoped for and dreaded simultaneously. #MehToo was trending again at number five – and from what she could see as she looked over his shoulder, the feedback was overwhelmingly positive.

'And you don't think—' she began.

'Clare, nobody will recognise you in that get up,' he said, removing her sunglasses in a way that felt strangely intimate. 'But I still reckon you should still think about – you know – coming out or whatever.'

'But Dan, this is never going to be my main job. My day job is pretty serious. Professional.'

'But who says?' he asked.

'Who says what?'

'Who says you can't be both? You're already a pretty good mother, I reckon.'

She snorted at this but said nothing.

'And you're nailing it at work, right?'

'Well, kind of . . .'

'Well, I can't see why you can't have this, too. Why do you have to choose? You've got a talent.'

'I know . . . I'm a poet, and I know it,' she quipped, partly out of embarrassment.

'No, it's more than that,' he said. 'You can speak to people. You can see how people are feeling and get it into verse. And the way you perform – it isn't the novelty that's keeping people interested. It's the message. It's the performance. Clare, face it,' he said, looking at her intensely. 'You're good at this.'

'But . . .'

'And no buts,' he said. 'You're the one showing everyone that women can have it all. That there's this "new movement" or whatever. Maybe it's time to listen to your own words.'

He was right, she realised. The only person setting limits was her.

Chapter Thirty

'So, the auction for the land and property in section B of the development plan takes place tomorrow,' Camberwaddle said, sliding a glossy brochure towards Clare over her desk.

'Right,' she said, looking at the small bungalow on its generous plot and trying to imagine the twenty-five houses Camberwaddle hoped to build in its place.

'I'll get my assistant to call you with the details once the transaction has gone through.'

'That's fine.' Clare was still at a loss as to why Camberwaddle had needed to tell her this information in person, rather than simply emailing it to her as usual. Looking at her top client, his silver hair looking slightly more unkempt than usual, a flush on his cheeks, she wondered if he was all right. 'Was there anything else?' she prompted after a few moments' silence.

'Sorry, yes,' he said. 'I've signed those contracts, so they've just gone to be countersigned by the head of commerce, then they'll be winging their way back to you.'

'Thank you,' she said.

Another silence.

'Is there anything else I can help you with?' she said again.

'Um . . . no, I think that's it,' he said, shuffling papers back into his leather satchel. Then, 'Oh!' he said, as if he'd just remembered something. 'I was going to ask how things are going for your husband. Quite a coup, him getting into frontline presenting as it were. Even if he is only doing a women's show.'

'Thank you,' she said, holding her tongue.

Camberwaddle suddenly grimaced.

'Are you all right? Do you want some water?' she asked. Please, don't let him vomit in my office, she thought. There isn't a window. It'll stink for weeks.

'No, no,' he said, straightening up and fishing a rather grey handkerchief from his pocket to mop his brow. 'Just a bug; I don't seem able to shake it.'

'Oh dear.'

'You know,' he said, once his colour had returned to normal, 'seeing as we're working together closely . . . well, perhaps it would be nice to meet up for a drink or something. Not just us of course, perhaps I could bring my wife, and you could, erm, bring Toby? Might be, well, a pleasant evening? We could talk to him about . . . well, his TV stuff?'

'Yes, that would be nice,' she lied, wondering how much sway he really thought the presenter of *Woman's World* TV show would have over the repurposing of greenbelt land, and whether he really thought he was being subtle.

'Great. Great.'

'Well, I'll wait for your call Stefan, on the properties.'

'And, um, yes, I'll contact you about that dinner,' he said, turning towards her as he left. 'See if we can't pencil something in.'

Yes, why not, she thought. Perhaps she'd invite Hatty as well – that could make for an entertaining evening. Friends in high places indeed.

Minutes later, Ann stepped in with a document for Clare to sign.

'Was Mr Camberwaddle all right?' she asked, leaning on

the desk conspiratorially. 'He looked a bit flustered when he left.'

'He said he felt a bit off colour; but I think he's OK.'

'Right. I was quite worried about him when I saw him walking through reception just now. He looked – I don't know – frail almost.'

Probably weighed down by the weight of his own subterfuge, thought Clare meanly. It was annoying that the client she thought she'd landed fair and square seemed to have his eyes on her husband rather than her. Having Camberwaddle in her corner was great – but she'd rather have him on the books because of her great legal brain, rather than her husband's great connections.

As it was, things with Toby were, if anything, looking more rocky than before. He *was* trying, he'd really started to listen to her, but this was the wrong time for him to notice her – he'd begun to worry what she was up to. And she didn't know how to tell him about Martha B. How could she begin to explain when she'd done so much behind his back already? Besides, it would all be over soon.

'It's just . . . all these phone calls. Sudden late nights. It's nothing to do with this Camberwaddle bloke, is it?' he'd said last night.

'What? Of course not!'

'I'm sorry,' he'd said. 'It's just . . . you never seem to tell me anything.'

'That's because you never listen!' she'd snapped.

'What do you mean?'

'I do tell you things, but you're always so preoccupied with your job you don't really listen to me,' she'd said, feeling tears prick at her eyes. 'Last time I told you about a work problem you told me I should make a lasagne.'

'Now come on! Your lasagne is legendary,' he'd said,

missing the point. 'I thought you'd be pleased that I liked it so much.'

'But I wasn't . . . I was telling you about a work meeting, not meal planning for the week. You just assumed I was talking about dinner. Probably because I'm a woman – that's what you think, isn't it? That I should be at home, in the kitchen.'

'How can I listen if you never talk! I don't understand women!'

'Coming from the presenter of *Woman's World*, that comment is pretty alarming.'

'But seriously, how can I understand how you feel,' he'd replied, more softly now, 'if you don't ever tell me?' He'd reached out and touched her upper arm, pulling her lightly towards him.

'What?'

'I know I've been a bit crap. Preoccupied. But I love you, you know. I do want to know how you're feeling. Even if I get things wrong sometimes.'

'Oh.' Telling him directly how she felt hadn't actually crossed her mind recently, she'd realised. She'd tried to show him instead. She'd felt her skin prickle – had she really become an online rap sensation simply because she was avoiding having a proper conversation with her husband? Was that a proportionate reaction?

Steph was right, she should have opted for a new lipstick, not a new identity.

'It's like that Martha B. character,' he'd said, suddenly.

Her heart had somersaulted. 'What?' she'd squeaked.

'Yeah, well, she's great, right? Women love her. She goes on TV, creates a furore, the whole hashtag thing, but when I actually want to contact her, to come on the show, for christsake, she's nowhere to be found. Like she doesn't really exist. Doesn't actually want to talk about it.'

'But . . . Martha B.?'

'Yeah, I contacted *The One Show*, and they gave me the number of a guy called Dan – her manager, or whatever. But he was really cagey when I rang him.'

'But why . . . why would you even want her on your show? Most of the time you speak to business leaders, lawyers, politicians . . . sometimes a film star.'

'Yeah, but she's like the voice for women at the moment. Hatty reckons she's going to be a big thing. That hashtag business. You know that women are suing their bosses now?'

'Oh.'

'Yeah, and it's like she's united all these women with problems. Not just the big take-your-boss-to-court problems. But the little problems that mount up. Being ignored. Overlooked for promotion. Being expected to do stuff that isn't really their job.'

'Right?'

'But what's the point of having this important message, if when people actually want to hear it, you're nowhere to be found?'

Clare was just beginning to look through the brochure that Camberwaddle had passed to her when she heard the sound of running footsteps. Ann burst into her office, glasses on a slant, eyes wide with alarm.

'Come quickly!' she said. 'It's Mr Camberwaddle! He's collapsed in the street!'

'What?'

'Yes! He had a glass of water in reception, got a couple of paces out of the door and just went! I've called an ambulance. They'll be here in a second, but I think it might be serious!'

Without really knowing what she'd do when she got there, Clare leapt from her chair and raced down to the reception area just in time to see her million-dollar client being wheeled away by paramedics.

'Can I do anything?' she said, rushing out of the main entrance. 'Can I call anyone?'

'Yes,' he squeaked, lifting up his oxygen mask for a second. 'Call Dawn. My wife.'

Chapter Thirty-One

'Left foot, right foot, spin and *jazz hands*!' Dan prompted, as Clare attempted to work her way through the routine for what seemed like the millionth time. 'Good! Good! That was almost there.'

'Almost there?' Clare panted. 'I thought I'd nailed it!' In all honesty, she'd nearly missed tonight's rehearsal. Surely if they'd just successfully performed on TV, they'd easily ace their imminent performance. And she felt pretty shaken after Camberwaddle's collapse. But Dan was a perfectionist. And for some reason she struggled to say no to him.

'We can't let up now,' he'd told her on the phone. 'This is our chance to be great – truly great.'

'I just feel . . .'

'I know,' he'd conceded. 'It must have been awful. But you know, endorphins.'

She'd known he'd get her on the endorphins. He was obsessed with them. Although he was right – a bit of movement was probably just what she needed.

He looked at her now, worried. 'Well, it wasn't bad,' he conceded at last.

'Surely it would be better if I just stood there and rapped and just danced a tiny bit, like last night.'

'But you heard what the guy at the studio said yesterday after the show, they thought the bits when we were more – I dunno – *together* were really cool. We've got to take it on board.'

'I know,' she said, looking at his hopeful face. 'Look, Dan. You do know that you lot will probably still make it now, don't you? After the TV thing? You've already had that agent on the phone. You've had the exposure you need.'

'Yeah, I know,' he said, his eyes full of yearning, 'but just imagine what might happen if we won the competition.'

'We kind of already did,' she said. 'I mean, we were on national TV. It's pretty much like having the prize already.'

'Yeah, but winning, getting on TV again . . . it's the start of something,' he said. 'I've had a music producer in touch too – just someone local, but he reckons we ought to lay down a track.'

She had the now familiar sensation of going over a speed bump too fast.

'Just . . . just don't get your hopes up too much,' she said. 'It's great, but I'm not sure. I still haven't decided if I want to carry on. Even if there *is* interest in us after the comp.'

'I know,' he conceded. 'But then I always think – what's wrong with having some hope? Even if it turns out badly, it's better to have believed in it for a while, isn't it?'

Carpe diem. Seizing the day. Making the most of opportunities.

She thought about her conversation with Stefan's wife, Dawn, the day before. 'He's collapsed; they've taken him to hospital,' she'd said.

'That stupid man.'

'Pardon?'

'I told him,' Dawn had said, her voice thick with angry tears. 'I told him to take it easy; but he wouldn't listen would he? You'd think after building up a multi-million property business he'd have taken a bit of time to enjoy his success. But no. It's an addiction.'

Later, Dawn had rung her back from the hospital. 'He's OK,' she'd said. 'But his heart . . . well, it was a close thing apparently.'

'I'm so sorry,' Clare had said, not really knowing what she was supposed to say.

'And me too. Sorry that I was a bit weird when you rang and told me. It was just . . . I suppose I've been waiting for that call for the last five years. Waiting for him to burn himself out – it does something to you.'

'I completely understand,' Clare had said. And she had. She could imagine exactly how frustrating it must have been to watch someone you love continue down a damaging route and not be able to get them to stop. Like Toby, she thought, suddenly. Steph was right – he had been looking peaky. And the weight loss, sure it was healthy that he'd got rid of his emerging gut, but maybe there was more to it?

'Stefan said you were nice,' Dawn said, before they ended the call. 'It's good to finally talk to you.'

Was she nice, though? She thought about the mountains of rubbish she'd had to wade through this morning just to exit the house. The fact that Katie's homework book had had ketchup stains on it when they'd finally found it on the kitchen counter. The fact that her husband – on the day he was recording his first show – had been forced to go to work wearing her underwear because she'd refused to wash anything that hadn't made it into the wash basket.

'It'll be good for you,' she'd giggled as he'd squeezed into her lacy knickers. 'Really putting yourself in a woman's position.'

'You know,' he'd said, turning this way and that in front of the mirror. 'These don't actually look too bad on me.'

Half an hour later, she and Dan had both had enough of her attempts at dancing. 'Suppose you're not a dancer anyway,' he'd admitted grudgingly, 'I mean, the rap's the thing, right?'

'We can only hope.'

'But you will practice?'

'I will,' she said. She meant it, too.

He'd kissed her then, on the cheek.

'What was that for?'

'Oh, you know,' he'd said. 'Just thanks for everything I suppose.'

Driving home, she'd found it hard to stop thinking about it. Why did Dan like her? He was only a few years younger than her, but it seemed as if he was from a different generation. He was so fit, so full of fun and dreams.

She reached briefly and touched the cheek where he'd kissed her. It was just a friendly thing, she told herself. She was overthinking things as usual.

Arriving home, the last person in for once, she picked up the coats from the hallway and hung them up; instantly feeling a little bit better. Walking through to the living room, she found Toby, sitting on a sofa that had been half cleared – evidently he was learning to troubleshoot enough to find somewhere to rest his bottom.

It wasn't much, but she clocked it up as progress anyway.

'Where're the kids?' she asked.

'Upstairs doing homework,' he replied. 'Or that's what they said, at least.'

'Right.'

'We cooked a pizza,' he said, looking at her as if for approval.

'That's . . . that's great.'

'There's a slice for you through there.'

'Oh! Thank you!'

'You're welcome.' He shifted slightly in his seat. 'How was your meeting?'

'Oh, OK.'

'And that Camberwaddle guy – still in hospital?'

'Yeah, but he's going to be OK, I think.'

'That's good.'

'Are you OK?' she asked, noticing his downbeat tone.

'Yeah. Well, kind of. It's not been the best day,' he replied.

'No?'

'No. Let's just say there was an incident in the loos.'

'Knickers?'

'Knickers.'

'Oh.'

'Yeah, and then when we went into the studio, Hatty saw the top of them poking out of my trousers and decided to, um, ping my elastic.'

'She didn't!'

'Yep.'

'What did you say?'

'I didn't know what to say. She's kind of my boss; I guess I'm going to have to put up with some of it.'

'You shouldn't . . .'

'Anyway,' he said, 'that's not what I wanted to talk to you about. After work I was walking to my car and, well, I'd taken my jacket off, and there were paparazzi . . .'

'Right?'

'And, you know. I bent to get in and . . . well, the knickers. Cameras.'

She nodded. 'Online?'

'Yeah,' he said, 'I daren't even go on social media right now.'

'Oh, Toby. But how about you make a joke of it – face up

205

to it? It could make for a fun discussion? Gender roles, that kind of thing.'

His brow furrowed. 'You know,' he said as if astonished, 'that's actually not a bad idea.'

'Thank you.'

'And you're OK, you know – physically?' she prompted.

'What do you mean?'

'I don't know – I guess you've been looking a bit pale recently. I thought maybe you were overdoing it or I don't know, a bit too stressed?'

'I suppose I am, a bit,' he said.

'Work stuff?'

'No. Well, yes that. But also . . . it's us.'

'Us?' She felt suddenly afraid. 'I mean I know things haven't been ideal, but . . . ?'

'I just wondered – is there something you want to tell me?'

She felt slightly sick. Had he recognised her on TV? She thought frantically of her Martha B. outfit, crammed into a carrier bag in her wardrobe. Maybe he'd found it. Maybe he'd put two and two together. She was going to have a lot of explaining to do.

'You just . . . well, you're late again. And I know you left work on time, I rang in and you'd already gone.'

'Oh!' She felt herself relax. He was worried she was having an affair. Not starring in her own rap group.

'Is there . . . is there something I need to know about?'

This was a difficult question to answer honestly. There was something she probably ought to tell him. But it wouldn't be what he expected. 'No, not really.'

'What do you mean, not really?' he paled.

'No, no,' she said. 'Seriously, nothing like that. I'm not

206

having an affair.' She sat down next to him, the sofa crink-
ling with plastic packets. 'Nothing like that.'

'Oh. So, what?'

'I'm not sure if I'm ready to tell you yet.'

He looked at her alarmed. 'Are you . . . are you ill or something?'

It was time. 'Look, I wasn't going to say anything – I
suppose I sort of wondered whether you'd put two and two
together after the TV thing. But I'm Martha.'

He looked at her with complete confusion.

'What?'

She couldn't do it, she realised. Not until she knew what
she wanted to do about it. He'd think she was completely
mad.

'I mean . . . I'm *like* Martha – you know, Martha B.
I want to . . . I'm just trying to do something for myself.
Something . . . well, different.'

'And you can't tell me about it?'

'Not yet. I will. It's just . . .'

'And you're not having an affair?'

'I am *absolutely not* having an affair,' she said, her mind
suddenly darting to a picture of Dan, his lips pressed to her
cheek.

'Then I guess I'll have to trust you,' Toby said, kissing
her gently.

'Thank you.'

'Now, let's get this sofa cleared off shall we? I think I got
a paper cut on my arse from that empty Pringle packet.'

Chapter Thirty-Two

'So you're sure you can't make the quiz tonight?' Ann asked as they sat together on a bench munching a lunch of shop-bought sandwiches.

One benefit – if there could be such a thing – of having a cupboard office that stank to high heaven was that she was breaking the habit of eating her lunch over her computer, Clare thought. Instead, she'd been out twice for a proper lunch this week, and today – to celebrate a rare moment of sun – she had chosen to hit the park with Ann.

'Not this time,' she said, her cheeks reddening. She wondered why she hadn't told Ann the truth about her busy evening. It wasn't as if her friend would misjudge her or laugh at her – hopefully. And she wasn't exactly going to ring up the clients and spill the beans.

'And you're sure everything's OK?'

Clare nodded, then said, 'Look, I can trust you right?'

'Of course!' Ann's brow furrowed with concern. 'I knew . . . I mean, I felt there was something up. Is it the office stuff? You're not feeling depressed? Look,' she reached and grabbed Clare's hand, 'whatever it is, we're in it together, OK?'

'Oh God, it's nothing . . . I mean, you don't have to worry about me,' Clare said, quickly. 'There's . . . I'm perfectly well, all things considered.' She felt a pang of guilt – had her economy with the truth made her friend worried? 'I . . . well, you know a few weeks ago, I took the day off sick?'

'Oh, the underpants day!' Ann grinned.

'That's the one! Well, I wasn't . . . it wasn't strictly true, I didn't have a sickness bug; I was so fed up with it all . . . and then I found myself . . .'

Ann nodded, her face full of sympathy and concern.

'Auditioning for *You've Got Talent* – the local round.'

'What?' Ann looked as if she thought she'd possibly misheard. 'An audition?'

'Well, yeah . . .'

'What . . . why . . . Why didn't you say anything?'

'Oh, I hadn't realised I was going to do it until I sort of found myself doing it . . .'

'How does that even happen?'

Clare explained about the bus. About getting on it almost on a whim.

'But . . . no offence, but what talent?' Ann said, her brow still furrowed. 'You don't play an instrument do you, or dance, I don't think?'

'You know my poems?'

'Well, sort of. You never let me read them, remember?'

'Yeah, well, I find it . . . it's just embarrassing, isn't it? The window into my soul and all that.'

'OK?' Ann was looking at her with a different kind of concern.

'It was . . . I mean, it wasn't planned. I just – the bus turned up at my usual stop, taking people to the auditions and I got on. I had my notebook and I thought, what the hell!'

'Good for you!' Ann said, her face splitting in an un-expected smile.

'Really?'

'Yeah. I mean, it's private isn't it – like asking to read someone's diary? But I always felt curious about your

209

writing, like it was a piece of you that you were ashamed of or something . . . so yeah. Good for you!'

'It didn't go as planned!'

It was a good thing, Clare thought later, that Ann had known her for a long time. Because coming out as an undercover internet rap sensation was not for the faint-hearted. When she'd brought up the YouTube footage on her phone to show Ann, her friend had been amazed.

'I saw that and thought how great it was,' she said. 'But I didn't recognise you at all! But it's obviously you – I can see it now!'

'Don't worry, nobody else has made the connection, thank goodness,' Clare said. 'You don't expect it do you?'

'You can say that again. I've always thought you were quite . . . well, shy really?'

'Shy?'

'Well, you know. You're great at your job, and confident – although maybe not corporately sexy,' quipped Ann, 'but when you've been to the quiz, or we've been out, you're always quite reserved, aren't you?'

Clare had always felt a little awkward – a remnant from her chronically shy schooldays. But she hadn't realised it was noticeable to anyone else.

'Oh,' she said. 'Really?'

'Yeah, don't get me wrong, it's not a bad thing,' Ann said. 'Better than being like Will and letting it all hang out.'

'Well, there is that. No Lycra unitards here!'

The pair of them grinned.

'I honestly didn't think you had it in you,' Ann said. 'Wow.'

'I don't think I do have it in me really. I'm sort of forcing myself to do it. You know, giving the boys their chance. It's nice – it's nice being up there when you're in the moment. And it's thrilling getting my words out there, I suppose. But it's not something I'm going to go forwards with afterwards.'

'Why not?'

'Well, who'd give up living *this* dream?' Clare said, brandishing her cheese and pickle sandwich. 'Corner office, great career, cheese-and-pickle for lunch.'

'You've got a point,' Ann smiled.

'And you don't think I'm weird?'

'I think,' her friend said, 'you are absolutely brilliant.'

Chapter Thirty-Three

Clare had driven to the theatre straight after work to meet up with Dan, get changed, and have a quick run through before they took part in the televised auditions. To the public it would be round one, but in reality they'd already been through two auditions to get this far. She'd never look at reality shows in the same way.

As she put the final touches to her stage make-up – ensuring she really looked nothing like Martha B.'s shy alter ego Clare, she noticed she'd had two missed calls from Toby. Poor Toby. She'd told him she had to go to some sort of lecture this evening but he hadn't looked too convinced.

She couldn't ring him back now – they were due to go on in ten minutes and everyone seemed to be almost rigid with stress about timings. A man with a clipboard called out the time every thirty seconds or so, and each time he did, different people went scurrying here and there in order to fulfil their various roles.

'I'm not feeling too confident,' she whispered to Dan.

'Don't be ridiculous. You can't back out now.'

'Want a bet?'

But he was right. Adrenaline pumped through her veins and she'd give almost anything to rush out into the street and get home in double-quick time. But she'd never forgive herself if she did.

Eezee Troupe were dressed in black trousers and white

T-shirts with an 'E' emblazoned on them in a bright yellow. Nadia had spent the last week printing out and ironing on special labels for the occasion.

The outfit she'd finally settled on for Clare — who, it seemed, didn't get a lot of say in it any more — was a pair of bright yellow jeans with a matching T-shirt. She'd stand out on the stage like a beacon. 'But no one will know it's you,' Nadia had reassured her, expertly applying make-up and helping her to fit her new blonde wig. 'So it doesn't matter, right?'

'Right,' she'd said, doubtfully.

They'd run through their routine a few times, and Clare was fairly confident she could get through the three-minute slot unscathed.

She looked over the piece of paper in her hand for the last time. She'd been reading it constantly ever since she finally managed to pen something in her lunch hour a couple of days beforehand. Dan had read it through and nodded. And the rest of the troupe had clapped when she'd rapped it out for the first time. She'd felt like a bit of an idiot, but at the same time, the applause had been quite gratifying.

'Five minutes,' said the man with the clipboard.

A young girl flashed past her, blue hair tucked under a cap, face fixed with concentration.

They were near the edge of the stage now, and she could see the presenters in their familiar get-up, laughing and joking as they did on TV. There was a screen displaying the footage, but there was no sound. She watched one of the judges wax lyrical about the guy on stage, an enormous smile on her face. Clearly he'd done well.

Then there was momentum. The previous act — a magician who'd managed to make a dove appear out of his zipper — walked off and winked at them as he went past. She'd heard

213

whispers that he was one of the hot favourites to win, and based on the audience reaction, was quite likely on track.

'You're on,' hissed a runner and Clare found herself propelled forward onto a stage, the harsh lights making it difficult to see the audience beyond.

The four judges sat in front of her, glossier and more groomed than she could have imagined.

'OK, darling,' said Steven Cruel, the main judge. 'What's your name and where do you come from?'

'I'm, um, Martha, I'm 36 and I'm from . . . Hertfordshire,' she said.

'And the boys?'

'These are Eezee Troupe,' Dan said, stepping forward, with a small bow of deference. 'Martha's backing dancers.'

'Great, great . . .' Steven glanced at the other judges. 'Well, best of luck.'

'Just three minutes,' she thought to herself. Three minutes of her life. Over in a flash.

The music began to play and the boys bounced out and took their positions. A spotlight shone on the centre of the stage – her moment. Propelling herself forward on legs that felt like jelly, Clare stumbled to the front and raised the mic to her lips.

'It's Martha B., here, yeah and I'm livin' it loud,
I'm calling to the women – girls, you oughta be proud.
Say what? You're over thirty and you feel like you've had it,
You're just in the beginning, come on ladies let's have it.
We're smashin' the glass ceiling, showin' that we're
*   contenders,*
It's time we stopped taking shit just 'cos of our gender.
Too right, we care for kids and yeah, we're excellent mothers,
But that's just one small talent, there are plenty of others.

214

We're wasted in our offices, ignored in the board room,
Well, tell the men to shift it, yeah, they need to make more
  room.
We ain't into knockin' men, but there's space for us all yeah,
We're not just into clothes, shoes, nails and styling our hair,
  yeah.
So what? I'm pushin' forty, but nah that shouldn't bore you,
I'm fit and bright and beautiful, and growin' in value.
My age ain't just a number, it shows that I've lived, right?
But if you say I'm past it, man you're in for a fight, right?
Here's Eezee Troupe, my boys they're here and backing me up,
We women should be visible, I'll tell you what's up.
This is a revolution, yeah all the women are risin',
You've kept us down for years, so this should not be
  surprisin'.
Don't take us for granted, yeah, the bar we are raisin',
Don't try to beat us, join us and it could be amazin'.
No more miss invisible – invincible more like,
If you don't like what you're seein' then just get on your bike,
  right?
It's Martha B. right here "mehtoo" but yo I won't accept it,
So get on board, let's change the world or man you'll regret it.'

As she fell into the agreed modified version of the splits (which basically involved her kneeling on one leg while sticking the other one out as straight as she could manage), the audience roared. Women stood up, waving #MehToo banners – one was wearing a T-shirt with a screenshot of Clare from the YouTube video. Another pair were wearing shirts that read 'We're Martha's Crew'.

Clare also noticed a woman towards the back waving a small sign that said 'Go for it!' It was Ann, Clare realised. How on earth had she got hold of a ticket?

She stumbled, slightly, as if in a dream. Then Dan was by her side, arm around her, holding her up.

They faced the four judges, whose faces were giving nothing away. 'Well, well, well,' said the younger of the female judges. 'I think you might have touched a nerve in here!'

Steven Cruel was shaking his head and smiling in a way he clearly hoped said 'I'm down with this female solidarity thing' while keeping his masculinity intact. 'It's a "yes" from me,' he said, leaning in to the microphone.

The other male judge nodded. 'What's not to love? You're keepin' it real and livin' it large, and you've certainly made an impression here!' he said, turning to the audience who whooped in appreciation. 'It's a "yes" from me.'

Three yesses would see them through. The crowd fell silent as the third judge – an actress and singer called Macey considered her verdict. 'Interesting,' she said. 'I hear what you say, but is this the best way to reach your audience? Are women actually going to take notice of a rap artist?'

She hesitated and in that moment Clare realised how much she actually wanted to get through, whatever the cost to her legal career. Was it all going to slip from her grasp; were they really going to get a 'no'?

After an almost unbearable silence, Macey suddenly burst into life. 'I say, YES THEY WILL!' she cried, standing up with a grin and pounding down on the gold buzzer. Confetti fell from above the stage and the boys began leaping and hugging each other.

Clare felt Dan's arms around her waist. 'Golden buzzer!' he said. 'It means we're fast-tracked to the live finals!'

'It does?' It had been a while since she'd watched the show.

Feeling as if she was in a film about her life rather than

actually on the stage being applauded for rapping in front of a live audience, Clare bowed and exited the stage waving with the boys.

'Oh my god, this is IT!' Dan was shouting. 'Boys we've made it!'

Backstage, sipping a glass of vinegary wine that a runner had shoved into her hand, Clare tried to call Toby back. There was no answer.

'Call for Martha B.?' one of the stage crew shouted, holding a phone aloft. 'Martha B.?'

'Here!' she said, raising her hand. The runner appeared at her side. 'Call for you,' she said, shoving an enormous phone into Clare's hand, then added, 'loved the act by the way,' before disappearing on her next errand.

Who would actually call her at the theatre? Who would know how to call her here? And who would actually ask for her by her stage name? As Clare put the phone to her ear, she couldn't imagine who it might be.

'Hello? This is, erm, Martha speaking...' she said, nervously.

'Hello Mrs B.? Or may I call you Martha?' The voice on the other end of the line sounded formal, but was somehow familiar.

'Martha's fine,' she said. 'Who is this?'

'It's Toby Bailey. From *Woman's World.*'

'Toby!' she gasped.

'Er, yes. I... well, usually my producer makes these calls. But we've been having some trouble getting hold of you so I thought perhaps I would... I knew you'd be at the theatre so...'

He doesn't realise, she thought. He really thinks he's talking to Martha.

'So, you're calling me, why?' she said, cautiously, changing her tone a little to sound less like herself. Was this a joke? Had he seen through her cover and was trying to reel her in to some sort of confession?

'Yes. I wanted to ... well, arrange a meeting – an interview, perhaps?' he continued.

'An interview?'

'Yes, you know, on *Woman's World*? I'd love to, eh, pick your brain about the whole hashtag MehToo movement.'

'Oh, I'm not sure I could ...'

'We'd ... it'd be so great for the show,' he said, almost pleadingly.

She felt her sympathy well up. 'Well, yeah, OK,' she said, wondering what on earth she was getting herself into.

'Great. Great. May I take a number? I'll get my secretary to ...'

'Sure.' Clare gave him Nadia's number. 'That's Nadia, she's, um, my stylist I suppose. Well, you can get a message to me through her.'

'Right. Don't want to expose your secret identity!'

'I'm sorry?'

'Well, you know. The mysterious Martha B. Who is she? Where does she come from?' Toby said.

'Yeah, ha!' Had Toby always been this abysmal on the phone? Or was it just when he was speaking to inspirational feminist middle-aged rap sensations? It was an unanswerable question.

'Right. Bye then,' she said, feeling slightly sick.

'Bye – and thank you.'

Chapter Thirty-Four

As Clare walked up to the front door late that evening, she felt a little like a teenage version of herself coming home too late from the pub on a Friday – nervous about inserting the key then finding her mother with a face like thunder on the other side of the door.

The curtain upstairs flickered as she opened the door and she heard Katie call Toby. 'Mum's here!'

Then Toby was standing there in the hall, not looking as different from her mother as she might have liked, hands on hips, mouth in a straight line. All he needed was an apron, a pair of slippers and a roll-up to complete the picture. 'Hi, Clare,' he said, as if he had caught her out, instead of simply found her arriving home at more or less exactly the time she'd said she would be there.

'Hi!' she said.

'Hi, Mum!' Katie said, bouncing into the hall like a puppy and giving Clare a squeeze.

'What's that in aid of?' Clare said, grinning at the unusual level of attention. 'And what are you doing up?'

'She couldn't sleep,' Toby said. 'Thought it wouldn't hurt if she waited up.'

'Aww, that's sweet,' Clare said, giving Katie a squeeze.

'She's been online. Reading that hashtag MehToo stuff,' Toby said.

'Yeah, do you feel like that, Mum?' Katie asked, head tilted to one side. 'You know, like we take you for granted?'

'Maybe a bit,' Clare admitted. 'Sometimes.'

'I'm so sorry,' Katie said, hugging her again. 'Because, you know, we do all appreciate you, Mum.'

'Of course we do,' Toby said, joining in after his daughter gave him a look.

'Good,' she said, frowning.

'Come on, put your mother down and I'll make her a cup of tea,' Toby said, taking Clare's bag as if caring for someone who was completely incapable of looking after herself. 'And get yourself to bed.'

'OK,' Katie said, working hard to appear reluctant. She was clearly exhausted.

'So,' Clare said, as Toby set down a cup of steaming tea in front of her on the breakfast bar.

They sipped in silence, before he spoke.

'How was it?' he asked, guardedly.

'What? Oh! The lecture? Pretty boring,' she lied.

'Pretty long too?'

'Well . . . yeah . . .' she felt a shiver of nausea. It was pretty obvious she was lying about something.

'You know, I do miss you,' he said.

'You do?'

'Yeah. We're barely in the same room for five minutes these days.'

'I know.'

He moved his hand along the counter to cover hers for a second. 'Things are a bit . . . well, things seem a bit weird at the moment, don't they?'

'Maybe just a bit.'

'I've got . . . I dunno. My head, it's all over the place,' he said. 'I am trying you know. Katie's been lecturing me about hashtag MehToo and it's clear she thinks I'm pretty crap.'

'She said that?'

'Well, not in so many words . . . I guess we've both been a bit preoccupied recently.'

'I know,' Clare said. She thought about the applause she and the troupe had received when the confetti had rained down. The flash of the cameras. The fact that the footage would be aired on ITV in the week leading up to the live final.

So, tell him! her mind urged. After all, Steph and Ann had taken it well. And he was her husband; they'd drifted a bit recently but he still had her back. But it wasn't so much what she was doing, but how much she'd already hidden from him. How could he trust her once she revealed all of this was going on? And how could she explain why she hadn't confided in him in the first place?

She felt almost sick with nerves as they climbed into bed and Toby switched out the light. It was ridiculous. A few hours ago she'd been rapping on stage and now she was scared to speak the truth to her husband.

'Toby?' she said, in the darkness.

'Yes?'

'I think . . . I think I'm ready to tell you . . .'

'What?'

'Look,' she said, feeling his arm snake around her back and pull her in for a spoon. 'I . . . well, you know something's going on, right?'

'Mmm hmmm,' he said, sleepily.

'Well, a few weeks ago, I took a day off work . . .' she said.

'Hmm?'

As she related the story to her husband she could feel the weight of her own subterfuge drifting away. She'd been ridiculous, she thought. She'd been so convinced that Toby didn't really care what was going on in her life that she'd underestimated him. And here he was, lying silent in the darkness listening to her every word.

'And guess what?' she finished. 'We're in the live final!'

Silence.

'Toby?'

Silence.

'What do you think?'

Her husband, whom she'd assumed had been listening intently all that time, let out a tiny snore in her ear.

'Toby!' she said, poking him harder in the ribs than she'd intended. 'Toby – what do you think?'

'Mmm?' he said. 'It's OK. Shhh . . .'

She lay awake for almost an hour, feeling a mixture of disappointment and anger. Because if Toby couldn't even stay awake when she'd make it obvious she'd be revealing something important, then he didn't care about her at all.

Chapter Thirty-Five

The phone rang at 9.30 a.m., meaning it was either a sales call, an emergency, or someone without the social grace to realise that it was FAR TOO EARLY to call someone on a Saturday.

Clare padded down the stairs, feeling groggy. Her muscles ached from the enthusiastic dancing last night and she could barely make it to the hallway. 'Someone had better be dead,' she muttered under her breath. 'Or at least seriously injured.'

'Hello?' she said, trying to sound bright and upbeat. She sounded more like an eighty-year-old man.

'Oh, hello, is that Toby?'

It was Hatty.

'No,' she cleared her throat. 'No, it's Clare.'

'Ah, sorry didn't recognise you there!'

'It's OK.'

'Well look, Bill and I have to pop down to Hatfield this morning – his tailor lives there. And I thought it might be fun to meet for coffee. Or even pop round, if that would be OK?'

'Oh. Of course,' Clare said, glancing frantically at the mess around her. 'What ... what sort of time?'

'I think we'll probably be with you in about an hour. That's lovely! Toodle pip!'

'Oh! That's a bit ...'

But the phone was dead.

In her foggy, sleep-addled brain, Clare had assumed Hatty would be suggesting two or three o'clock in the afternoon at the least. Were they seriously going to drop in on them in just an hour?

'Kids! Toby!' Clare yelled. 'Come here!'

To get things anywhere near straight enough, they were going to have to work as a team.

An hour later, exhausted but triumphant, Clare opened the door to Hatty and Bill with a smile. The hall behind her was spotless. The coffee was brewing. The kids were making themselves scarce. And as long as nobody opened the cupboard under the stairs she was pretty sure they could pull off the illusion of being enviably clutter and mess free.

'I didn't realise,' Alfie had panted at one point, 'how difficult it is to clean up.'

Clare had nodded, although in truth this was a particularly epic tidying up session, bearing in mind nobody had cleaned up properly for about ten days and the rot was definitely setting in.

'Sorry,' he'd added. 'I'm crap, aren't I?'

'You'll learn,' she'd replied, ruffling his hair and realising that what she'd thought was a messy mop was actually carefully coiffed and covered in product.

'Hatty! Bill!' she said, now, taking their coats. 'Can I get you anything?'

'Oh, just a coffee. Smells lovely.'

'Ah, Toby!' Hatty added, as she entered the kitchen. 'How are you? Awful business yesterday.'

He shrugged.

'Yesterday?' Clare asked.

'Yes, didn't he tell you? Oh, that's so like Toby! Not wanting to upset you.'

'But what happened?' Clare studied her husband's face.

224

'Oh, just some of these MehToo women. Waving placards during my interview, that sort of thing.' Toby's cheeks began to flush slightly.

'Oh.'

'And, well . . . Yelling things about me in the street.'

'Oh.'

'And yesterday, well, they flew a blimp outside the window in the studio during filming,' Toby reddened even further. 'It was supposed to be me. Wearing high heels, lipstick and knickers – you know, after that photo of me went viral. They're angry about the *Woman's World* thing. It's all over the internet.'

'Oh Toby!' She hadn't had a chance to watch anything – in fact, she'd avoided the news, not wanting to see any clips of the show that had now – again, according to Dan's texts – gone viral.

'But I've got it in hand,' Toby said, slipping an arm around her waist.

'Oh?'

'Yes, believe it or not, I managed to get through to the woman herself on the phone last night. Martha B.,' he grinned, his ears reddening.

'Oh, that's amazing!' Hatty said.

'Yes, she's agreed to have an interview with me – hopefully this week. I hope we can get a handle on this thing.'

'Right. How?' Clare said, a little too sharply.

'In fact, I was going to speak to you later,' Toby said, reaching for Clare's hand and squeezing it earnestly. 'But I really hope you'll come with me to the interview. You know, a bit of solidarity, moral support. You can stay in the green room – maybe even meet the woman herself!'

In any other situation, she would have, but this was tricky. 'Well . . .' she began.

'I think it'll look good, you know – play out well in the media,' he added.

'Well, work's quite busy . . . but . . .' stammered Clare. 'I'll try.'

'That's a girl!' Hatty said, winking.

Clare broached the subject again after Hatty and Bill had left. 'Toby,' she said.

'Yes?' he looked up from the crossword he was attempting.

'Do you . . . did you hear much of what I said last night?'

'Last night?'

'Yes. Um . . . I told you something, in bed?'

'Oh.' His cheeks flushed. 'Sorry.'

'It's OK.' She noticed again that her husband's face looked a bit pinched and tired. 'Are you OK?'

'I'm . . . yeah, I guess.' He looked awkward and shifted slightly in his chair.

She'd been angry about his dropping asleep on her, but looking at his face now, she was more concerned. 'Why do you think you're so tired?'

'Not sure,' he shrugged. 'I guess, irregular hours. They say that's pretty crap for the constitution.'

'Is the job worth it, Toby?'

'Yes, yes,' he said. 'If anything, being on *Woman's World* should mean that things will get a bit more regular now. No news reports – or very few. Mostly arranging things at more sociable hours.'

'OK.'

'And you know, the worries – about the protest and that. I hope . . . I think I can get on top of things. The Martha B. interview might help. And Hatty's going to advise me a bit on language.'

'That's good.'

'So,' he said, looking at her. 'Sorry I fell asleep ... I'm awake now – I think!' he smiled sheepishly. 'What did you want to tell me?'

She couldn't do it, she realised. She couldn't blow her cover – he needed Martha to rescue him first.

Chapter Thirty-Six

Clare let herself into the meeting room cautiously, not quite sure what she'd find behind the door. To her relief, Nigel and Will were – at least at the moment – dressed in their normal office wear. And there wasn't a leotard in sight.

A few other staff members were there, including Ann, who'd been waiting for her this morning with a bunch of flowers. 'You were amazing!' she'd said.

'I can't believe you came!'

'Where else would I be!' her friend had said.

Clare took her seat next to Ann and they grinned at each other. 'No live performances tonight then?' Ann quipped.

'Never can tell.'

On the whiteboard at the front of the room, someone had scribbled 'Are you feeling Corporately Sexy?'

'Hi, hello,' Nigel said, a few minutes later when it was clear that this was the sum total of attendees. 'How are you feeling today?'

'Fine thanks!' Clare said, at the same time as everyone else chanted out 'corporately sexy!'

Nigel shot her a look. 'Did you, er, not get the email?'

'Sorry,' she said, 'I haven't had a chance to check through my inbox this morning.'

'Right,' Nigel said, disappointedly, shuffling some papers. 'Well, today's workshop is about positive mantras. Will?'

Will stepped forward, clearly in his element. 'Thanks,

Nigel,' he said, as if he was a TV news reporter receiving a handover from the studio. 'Well, thank you all for coming today. I think you'll find this session particularly useful.

'Hans Hankerton writes in chapter thirty of his book *Be Your Own Guru*, that in order to be corporately sexy, we must embody the concept. We must become one with our business; must allow ourselves to be completely absorbed with becoming the best employee or business manager we can be.

'And this involves mantra recital,' he continued, scribbling 'mantra recital' on the board. 'Each morning at the start of a workday, I recite the following mantras to myself, so that I truly take on the character of Successful Lawyer Will – a Corporately Sexy Businessman.'

All this without a hint of irony.

Will closed his eyes, moved his legs into the widest power stance possible and took a deep breath through his nose, allowing it to gush out of his mouth in a torrent.

'I am sexy, I am sexy, I *am* sexy!' he chanted.

'I'm a winner, I'm a winner, I *am* a winner.

'Will is successful, Will is successful, Will *is* successful!

'Today, will be a *sexy* day.'

He opened his eyes and looked around the room so confidently that they all felt obliged to clap. 'Thank you,' he said. 'Now we all know our strengths and weaknesses. We all know the elements of our work selves we need to address. I spent months working on my mantras, so don't feel too much pressure to come up with the right words straightaway. But what I want you to do is jot down some phrases that, over time, will become as effective as mine.'

At that moment, Elaine, the office manager, walked in with a platter of sandwiches, admittedly one of the meeting's main draws. They'd been ordered from a local delicatessen and were stuffed with smoked salmon, avocado and all things expensive and on trend.

'Not yet, not yet!' Will admonished, as they all reached forward. 'Mantras, then sustenance. For as Hans Hankerton says, if we do not nourish the mind, how can the body ever be fed?'

Clare took a glance at Nigel to see whether he was having second thoughts about the whole mantra thing. She'd known him for almost a decade and until recently he'd hated corporate speak. And he wasn't the sort of guy who'd usually be taken in by this weird, self-help language.

To her horror, he was sitting there, gazing at Will practically entranced. She vowed to google Corporate Sexiness later, just to see whether it was linked to some sort of brainwashing cult.

'Work hard,' Clare jotted idly on her pad. 'Get paid.' She glanced over at the others. Half were sitting looking slightly confused, others were scribbling diligently. Ann seemed to have written a couple of lines and was now drawing a picture of a sandwich.

Clare found her mind wandering once again to the weekend; to Hatty and Bill's surprise visit. It had been nice, actually. Once she'd actually got her breath back from the frantic cleaning.

At one point, Toby had taken Bill for a look at their garage extension – the only part of the house he'd decorated himself. He was particularly proud of it, and actually it wasn't bad. Hatty had sipped her coffee and regarded her for a moment over the top of it.

'How are you, you know, with Toby's promotion?' she'd asked, suddenly.

'Me? Well, I'm delighted of course,' Clare had said, automatically.

'Are you sure? I see how busy things are for you and I wonder whether I've actually done you a disservice,' Hatty had continued. 'I mean, Toby's very talented — I wouldn't have put in a good word otherwise. But with two children at home, and his needing to be in London more. Well, it's obvious who's going to end up picking up the slack.'

Clare had grimaced. 'Well, you know how it is. I mean, I don't mind. He's very supportive of my career. And the kids are older now.'

'But it's hard.'

'It can be.'

'And it's not as if you have a lot of time on your hands. I imagine you're up to your neck at work sometimes.'

'Oh, just every day!' Clare had grinned.

'Well, I really hope I haven't made things harder.'

'Oh, no. Honestly, it's not so bad. It's . . .'

'It annoys me though,' Hatty had said, decisively, setting her cup down and accidentally splashing coffee on the kitchen table. 'Because, well, it's the assumption of it, isn't it? The way men can take on more in their jobs and we're all meant to celebrate. But when we want to, we end up apologising for it.'

'Well . . . yes.' Clare had thought of her nights out with Eezee Troupe and how difficult it had been to find the time. Whereas Toby would call to say he'd be late and know that she would cover for him without question.

'I missed my chance, you know,' Hatty had said, her eyes looking suddenly misty.

'You did? But you've got a great career.'

'Yes, but it's someone else's great career. Not what I . . . well, not my first choice.'

'Oh.'

'I loved presenting,' she'd continued, 'loved the interaction,

231

the buzz of live TV. And I was good at it, too! Then a few years off raising the kids, a bit of part-time work, the breakdown, which I'm sure you saw splashed in the papers. It was postnatal depression actually, but people weren't quite as "woke" when it came to mental health a decade ago. And suddenly when I came back, with a few more wrinkles and eye-bags than they preferred, I was shoved to the side. Promoted off people's screens.'

'I'm sure that's not—'

'Oh, believe me. It was made pretty clear to me when it happened. They appreciated my talent, my eye for a good story. But didn't want this old bag to deliver it.'

'That's awful!'

'There was a moment the other day,' Hatty had said, 'when I thought . . . Well, when the director asked me for ideas of who might make a good presenter. And I thought he was asking me in a roundabout way. You know, seeing if I'd be up for the job!'

'Oh, you'd be brilliant at it!'

'Tell them that,' Hatty had said. 'Toby's great. He deserves a break, I really believe that. And I'm pleased for him. But I suppose I hoped they'd give me a shot at it.'

'And you didn't say?'

'I hinted as much as I dared.'

At that moment, the men had clattered back into the kitchen. 'Three coats of emulsion!' Toby had been saying, as Bill shook his head in apparent amazement.

'Are you OK?' Bill had said, noticing Hatty's slightly red eyes.

'Oh yes, don't worry about me,' Hatty had said, suddenly back to her old self. 'Just talking about . . . well . . .'

'Women's problems,' Clare had interjected, truthfully.

'Ah.' Both Toby and Bill had looked uncomfortable and

for a moment Clare had been tempted to mention uteruses or periods or vaginas just to make them squirm.

But she wasn't that petty. Not quite.

Later, when they'd washed up together before popping out for lunch, Toby had asked her if she'd support him.

'I do support you,' she'd said, quite affronted.

'No, I mean . . . next week. With this Martha B. character. She's agreed to meet me. And to be honest, Clare, I'm terrified.'

'Terrified?'

'Yes, she looks so intimidating, so confident you know? All that colour. That, that hair. All the hashtag business.'

'Really?'

'Yeah, and her music. Her lyrics really speak to people. It's like meeting Madonna, you know? Or Beyoncé, or, or . . . Big Narstie.'

'Big Narstie?'

'Yeah, you know. Powerful, right? But kind of . . . well, sexy at the same time.'

'Oh.'

'So, will you come?'

'I'll think about it . . .' she'd said. Which at least was true. She'd be thinking about it most of the week. What would she say? Would Toby recognise her close-up? And could she get out of it somehow?

'Sandwich?' Will asked now, appearing at her side and interrupting her reverie. 'Looks like you've made a good start.' He nodded at the desk.

She looked down at the pad on which she'd been doodling subconsciously and saw the words.

Go to work. Get paid. Powerful, but sexy.

Chapter Thirty-Seven

'Hello, Stefan, how are you?' Clare asked nervously after Ann put the call from Camberwaddle through.

'Not too bad, thank you,' he replied in a voice that didn't quite sound as robust as usual. 'Still in the hospital, of course. Having the pipes flushed out this afternoon, apparently.'

'Oh, I see . . .'

'Arteries, I mean. Bypass apparently.'

'Right.'

'Too much good living, my wife says, heh.' He tried to laugh but was stalled by a coughing fit.

'Gosh,' she said. 'Well, we'll all be thinking of you here. But should you really be on the phone? I'm sure your assistant said—'

'Yes, yes, I know the conveyancing's all under control,' he said, 'but I was going to ask you about your litigation team.'

'Right?'

'Yes, I mean, I'm not a litigious man, per se. But this whole brush with death business has left me, not angry as such, but well, *indignant* as a consumer.'

'You want to sue the hospital?'

'Oh, no. They've been marvellous. Got the ticker restarted, all that. I mean the bastards who got me in this shape in the first place.'

'Who are . . . ?'

'It's more of a question of who it *isn't* than who it is. Crisp manufacturers, oil producers, chocolate makers, bakeries, pizza restaurants, that clown chap – you know – Ronald . . . the list is extensive!'

'But . . . what would you be suing them for?'

'For clogging up my arteries of course. And do you know the beauty of it, Clare?'

'The beauty?'

'It's a limitless suit. Imagine when I win how many other suits we can line up. It'll be the ultimate class action. We can set up phone lines, take the bastards down.'

'The crisp manufacturers?' she said, a little faintly.

'All of them.'

'Well, I'm not sure—'

'Yes, yes,' he said, hastily, 'I realise you're not a *litigator*, but I have reason to believe your firm has quite the litigation department. My last piece of litigation, well, it didn't work out. And I'd rather have all the legal stuff done under one roof, so to speak. Anyway, I was wondering if you could introduce me to William Spence?'

'Will? Of course . . .' she said. 'Shall I put you through to him now?'

'Oh, do you think he'll take my call? I'm sure he must be very busy,' replied the man who had once phoned her at three in the morning to talk about garage access. 'Wouldn't like to disturb.'

'I'm sure he'll be delighted,' Clare replied through gritted teeth.

'Well, if you're sure. I must say, I'm impressed with his work.'

'His work?' Was there a chipped-tooth class action being filed that she hadn't yet heard of?

'Yes, well, the way he's really there for clients – in their time

235

of need so to speak. I was resuscitated, you know. They've probably told you. Anyway, my only lasting memory of the whole process was looking up at those defibrillator things and reading the words "Tell someone who cares" – and the details of Mr Spence at your firm. It was like a message from God – a higher power showing me the way forward!'

'Right . . .' she said.

Will poked his head in her office an hour later grinning from ear to ear. She squinted as the light bounced off his bared teeth and straight into her eye. 'Thanks for the recommendation,' he said. 'Do you know, he's already offered me a retainer. Nigel's put the champagne on ice!'

'That's great,' she said, trying to smile.

'Look, it's nearly finishing time. Do you fancy nipping out for a drink?'

'Oh, I'd better not.'

He looked suddenly crestfallen. 'Look, I hope you don't mind me saying. But I feel as if we've never really . . . well, connected. I hope . . . I mean, have I upset you in some way?'

She looked at him, his little gelled quiff and designer suit. His even white smile. His manicured nails. 'No, of course not.' Because he hadn't, had he? It wasn't his fault that Nigel had marked him out for future greatness on account of his killer combination of penis and litigious tendencies. It wasn't even his fault she was stuck in a cupboard while he rested his buttocks on the most comfortable chair she'd ever had the pleasure to sit in.

'So, how about it? Quick gin and tonic? My treat.'

'OK,' she said, sliding the contract she was reading back into its cardboard sleeve. 'Why not?'

Her first instinct had been to say no – but something had stopped her. After all, Dan had given her and the boys a night off rehearsals. 'We'll have to get back into it though?' he'd warned. 'Can't let timings slip now.'

As they left the office building, Clare paused outside The Duck and Dive, a gastro pub she'd been to a couple of times with Ann. 'How about here?' she said.

'Do you mind if we don't?' Will said now. 'Not sure I like the atmosphere in there. Full of old people.'

'So, where?' she said, feeling a little impatient . . . and old.

'I know a great place.'

She followed him, having to take a little skip every three steps to keep up with his enormous, confident strides and almost losing him when he suddenly cut down an alleyway that led to a bar she'd never seen before. Through the window she could hear the sound of music beating away, and the signage was all glass and chrome.

He held the door open and nodded her through, grinning.

Inside, the place was heaving with young men and women in sharp suits, sporting slick haircuts. A few sat on bar stools, drinking shots. Others clustered together at tables talking shop.

She felt a shiver of recognition. She had literally walked onto the set of *Legal Minds*. On the show, the best lawyers all seemed to flock to the bar to drink tequila shots and have innuendo-soaked conversations with renegade FBI agents. Toto, we're not in Hatfield any more, she thought.

'What are you having?' Will asked. 'Vodka martini? Whisky sour? Glass of wine?'

Before Clare could answer, a ridiculously attractive-looking woman, her silky hair tumbling around her face, her make-up immaculate, came up to Will.

'Hey, well done in court today,' she said, in an American accent. 'Good job.'

Will raised his glass. 'Better luck next time, Tabitha.'

'So, will I see you later?' she pouted.

'Not tonight,' he replied and turned rather abruptly back to his drink. Clare met the woman's eye for a second and was rewarded with a scowl. Whisky sour indeed.

'Defendant's counsel,' Will said to her in lowered tones. 'Had quite a whipping in court today in the case of Smith vs. Hastings.'

'Remind me?'

'Ingrowing toenail op. Removed the wrong nail. Quite a nasty suit.' Will sipped his drink and looked darkly into thin air. Thinking. Remembering. 'Took three months to grow back, and even then it was bruised.'

'Goodness.'

He looked over his shoulder and scowled briefly before turning back to Clare and furtively whispering. 'Here's trouble.'

'What?'

'See that chap over there,' he continued. 'Police. Better watch our units tonight.'

'Right.' She glanced over and took in a muscular man, hair slicked back with wax, leaning on the bar. Catching her eye, he winked and she looked away, hastily.

She was about to ask Will about the Camberwaddle litigation, when another man wearing a cap, his face peppered with stubble, sidled up to the bar. He placed an envelope next to Will's glass. 'Phone records,' he hissed out of the corner of his mouth. 'But they didn't come from me, right?'

'Isn't that the guy from the chip shop?' she said, incredulously, when he'd disappeared.

'Best not to discuss it in here,' Will replied, glancing around. 'This could break the whole case.'

'The toenail case?'

'I've already said too much.'

'Tequila?' asked the man behind the bar, lining up a couple of shot glasses in front of them.

Will glanced at Clare.

'I'd better not,' she said. 'I've got a cottage pie in the freezer. I'll just have, um, a small white wine please.'

'I get ya,' Will said, winking as if cottage pie was code for something far more glamorous or important.

When she emerged into the early evening air half an hour later, leaving Will to live his life as a sexy lawyer in the parallel universe that clearly existed in his favourite bar, she stumbled slightly. It wasn't the wine, or at least she didn't think so. But the strangeness of it all. First Friday night. Now this.

She hadn't intended to drink anything at all – but the white wine meant that now she had to leave Claudia in the work car park. Waiting for her cab at the side of the road, she suddenly felt close to tears. When had life got so complicated? All the lies, the exhausting rehearsals. All the frickin' taxis.

Then, just as she felt herself begin to get slightly teary, she noticed a limousine with blacked-out windows purring towards her. It pulled up to the kerb in front of her and the window descended to reveal Toby's rather flushed face.

'Can I give you a lift m'lady?' he said, with a wink.

'Toby!' she said, although part of her was still struggling to register that this was in fact her husband. 'What are you . . . why are you . . . ?'

'Studio hired it for a celeb who didn't show,' he grinned. 'Shame to waste it. Anyway, was just going home and suddenly there you were.'

Sure, she was a feminist. But at that moment, galloping up on his steed, Toby had become her knight in shining armoured car.

And she didn't mind one bit.

Chapter Thirty-Eight

'Morning!' Will stepped confidently into her office the next day – hair even more coiffed than usual – and smiled.

'Hi,' Clare replied. 'Good night?'

'Not bad,' he replied, with a wink that was clearly meant to suggest that there may have been a bit of action from the ladies. 'You know how it goes!'

'Great,' she said. 'Have a good day.'

'You too!' He turned on his highly polished heel and clipped off down the corridor towards Nigel's room.

She thought about Camberwaddle, whose surgery had apparently gone well, but who would be off the radar for a few days – that's if his doctors managed to wrestle the mobile from his hand. Unless his desire to sue half the food industry through Will had been some sort of illness-induced madness (and it was possible), she'd now be sharing her biggest client with her newly qualified colleague.

It sounded mean, she knew it did. Will had won the business; he had every right to take on a new client, especially if a lucrative offer landed in his lap. But she was pretty sure that the next time Nigel decided to make someone partner it wasn't going to be her.

Was she fundamentally unlikeable? she thought. Or was it her work – a steady stream of healthy income, sure, but not the most interesting area of law. Form filling, paper-pushing, and aside from the odd argument over boundaries, pretty much the same transaction over and over.

It just wasn't sexy enough.

But why was she so intent on getting made partner in Nigel's firm anyway? Sure, she'd earned her stripes here, had gained valuable knowledge. And Nigel had been the one who'd taken her on when she only had limited experience. But why was she still trying to get his attention when his passion for law clearly lay in another direction? She was like a schoolgirl with an inappropriate crush on a popstar. No matter how much she tried, she was going to be overlooked.

'Bailey & Partners' she wrote idly on her legal pad, doodling flowers around the edge of the lettering until they were almost invisible. Dare she start her own firm? Conveyancing specialists, and not a trip and fall in sight? No more seeking favour from a boss who was quite happy to add her wins to his profit margin but had no interest in the work that went into getting the money in the first place.

The phone rang. 'The funds are in for the Smithson purchase,' Ann said.

'Great,' she replied, making a note on her pad. Completion could happen tomorrow – they'd be over the moon.

'Can I nip off early today?' Ann asked. 'Doctor's appointment.'

'Of course!' Clare replied. 'Everything OK, I hope?'

'Oh, nothing serious,' Ann replied. 'Just a check-up.'

'Glad to hear it.'

Once Ann had left, Clare marked the competition date in her diary and wrote a quick email to Mr Smithson. It felt good to be the bearer of good news to a client; her job might be boring, but she'd never tired of that.

Then, in the diary, she saw another scribbled appointment on tomorrow's date that made her blood run cold. 'Toby

241

meeting Martha B.?' she read. She'd meant to do something about this before, but had pushed it to the back of her mind. She'd hoped at first to be able to go – boost his status maybe. Help him. But the idea of more subterfuge felt suddenly too exhausting. He'd be OK, wouldn't he, without her help. Things would die down.

She typed 141 into her phone to disguise her number and rang a familiar mobile.

'Toby Bailey?' he said, with an inflection at the end that made it sound as if he wasn't quite sure who he was.

'Hello, em, Toby . . . it's, well, it's Martha B.,' she said, feeling her cheeks get hot.

'Martha!' he said, using the same tone, she noticed, as he did when speaking to her mother on the phone. 'How wonderful to hear from you!'

'Thank you. But I'm afraid I have some bad news.'

'Bad news?'

'Yes, I'm not going to be able to meet up for that interview after all; rehearsals are overrunning.'

'Oh.' His voice was flat. In the distance on the line she could hear the faint sound of chanting.

'What's that in the background?'

'Oh, you know,' he said, 'just a few protesters.' He laughed nervously. 'They seem to come every day now. I'm not really sure what I'm meant to do about it,' his voice sounded suddenly boyish. 'To be honest, Martha, I think I'm out of my depth.' He seemed to remember himself then. 'I mean, of course I know what to do about it! It's just . . . I mean, it's not ideal.'

'No,' she said.

'Look,' he said, his voice lowering, 'are you sure you won't be able to make this interview? It's just well . . . I didn't want to say anything, but my wife and daughter – they're absolutely huge fans of yours. And I'm afraid I might have promised them your autograph. It would be so appreciated if you could help me.'

'They're fans?'

'Yes. At home, it's all they talk about.'

'Really.'

'Besides,' he added, 'you'd like my wife. She's ... she's an incredibly successful lawyer. Really, well, the embodiment of an empowered woman.'

'Oh really?'

'I'm sure if you need any legal advice she'd be more than willing to help you.'

'That's very kind of her.'

Part of her was angry at Toby, but part of her felt sorry for him too. Holed up in his dressing room, forced to pass rather vehement protesters outside, pretending not to hear their shouted comments as he scuttled away to his car, her husband was drowning.

And while he might not have spoken to her directly about it, clips she'd seen on the news, the odd comment, and now his defeated confession to 'Martha B.', were about as close to a cry for help as she'd ever heard.

'Look,' she said, 'let me see what I can do.'

'Really?' his tone went up an octave and he coughed it back into place. 'I mean *really*?'

'Yes. Look, I'm not sure I'll be able to meet your wife and daughter ...' she added, because if she was going to engage in this lie she might as well get herself out of trouble at the same time, 'but perhaps we can meet for a pre-recorded interview?'

'That would be ... Oh! Martha! I mean Miss B. I mean Mrs. I mean Ms ... Mrs ... Ms ... Miss?'

'Martha is fine.'

243

On the way home, running early for once, she pulled into a layby outside an estate agent and nervously went in. The man on the front desk beamed at her as she entered. He looked to be about eighteen – half man, half boy, with the downy moustache to prove it.

'Hello, madam,' he said. 'I'm Ben.' He held out his hand for a shake and she duly obliged. His hand was small and hung limply in her grasp. 'Agent Ben, at your service,' he said, with a mock salute and a grin that made her warm to him.

'Hi, Ben,' she said. 'I'm interested in finding out about any commercial property you might have for rent. Just a small office space, really, at this stage.'

'Sure, I'm afraid there isn't much at present.' He turned his back on her and rifled in a filing cabinet, pulling out a sheaf of stapled papers. 'The ones in red are gone,' he said, 'but there are a few others left.'

'I'm thinking of starting my own business,' she said, needing to hear how it sounded out loud.

'Ah, you're one of *them*,' he said, knowingly, nodding his head as if identifying her as a member of a secret society or special cult.

'One of them?'

'Yeah, one of them MehToo women, right?'

'Well, sort of, I suppose.'

'Do you know, since that thing started, I think we've let more offices to women than we had in the year beforehand?'

'Oh, wow, really?'

'Yeah, I mean it's great,' he said, then seemed to check himself. 'I didn't mean great for the agency – well it *is* great for us, too, but that's not what I meant. My mum, she runs her own business and she says it's about time more women took the plunge,' he said, reddening slightly.

244

'Your mum sounds like a wise woman.'

'Don't tell her that!' he grinned. 'I'll never hear the last of it!'

Clare thanked Ben and took the papers back to her car, flinging them on the passenger seat. 'Fasten seat belt,' Claudia instructed. 'Fasten seat belt.'

She duly buckled up.

'Fasten passenger seat belt!' continued the car hysterically. 'Fasten passenger seat belt!'

Really? Usually this was only activated when someone was in the seat. Did the car really think this wodge of papers was a human arse? She moved them slightly with her hand and started the engine.

'Passenger is unsecured! Passenger is unsecured!' cried the car. For the first time, Clare realised how much like a Dalek the automatic voice was. Exterminate!

Rather than push the papers onto the floor Clare duly leaned over and fastened the passenger seat belt.

'Happy now?' she asked the car as she drove off.

But even the car seemed to be oblivious to her presence.

She reached home, switched off the engine and sat in the car for a minute looking at the house. Since their frantic cleaning spree before Hatty and Bill had popped in, it had started to look dishevelled again. Plates had begun to pile up near the sink and next to Alfie's bed.

She'd left before the kids this morning – goodness only knew what would be waiting for her inside.

But as she opened the door, the overwhelming stench was not of mildew and festering food, but lemons.

'Kids?' she called, feeling oddly nervous.

'Yeah?' Katie called from upstairs.

'Have you tidied up?' she asked, noticing all the coats hung on pegs and shoes placed in pairs by the door.

'Well, a bit.'

'Oh, thanks Katie!'

'No, I mean. It was already pretty much like this when I came home,' came the reply. 'Mum, it was Alfie.'

'Alfie!'

'Yep. He's gone to Sam's house now. But when I got in he was hoovering.'

So it was true. Everyday miracles could sometimes happen.

Leafing through the estate agent's papers over a coffee, waiting for the baked potatoes to crisp up, Clare couldn't help but feel a little frisson of pride whenever she saw a listing marked as 'Let'. Of course, it wasn't really likely that the whole Martha B. thing had woken up a generation of would-be entrepreneurial women – but if what Clare had done had influenced even one woman to take a risk then that was pretty good.

Chapter Thirty-Nine

'I want to talk to you about something in a bit,' Clare said to Toby as he hacked determinedly into his baked potato later, his face grim.

'Yes?' he said, looking up. 'What about?'

'Not now,' she said, nodding at the kids. Alfie, who had devoured his first baked spud and was covering the second with cheese, and Katie, who was diligently scraping all of the soft white contents onto a plate and discarding the skin on the tablecloth in disgust.

'Go on, Mum,' Katie said. 'We all want to hear what you have to say!'

'Katie! Will you stop with that MehToo thing?' Alfie said, mouth full of cheese and chewed potato.

'What do you mean?'

'It's all "listen to Mum" and "women this, that and the other",' he moaned.

'So, I think it's important!' said Katie, primly.

'Come on you two, leave each other alone,' Clare said, feeling simultaneously proud of Katie and protective of Alfie. Her boy had cleaned today. He had turned an almost unimaginable corner.

'But . . .' Katie continued.

'Yeah, well . . . you know. If she doesn't want to say it in front of us,' Alfie said, nodding meaningfully at his parents, 'it's like . . . well, it could be a *sex* thing.'

'Alfie!' Clare said, not knowing whether to be angry or burst into laughter.

'Well,' he said reddening. 'You know. It might.'

Katie continued to scrape potato from its skin, her ears red. 'OK,' she said. 'Maybe tell him later, Mum.'

'Kids!' Clare continued, 'it's not about . . . Look, I was just going to tell your father that I'm thinking about opening my own firm.'

'Your own firm?' Toby said, with a bit more incredulity than she'd prefer. 'Are you sure?'

'Well, no, not completely. But I think it could be a good move for me,' she said.

'I think you should go for it, Mum,' Katie said, loyally, finally forking her first appropriately doctored bite of potato into her mouth. 'You can do anything.'

'Yeah,' Toby said, sounding less sure. 'It's . . . it's certainly an interesting idea.'

'Mum,' Alfie said, stopping mid-chew.

'Yes, love?'

'Is there any more cheese?'

Later, when Alfie was in his room gaming with a mysterious stranger online, and Katie was taking selfies in front of the mirror — both activities that Clare was a little unsure of but equally wasn't sure how to tackle — she and Toby sat on the miraculously litter-free sofa and turned on the TV.

'Shall we avoid the news tonight?' Toby said. 'Maybe try something else? A film?'

'We could do both?' She always liked to at least watch the headlines, just so she could be sure that she wouldn't come a cropper conversationally at work or with a client.

'Yeah, but . . . you know. The news is so much like work for me these days!' Toby said, his neck starting to develop blotches in such a tell-tale way that she was almost desperate to put the TV on to see what he was trying to avoid.

'OK, just the headlines,' she said, pretending to be oblivious to his panic.

The opening credits were just finishing when she finally clicked on the television. 'But first, women were out in force today protesting at the appointment of popular TV host Toby Bailey as presenter on *Woman's World*,' the newsreader began.

Clare glanced at Toby, who was staring fixedly at the screen. 'Scores of women pursued Mr Bailey as he made his way to the studio this morning – brandishing placards that suggested he was undermining women and setting back gender equality by decades,' she continued.

'Oh, Toby,' Clare said. Why had she not heard about this? Why hadn't Toby said anything?

'One woman even threw a bra onto the windscreen of his car, almost causing the Mercedes to crash into a wall,' continued the newsreader, as the screen cut to a shot of a woman running alongside the car and flinging a large pink bra onto the windscreen. It caught on the windscreen wipers where it flapped like a flag.

'Protesters are angry at the appointment of a man into a role that is seen as one that only a woman can fill, in what has already been criticised as a toxically male environment,' the report continued. 'But the director of staff at ITV insists that we live in a society where gender should not and will not influence employment policy. The studio also provided the following statement: "While we sympathise with the protesters, we stand by our view that presenting roles should be issued on merit, rather than based on a person's gender."

'Much of the current protest has been attributed to the deep dissatisfaction ignited by the so-called MehToo movement, inspired by popular rap star Martha B., a *You've Got Talent* contestant whose recent appearance on *The One Show* captured the hearts of the nation,' continued the report.

The camera then cut to a view of the crowd, with several placard-waving women standing at the front. 'We're here for Martha,' one of the women said. 'She's right – women need to tell it like it is and start making real change.'

'Martha B.! Martha B.! Martha B.!' the women chanted.

Back in the studio, the newsreader looked into the camera. 'While fans look forward to Martha B.'s next performance, those in ITV must face the difficult question – has a mistake been made?

'Mr Bailey was unavailable for comment.'

Clicking off the TV, Clare looked at her husband, who stared dismally at his reflection in the black screen. 'Oh Toby,' she said. 'I'm so sorry – I mean, I knew there was . . . I knew not everyone was thrilled, but this is . . . Do you know what you're going to do?'

He shook his head, sadly. 'The worst thing is,' he said, 'Hatty's completely avoiding me now – ever since . . . well, you know. She was my guide in there. That place – it's toxic. And once you've got bad press, people don't want to be associated with you anymore.'

'Avoiding you?'

'Yep. Pretty sure.'

'Oh.' She thought back to Hatty's tears, her desire to be in front of, rather than behind, the camera. 'Have you tried talking to her?'

'I'm not sure she'd listen at the moment.'

'Look, Toby. I said . . . I promised I wouldn't say anything, but Hatty doesn't feel quite right in her job either.'

'Oh?'

'Yeah. She'd rather be presenting . . . I think she was rather hoping that *Woman's World* would be her gig.'

'Really? But she recommended me! Why would she do that?'

Clare shook her head. 'I think she just hoped . . . But she thinks, well, it's an age thing. You know – women of a certain age, getting overlooked.'

'But Hatty was a brilliant presenter. And she's an ace producer!'

'I know. But maybe that's not how everyone sees it.'

Toby began to chew a nail thoughtfully, before checking himself. 'Oh,' he said. 'Poor Hatty.'

'Yeah. But look, it's not your fault. I've seen you present and you're brilliant. I mean, you deserve that job.'

'Do you think? Even if I'm man?'

'Even if that's the case,' she grinned.

He laughed. 'You know what I mean,' he said, giving her an affectionate dig in the ribs.

'Ha,' she said, giving him a dig back.

'Anyway, I'm hoping as far as these protests go, the Martha interview might help.'

'I hope so,' she said, gently. She felt loyal to Martha, to her cause. Toby would have to play his cards right in the interview.

'Yeah, I want to show women that I am on their side. Despite . . . well, despite having a penis.' He looked at her then. 'I love you, you know Clare.'

It had been a long time, she realised, since either of them had said that.

'You too,' she said, 'although I'll love you even more if you get me a biscuit.'

Chapter Forty

'I'm Martha B. – remember my name!'

It was the first time they'd rehearsed for a few days and as she dropped into her final pose, Clare could feel each and every muscle straining.

'Great, great!' Dan said, jogging to the front of the group, hardly affected at all by the fact that he'd just carried out an incredible demo for the boys, in which he'd backflipped four times and landed directly on his crotch. 'Except . . .' he said, looking at Clare apologetically. 'Could you try to, well, smile a bit?'

'Sorry, it's just I'm concentrating.'

'I know, I know. It's just I think it'll look a bit weird if the boys are all dancing around behind you and you've got that . . . that look on your face.'

'Sorry,' she said again, feeling a bit like a child being told off. 'I am trying.'

'I know. Maybe a bit too hard,' he said with a shrug. 'Just feel the music. Let it flow through you. You're overthinking it.'

She'd always liked music. As long as someone else was performing it. As a child, she'd taken piano lessons for a bit. But that was as far as it went. Of course, she'd had the odd dance in public – she'd done a bit of clubbing in her time, but that was when she'd had a few too many vodkas and nobody was really watching.

The performer in her came from somewhere else. Something natural that flowed through her when she lost herself. She couldn't let her inner critical perfectionist override this, or she'd end up getting it all wrong.

'And you think the rap will be ready in time?' he said.

She'd used her old lyrics for the rehearsal – she'd had a bit of block, so she'd told Dan she was just tuning things up and wasn't ready to reveal her latest lines.

'Yeah, I'll bring it along next time.'

'Good,' he said, slapping his hands together like a teacher. 'So, what do you reckon guys? One more time from the top.'

'Yeah,' they replied, so scarily in unison that for a moment she wondered whether they might be an army of tiny clones.

She dialled Steph from her hands-free car phone on the way home. 'Attention to the road,' the car reminded her helpfully. 'Avoid distracting calls.'

'Hello?'

'Hi, Steph, it's Clare.'

'Oh, hi, how you doing?' In the background Clare could hear the relentless chirping of cartoons. She recognised a theme tune from years ago.

'That's *Teletubbies*, right?'

'Yup. I can't imagine he knows what he's watching. But it seems to keep him quiet,' Steph replied.

'John or Wilbur?'

'Very funny.'

'Anyway, just thought I'd ... well, I need some advice really,' Clare went on. 'I'm in a bit of a situation, I suppose.'

'Again?'

'Well, you'll laugh, but Toby's arranged some sort of

televised interview with Martha B. He's hoping, I think, that meeting her, me, her will help him with all the protests. But I'm not sure I can go through with it. I mean, it's not as if I'm wearing a rubber mask. Will he really not recognise me, in the flesh, despite the wig and shades?'

'Crikey – you do know how to make a drama into a crisis!'

'Yep, that's me! But, seriously, what shall I do?'

'What do you mean?'

'Well, if I pull out of the interview, Toby will be gutted, and might struggle with the whole movement business. But if I tell him who I am he might not want to go through with it – because it will look staged, won't it? And I can't pull out of the talent show thing – those boys are depending on me. But what I really want to do is go into hiding, to crawl under the duvet and pretend it isn't happening!'

'I can understand that.'

'But I also kind of . . . don't.'

'You've lost me.'

'Well, I don't know. I kind of . . . like rapping. I'm even starting to like dancing!'

'Oh!'

'Oh, and I'm thinking of setting up my own firm, but it's really scary – I don't know whether to hand in my notice and then try to do something from home, or go all in and hire offices.'

'Wow.'

'Or really go for it with the Martha B. act, you know? See where it might take me.'

'Really?'

'Yeah. No idea what I'm thinking, what I want!' Clare said, her head spinning with it all. 'So, what do you reckon?'

'Just wow.' In the background, Wilbur had started to cry.

'But what should I do?'

'Look, sis,' Steph said, carefully. 'I love you, you know that. And I'm here for you. And I want you to ring me up when you're having problems.'

'Right?'

'But when I've been at home all day wondering what on earth to do with my life . . . When Wilbur's been teething and crying and filling his nappy every five minutes . . .'

'Uh huh?'

'Well, to have you ring me up with the terrible problem you're worried about because you've created this ridiculously popular character, who has somehow united most of the women in Britain . . . And how are you going to manage to do that while starting your own law firm . . .'

'Yes?'

'Well, two things. First of all, have you thought how it makes me feel? A bit shit, that's how. Because my sole achievement this week has been to catch up with the washing on Wednesday morning.'

'Oh, Steph.'

'And the pile's enormous again, so that was a short victory.'

'I'm sorry.'

'Don't be, don't be,' her sister said, 'but try not to see all these things as problems. You're having an amazing adventure. It's a bit weird, true, but then that's normal for you!'

'Hey!' Clare laughed.

'And you know how you were worried about being invisible?'

'Yes.'

'Well, you're not.'

'You don't think?'

'Clare – you're a national celebrity and soon to be senior partner of her own law firm.'

'But am I though? It's not me, after all. It's Martha.'

'What?'

'It's Martha who's the celebrity – not me.'

'But it doesn't have to be in disguise – that's all been your choice.'

'True.'

'And you know, if you really want to find an invisible woman, you wouldn't have to look too far away.'

'What do you mean?'

'Me! Clare, I love you, but do you ever think what *my* life is like? John working all the time. Wilbur never seeming to want to sleep, or be put down, or give me a second's break to – I don't know – go for a pee?'

'Oh, Steph . . .'

'It's pathetic, I know,' Steph continued, voice thick with tears. 'But sometimes I just want to get in my car and drive and drive and drive . . .'

'Steph, you don't mean that.'

'Don't I?'

'Do you?'

'No, I suppose not,' Steph continued, clearing her throat. 'Just ignore me – having a moment.'

Steph was right, Clare realised, after she'd hung up the phone. She might have felt invisible, but she'd also been part of the problem – she hadn't seen that the most important woman in her own life was struggling.

Chapter Forty-One

'Could you sit down for a minute?' Clare asked when Ann poked her head around her office door the next morning. 'Nothing to worry about,' she added.

'Phew,' Ann grinned. 'You scared me for a minute!' She closed the door and sat down in the seat across from Clare's. 'You sounded so formal. I thought you were going to tell me to stop eating so much chocolate at my desk or something.'

'Never!' Clare laughed. 'I know you're fuelled by chocolate.'

'True. So, what's up?' Ann smiled.

'Erm,' she said, clearing her throat.

Ann looked at her patiently, her smile becoming a little strained.

'Sorry. I just wanted to ask you something, in confidence . . . and it mustn't go beyond these doors – at least for now,' Clare continued.

'OK?'

'I'm thinking – and it really is only in the very early stages – of starting out on my own.'

'Your own firm?'

'That might be a bit of an oversell, but yes, a very small firm. Me, one other partner perhaps, admin support.'

'Right . . .'

'And I wanted to ask you – hypothetically – if I decided to jump ship, whether you'd want to come with me?'

'Oh!' Ann's cheeks reddened slightly.

'Yes. I mean, when I say "jump ship" – I'd do it all properly. Proper notice period, that sort of thing. Wouldn't leave Nigel in the lurch, or the clients, although I won't be stopping any clients who decide they'd like to come with us of course!'

'I see.' Ann was giving nothing away.

'I could match your salary – I'm afraid I couldn't offer more at the moment. It's going to be a squeeze at first. And of course, with any start-up, well there's a risk it won't work out. Which is why I want to be totally up front with you.'

'OK.'

'But I would hope that in time I could reward your confidence in me – bigger salary, more responsibility, that kind of thing. I mean, I think at this stage you could probably do most of the transactions in your sleep.'

Ann grinned. 'You could say that.'

'Anyway, I'm not asking for an answer now – I don't want one yet. I want you to think about it properly. And don't worry about upsetting me if the answer is no. I've decided to take a risk – but I completely understand if it's not for you.'

'Thank you,' Ann got to her feet. 'And thank you, you know, for offering . . . for having faith in me . . . Martha.'

'Shhh.'

Once Ann had left her office, Clare looked at her watch. It was 11 a.m. She glanced involuntarily at the bag in the corner. Alfie's old gym bag was stuffed with Martha B. get-up. Wig, hat, sunglasses, more make-up than she usually wore – and a tracksuit that Dan had assured her looked 'fly'.

In two hours she would be walking into a small studio and sitting down with her husband for a media interview. How on earth she would do it without being recognised, she didn't know. She was just relying on the fact that it wouldn't occur to anyone that Martha B. might be Toby's wife in disguise. And wouldn't put two and two together even if she looked a little 'odd'. After all, everyone knew that Martha B. was a persona . . . they just didn't know whose.

She laughed briefly to herself, realising that for once she hoped her husband wouldn't notice her. That his habit of being wrapped up in himself – his work – would stand in her favour for once.

The taxi arrived, as arranged, outside the shop on the corner, and she slipped inside. 'ITV studios,' she said to the driver.

'Right you are . . . Hey, are you that rapper?'

'That's me.'

'Me and the girls,' said her driver, looking in the rear-view mirror and catching Clare's eye, 'we love your stuff. Amazing. And so glam!'

'Oh! Thank you.'

Half an hour earlier when she'd sneaked into a toilet cubicle at the public loos to change, it hadn't felt very glamorous. She'd changed as cleanly as she could and stuffed her office clothes into the backpack, all the while trying to avoid a suspicious wet patch on the floor. Transformation complete, she'd exited the loo like superman from a phone box and walked towards the newsagent to wait.

Almost instantly she'd been noticed. Whether people recognised her, she wasn't sure. Perhaps they just thought she was weird. But she'd definitely begun to see people giving her second glances. One woman had lifted her mobile phone for a snap.

This, she'd thought doggedly, as she'd tried to avoid eye contact, is what it is to be very, very visible.

After they'd whipped through the traffic in record time, she paid the extortionate fare – hoping Toby wouldn't question it when their joint bank statement came in later that month. 'Well, good luck!' said the driver, whose name was Gloria and who, she'd informed Clare in great detail, was having trouble with her boyfriend, Clive.

The taxi had pulled up outside the main entrance, but it was impossible to ignore the cluster of about twenty protesters standing with signs reading 'Women for Woman's World' and 'Bog off Bailey' standing nearby. Their attention seemed to be focused on a window, whose half-opened blind revealed someone wearing an orange shirt.

'Come down here and have it out!' someone shouted.

'Yeah, man up!' another said, and the group dissolved into laughter.

Hoping not to be seen, she walked quickly towards the entrance with her head down, but just as she reached the revolving doors she heard a cry of 'It's Martha B.!' and a thunder of footsteps. Luckily, she slid past the security guard on the front door in the nick of time, leaving protesters with their noses pressed to the glass like sperm around an already fertilised egg.

Sure, the protesters were on her side, but Clare didn't know how they'd react if she told them she was here to be interviewed by the enemy.

This is the test, she told herself as she spoke to the girl on the front desk and a runner met her to take her to the right place. This was when she'd really know whether her disguise held up.

When she was shown into a small studio, with two chairs facing each other flagged by screens emblazoned with 'Woman's World', she felt her stomach rumble in protest. How could Toby not recognise her if she was sitting so close to him? Her voice, her mannerisms, the small part of her face that was visible, albeit covered in make-up?

The cameraman strode over, his hand extended. 'Neil Down,' he said, shaking her hand profusely. 'Great to meet you.'

'Do you know where Tob . . . where Mr Bailey is?'

'I think he's on his way. Just setting up.'

'Right.'

'And this is George, he'll be doing a piece to camera just before you have your . . . your chat with Toby,' Neil added.

'Hi, George.' This time she remembered to use her slightly altered 'Martha B.' voice – a little lower, with what she hoped was a slight northern accent.

Neil looked at her for a moment, clearly clocking the change in pitch, then carried on adjusting his camera.

George, who looked to be about eighteen, shook her hand. 'Big fan,' he said.

'Thanks.'

Then the door opened and suddenly Toby – wearing an astonishing orange shirt – strode into the room, looking more confident than she'd ever seen him.

'Good afternoon, all!' he said, in a rather loud voice. Clare noticed he had a couple of red patches on his neck. Despite his manner, her husband was nervous.

Afterwards, on her way back to the public toilets in which the transformation from Clare to Martha had to be reversed, she reflected on how it had gone.

Was it good, she wondered, that Toby had seemed not to recognise her at all? In fact, still emphasised the fact that his wife was a 'big fan' and asked for her autograph. 'Dear Clare,' she'd written. 'Hope to meet you one day, Martha B.'

'So, what's your message to women out there?' Toby had asked, once the cameras had started rolling.

'The message isn't so much *for* women,' Martha B. had

replied. 'The message is for all of us – how we need to see each other more; understand and recognise the part we all play in each other's lives. And that includes women – many of whom feel overlooked even by the people who ought to champion them.'

'Right.'

'And we're all guilty of that . . . We can all become pre-occupied with our personal journey and forget to see others.'

'Yes,' he replied, 'yes, I see that. Can I ask you something, Martha?'

'Of course.'

'You'll know that there have been protests about my . . . my role on this show. But having met me – seen how it all works – would you say that I'm suited to this position?'

It was quite an ask. On the one hand, she had wanted to say yes. But thinking of Hatty – more experienced, more suited to the job – had made it difficult.

'Well,' she'd replied carefully. 'On the face of it there's no reason why a man can't perform this role, provided he is prepared to listen and come to understand the issues that women face, in the workplace, in the home and beyond.'

Toby had visibly relaxed at her words and she'd realised how much importance he must have placed on this weird interview.

'But,' she'd said, watching him pale, 'I do wonder whether it would be better to have female input too.'

'Oh.'

'I mean, wouldn't it be great to have both? A male pre-senter – like yourself. And maybe . . . maybe a female host, someone experienced,' she'd said.

Overall, it hadn't been too bad, though, she thought, changing out of the Martha B. tracksuit then having to climb back into the bottoms after dropping her work trousers in a puddle of wee on the toilet floor. They might well cut the last bit, but she'd got her point across. She was all for Toby having his shot at the limelight, but the fact that Hatty – or another woman – would add something more to the show was undeniable.

Chapter Forty-Two

Clare leaped out of bed and was almost in the shower before she realised it was Saturday and retreated back under the covers. Toby was asleep by her side and she stroked his hair, only to feel the crispy texture of hair gel in his once-soft barnet.

She was just about to relax back for a bit more of a doze when she suddenly realised the significance of the day. If it was Saturday, that meant the audition shows were on TV tonight. She had to think fast or her cover would be well and truly blown.

'So,' she said a little later, as Toby sipped the cup of tea she'd brought him in bed. 'The weekend! I thought we could maybe go out for a meal this evening.'

'What, like a date?' he said, eyeing her with a mixture of interest and suspicion.

'Well, not really, although that sounds lovely, too,' she said, hurriedly. 'I thought all of us – you know, the whole family.'

'On a Saturday night?'

'Yes, why not?'

'Do you think the kids will be up for it?'

Clare pondered for a second. 'Probably not. But you know, maybe we ought to encourage them to come anyway. It's been so long since we did anything as a family.' *Plus I'm going to be on national TV and don't want either of them to see me.*

They didn't always watch TV on a Saturday night. Sometimes they went out, sometimes had a takeaway. But there was every chance that if she didn't remove her family from the house someone might just click on the TV to see the auditions show. On which, she'd been reliably informed, there would be a rather big segment on the heart-warming story of a dance troupe who'd found their way to fame with a mother figure known only as Martha B. The gold buzzer would be activated. They would be the main feature of the show. She had to keep her family away from the TV at all costs.

'So, what shall I book? Pizza place?'

'I thought maybe the Rose and Crown? They do a great menu, apparently.'

'OK, done,' he grinned. 'It'll be nice to all be together.'

He looked so pleased about it that she felt guilty.

Predictably, the children were less than thrilled about going out, especially Katie, who had a long-standing Saturday night date arranged around her best friend Tessa's house (where the pair of them ate chocolate and – as far as Clare could work out – did each other's make-up). But Clare insisted – she happened to know that Tessa's family liked to keep a TV in every room, and there was always something on in the background.

Most likely, on Saturday night, it would be *You've Got Talent*.

After she'd bribed Katie with the promise of a future sleepover to make up for it, she tackled Alfie, who was in his room playing some sort of shoot-and-kill game with a disembodied voice that sounded American and female.

265

'What?' he said, distractedly, when she came in the room. Then, 'sorry, Mum.'

'Oh, is that your mommy?' the American voice responded. 'That is just soo cute!'

'Not exactly,' Alfie said. 'What?' he said again.

There was a silence when she momentarily forgot why she'd come in the room in the first place. 'Oh, yes!' she said. 'We're off out to dinner tonight at the Rose and Crown.'

'Great,' he said.

'Great?'

'Yeah. Great.'

'So, you'll come?'

'Oh. I didn't realise you meant . . . me. But yeah,' he said with a shrug, 'count me in.'

'Aww, a date with your mommy?' said the voice again.

'Shut up.'

It was almost too easy.

The Rose and Crown was labelled a family friendly pub, due to its generous playpark and beer garden. None of which was very useful to them on this particular evening with its biting wind and tiny prickles of icy rain.

Inside, the bar was heaving, and by the time they were shown to the small corner table that Clare had booked, she'd already removed two of her outer layers and was debating whether her silver and lace bra would pass as a crop top if things got any warmer.

She decided to keep things decent, after all, this was a family establishment and as Toby's wife she was a woman in the (semi) public eye – the last thing she wanted was for someone to tweet a picture of her, leading to tabloid outcry and the discussions on morning TV that – by law – have to occur every time a well-known woman appears in public with a questionable outfit choice.

Even though they were there with their children, and even though they'd ridden in near silence in the car, it was actually nice to be out with Toby. They'd used to do date nights once in a while; when had they stopped? She reached down and instinctively grabbed Toby's hand and to her surprise, he gave hers a little affectionate squeeze.

The big TV in the corner of their annex was showing some sort of football results programme with a bar of scrolling news underneath, and Clare noticed almost instantly that Toby's eyes were glued to the screen. Which was weird, as he didn't follow football particularly.

'Toby,' Clare said, noticing the waitress hovering at his side. 'I think she's waiting to take your drinks order.'

'Sorry, sorry,' he said, smiling at the waitress in such a friendly manner that Clare's stomach began to knot a little. 'Just keeping an eye on the news,' he said. 'Wondering, well – you know – if there's been any developments with the . . . you know, protesters.'

'They're still there?'

He shrugged, 'probably.'

After they'd ordered their wine and a couple of Cokes, Clare glanced around the table at her family. Toby's eyes were still intermittently creeping across to the scrolling news. Alfie had his phone on the table. Katie was sitting playing with a small packet of sugar that someone had left. 'Well,' Clare said, brightly, 'this is nice! But put your phone away, Alfie.'

'Just on Twitter,' he said. 'Not messaging anyone.'

'Still.'

'I'm waiting to see if the new codes have been released.'

A gaming thing. Clare sighed – she knew if she banned his

phone from the table he'd be sneaking off to the loo every five minutes to check. She wondered, briefly, whether her son was an addict. All this obsession with levels and points and when the next gaming codes were out on the net. She'd worry about it later.

'OK,' she said. 'But just check it once in a while – and no messaging.'

Across the table, Alfie gave her a mock salute.

'I'm starving,' Katie interjected. 'We've usually eaten by now, and we haven't even ordered.'

The waitress arrived with their drinks. They all made their food orders then sipped happily for a few seconds.

'Nice wine,' Clare said, wondering why it was she seemed to have nothing particular to say to her family – the most important people in her life. She glanced up at Toby and was annoyed to find his gaze once more directed to the TV. 'For God's sake! Can't you switch off from work for a minute!' she snapped.

'Sorry, sorry,' he replied. 'It's not work any more; they've switched the channel. And it's just hard to keep my eyes off the screen with that weird bloke on it.' He nodded towards the TV and Clare turned to look. On it, there was a man dressed in a long, rather grubby raincoat, standing on a stage with a look of panic in his eyes. 'Just wondering if he's about to get himself arrested.'

She recognised that grubby mac! 'Mr Flasher,' she whispered to herself, watching the man as he flung off his raincoat of restraint and did a delicate twirl in the sequinned leotard he was wearing underneath. 'Oh shit,' she muttered. Because if Mr Flasher was on TV, that meant the talent show was on TV. In the pub. On the big screen.

And if they were showing the talent show in the pub, that meant that in about half an hour, she was going to be projected onto the screen – the screen her family seemed unable to avert their eyes from – performing a rap in front of thirteen young backing dancers.

She realised then that she'd made a terrible mistake. Because she could have controlled the environment back at home. She could have outed the power or insisted on watching something on the other side. At the very least, she'd have been able to distract anyone watching at the pertinent moment.

Here, she was a sitting duck.

A duck whose secret rap star identity was about to be exposed.

To make matters worse, one of the men leaning on the bar walked over to the TV and turned on the subtitles. 'Can't hear a feckin' thing,' he said to them as he walked back.

'Any chance of flicking back to the news in a bit?' Toby asked him. 'Just . . . well, I'm expecting some news. On the news. You know?' He winked at the man conspiratorially.

The man looked at him with a furrowed brow. 'There's always news on the news,' he said slowly. 'That's why it's called the news.'

'I know,' Toby said, patiently. 'But tonight, I think there might be some *news*. You know . . .' he winked again. 'Actual *news*.'

'Right . . .' The man clearly wasn't a fan of *Woman's World* and had no idea what Toby was going on about.

'Could I?' Toby made to get up, but the man shook his head.

'Sorry mate, boss wants it on – his wife was in the audience apparently.' He nodded to the bloke behind the bar, who gave him a thumbs up. 'We can switch over after?'

'OK, thanks.' Toby shook off his disappointment then

turned to the family. 'Sorry about that,' he said. 'I think I rather intimidated him, don't you?'

'Oh, look!' Clare said brightly, hoping to distract everyone from her imminent TV debut. 'Our food has arrived!'

On the screen she saw a man in a bear costume. The subtitles across the bottom of the screen read: 'I'm sixty-nine you know!' 'Audience gasps.'

'Sixty-nine!' Alfie said. 'That's amazing!'

'Don't be daft, Alfie. Sixty-nine is nothing. Grandad's sixty-nine for a start and you don't see him getting dressed up as a bear and parading himself on TV, do you?' Toby said.

'He could if he wanted to!' Alfie replied, defensively, missing the point entirely. He looked at his phone and laughed. 'Someone's saying he looks a bit like Keith Lemon,' he said, delighted. 'He does, doesn't he?!' He clicked on the *You've Got Talent* hashtag. 'Oh, he's a grandad to four.'

'Leave the phone,' Clare said.

He pushed it slightly away from him. 'Sorry.'

Glancing at the screen again, she felt a shudder of recognition.

'So,' she said, desperately trying to distract their attention from the screen. 'Would anyone like to try one of my garlic mushrooms?'

'Look at this woman,' Alfie said. 'Looks a bit like Aunty Steph, I reckon!'

'That,' said Toby, 'is Martha B.' He nodded at the screen. 'I interviewed her.'

'I know, Dad,' said Katie. 'Even if Alfie's clueless as usual.'

Clare turned and was confronted by herself in her full Martha B. garb. She felt her cheeks get hot.

But nobody seemed to have recognised her. Perhaps she'd dodged a bullet.

'God, big reaction!' Alfie said, glancing at his phone

again. 'People saying about it being refreshing or something. Weird.'

'Alfie,' Toby admonished. 'Your mum said no more phones.'

This was the moment when he decided to back her up?

'Bloody hell, Macey gave them the golden buzzer!'

'What else does it say?' Clare said, grabbing the phone for a look.

Love the ridiculous suit #You'veGotTalent

Are those all her kids? The slag! #You'veGotTalent

I agree with her – fed up with being judged for my looks #You'veGotTalent

Martha to win! #MehToo

Lovin the Eezee Troupe #MehToo

As the hashtag gathered pace once more, Clare realised that rather than feeling shocked or alarmed, she actually felt just a little bit proud.

Chapter Forty-Three

Sipping her flat white, Clare looked at her watch again. Steph was now officially ten minutes late.

They'd spoken briefly on the phone on Sunday and her sister had seemed all right. She'd mocked her for her *You've Got Talent* appearance and been completely stunned that none of Clare's family had noticed more than a passing familial resemblance.

'Lord, I know you said you were invisible, Clare,' she'd said, 'but now I'm starting to believe it.'

Then they'd arranged lunch. But it looked as if Steph had stood her up.

It didn't matter, really. She remembered how difficult it could be to leave the house with a baby; but at the same time if her sister was much later, she'd only have about twenty minutes to chat before having to head back to the office.

She called her sister's phone again, but it went straight to answerphone. Probably Steph was driving or rushing along with a pushchair and just about to fly in the door.

Another sip, another glance at the watch, another feeling of elation as the door opened and disappointment when it revealed that the latest customer wasn't Steph.

In the end, she phoned her sister and left a message: 'I'm really sorry, Steph. I've had to go back to the office. Hope everything's OK. Give me a call.'

Walking back, she tried to shake off the feeling that she should have waited a little longer or done a little bit more.

Soon though, she was on the phone to a client, buried in work and any thought of Steph or where she'd got to had been filed at the back of her mind.

Half an hour later, when she'd finished speaking to Mrs Jones, who was digging her heels in about the possibility of leaving the fitted curtains for her buyers, Nigel burst into her room without so much as a knock.

What if I'd been practicing my corporate sexiness? She wanted to say. *I could have been sitting around in my knickers.*

'Just got your holiday form,' he said, waving it at her as if she'd demanded evidence. 'Another half-day off! Becoming quite the part-timer, eh! Ha, ha.'

'Um, yes,' she said. *Although before these two measly half-days I've had off recently, I've literally put all my waking hours into the firm.*

'I'll get Will to oversee Ann for the morning,' he continued.

'Oh, you don't need to do that!' she said. 'Ann is fully briefed.'

'Even so,' he said. 'It's good to have a proper solicitor on the case, I find.'

If she did make the jump and start her own firm, she decided, she'd always value experience over qualifications. Will might have the recent paperwork, but he knew zilch about conveyancing, wasn't familiar with any of her clients or cases, and wouldn't know a property information form if it hit him in the face. Yet when Ann successfully managed her workload while Clare was away, it was Will who would get all the credit.

'And will we see you later on?' Nigel asked, sinking uninvited into one of her plastic chairs and leaning back, before once again losing his balance and grabbing frantically at the desk to right himself.

'Later on?'

'Yes, the training session,' he continued, looking quite aggrieved. 'Stage six of the ... the corporately ... corporately *sexy* training.' He had, at least, the decency to blush.

'Actually,' she said. 'I've got an appointment after work.'

'Oh.'

'But, look, I'll practice my mantras.'

'Well, that's good. Although I must say I would hope that the more senior staff would lead the way on this,' he said.

'Nigel,' she replied, trying to keep her voice calm. 'I've worked with you for almost a decade. I've turned over consistently high profits for the firm. I work more hours than any of the other senior members of staff. I was the one responsible for bringing Stefan Camberwaddle on board in the first instance. It's great that you're, er, trying something new. But don't you think that maybe not everyone needs to improve their work performance?'

He was silent for a moment. 'Is this about the MehToo thing?' he asked.

'The what?'

'You know, these women's rights protests or whatever.'

She bristled. 'It's about fact, Nigel. I don't need to put on a unitard and let my flaws hang out. I don't need to tell myself I'm corporately sexy or that I'm going to conquer the world or whatever. I'm just getting on with the job and doing a bloody good one at that.'

After Nigel had made a bumbling apology and exited the office, she waited for her heart to stop pounding and picked up the phone. 'Toby?' she said, when he answered. 'I'm going to do it!'

'Do it?'

274

'Yes, I'm going to start my own firm. I've decided.'

'Oh.'

'You don't sound sure about it.'

'No, no, I think it's great. It's just . . . well, the money aspect.'

'Honestly, I think it's worth the risk.'

'But what if I lose my job?' he asked, his voice sounding slightly squeaky.

'Lose your job?'

'Well, you know my interview with Martha B. . . . it went well. But, well, I heard the director is looking at my role. They hate the controversy, you know?'

'Toby, they're not going to fire you! At worst they'll, well, reassign you,' she said, feeling guilty for her possible part in things.

'I suppose . . . well, yes go for it. We'll manage,' he said.

'Thanks, love.' Because he meant well, even if he so often seemed to get things wrong.

'And, congratulations!'

'Pardon?'

'Congratulations! It's . . . well, you should be really proud of yourself.'

As soon as she hung up, ready to tackle the mountain of work on her desk in record time so she could go through listings and make sure she had everything in place for viewing office space on her hard-won 'day off', her mobile beeped.

This time, it was a text message from Dan. *Martha B. trending on Twitter*, he'd written. *Take a look*.

Lost in her work at the office, she'd forgotten to even tune in to *Woman's World* and watch her interview with Toby being aired. Or perhaps she'd wilfully ignored the fact her alter ego was going to be beamed to the masses over lunch. Either way, she hadn't seen it yet.

As Dan had said, the hashtag #MarthaB. popped up in the top ten trends on the side of her screen. Heart in mouth, she clicked on the link.

#MarthaB. telling it like it is! said a Tweet. *You go girl!*

#MarthaB. schmoozing with @Toby on #Woman'sWorld said another, adding a vomiting emoticon for good measure.

Scrolling down, it seemed that most of the references were positive. That she hadn't let the side down, even though she'd tried to swing public opinion a little more in Toby's favour.

'Bodes well for the live finals on Saturday!' she replied to Dan. After which, she thought to herself, everything would be different.

'You're amazing,' he replied.

She spent the afternoon getting her files as up to date as she could, and arranging as much as she could in advance to make sure tomorrow went well.

Then, just as she was stuffing paperwork into Alfie's half-ripped gym bag, the phone on her desk trilled into life.

'Clare Bailey speaking.'

'Hi, Clare, it's Will.'

'Hi?'

'I've got Stefan Camberwaddle on the phone; he wants a quick word, if that's OK?'

'Sure, thank you.'

'OK, putting him through.'

Clare waited for the familiar click on the line. Then, 'Hello?'

'Hello, Clare, it's Stefan Camberwaddle here,' he said, unnecessarily.

'Stefan! How are you?'

'Fine, fine, thank you. I just wanted to run something by you quickly.'

276

'Yes?'

'Well, your ... this Will chap ... he's started work on my litigation, which seems to be fine.'

'Great ... good news.'

'But he's ... he seems quite excited about a client of yours named Hans something.'

'Oh,' she said.

'Yes, I just wanted to know ... well, he invited me to some sort of training session he thought might benefit me in some way.'

Clare's heart sank. 'Oh, did he?'

'Yes. He ... he, um, said it would help me to be more ... attractive, or something,' continued Camberwaddle. 'I just wanted to ask, I suppose. Whether he's ... is he as good a lawyer as I thought?'

Clare thought about Will. His constant smart appearance (except when working out in a leotard or underpants); the fact that he was always on time; that he won many of his cases, despite their rather trivial nature; the bizarre but ulti-mately probably useful contacts he had in the underground world of American law drama that seemed to exist in his favourite bar.

'He's ... he's hardworking. Yes, I think he's a good lawyer,' she said at last. 'He's just trying a new strategy ... which I suppose is a bit on the alternative side. But otherwise, he really is sound.'

Camberwaddle sounded relieved. 'Right, thank you,' he said. 'It's good to have a solicitor whose opinion I trust.'

She hung up the phone hoping that she'd made the right decision, and that Camberwaddle wouldn't be leaping into her room in a shiny all-in-one next time they had a meeting.

Picking up her bag, she checked her office desk once more

to ensure everything was laid out clearly and neatly, then picked up her bag.

'Oh, Ann,' she said, passing her desk. 'Aren't you off yet?'

'Just finishing this.'

'You don't have to you know.'

'I know. But I want to be on it for when His Highness Will is watching over me tomorrow morning.' Ann's tone was light, but her voice had an edge to it – she really was dreading being overseen by the firm's rising star.

'Sorry,' Clare said. 'You know it wasn't my idea, don't you? I think you could handle this lot standing on your head.'

'I know,' Ann replied. But her tone had softened. Perhaps she hadn't been sure. 'By the way, good luck tomorrow.'

'What, with the *house hunting*?' Clare said, with an elaborate wink.

'Yeah, make sure you find something with a view.'

'Definitely.'

'And Clare?' she called, as her boss began to turn away.

'Yes.'

'Don't forget your power stance.'

Chapter Forty-Four

'I'll take it,' Clare said, decisively.

Ben nodded and scribbled on his pad. 'Great choice,' he said.

It wasn't much, sure, but it was a start. The second floor of a Victorian terrace on the high street; clearly once someone's home, but now converted into offices. A small insurance firm situated on the ground floor, and Bailey and Associates (although who the associates would be at this stage she had no idea), would be tucked away above them. The shared reception area was a bonus, and she hoped to have a chat with the woman who managed the insurance company to see whether they might share reception support.

She'd yet to hand in her resignation at work; yet to even mention it to Nigel – although she'd been tempted once or twice, particularly when he'd been only half listening to what she was saying. Would he even hear her properly? Would it make him sit up and take notice?

But she wasn't doing this to score points. She was making a positive change for herself; and hopefully for Ann, too.

'So, you'll need to pay three months' rent up front and fill in a bit of paperwork,' Ben continued, as she fantasised about the type of furniture she might buy for the modest carpeted room with its tiny corner office, central desk area and a toilet that was located in what had clearly once been a kitchen. At least it beat her cupboard office.

'No problem,' she said, although it would be a bit of a squeeze. The rent was slightly higher than she'd anticipated, which might make money tight for a while.

'Are you OK?' Ben asked, and she realised she'd been staring, trance-like, out of the window as the thoughts had run through her head. Her eyes snapped into focus and she suddenly realised that the window of the office looked directly into a flat above the newsagent over the road. Through the window a young man, wet from the shower and wearing only a towel, was looking back at her.

'Yes, sorry. I mean, I wasn't looking at ... I was thinking about the company, you know?' she said, flushing.

'Sure, I believe you!' winked Ben, misreading the tone. 'Now I know why you wanted *this* office!'

Her look brought him up short. 'Sorry,' he said. 'I'll get the paperwork shall I?'

She only just made it to the office by 3.30 p.m., having stuffed most of the paperwork into her bag and promised to drop it in to Ben on the way home. She hadn't called ahead, which of course meant that Nigel had decided this was the one day he had wanted to discuss something with her straight after lunch, and had been pacing up and down the corridor waiting for her to arrive.

'Hello, Nigel,' she said.

'Hello,' he said, looking at her suspiciously. 'Long lunch?'

'Lunch meeting overrran.' She shrugged in a 'can't be helped' kind of way and he visibly relaxed.

'Oh right,' he said. 'Camberwaddle?'

She smiled and avoided the question. Not that it was any business of his, really, where she'd been – she was only an hour late for the start of the afternoon. The number of times she'd worked an hour or two after the office closed, or popped in on a Saturday morning without comment. He probably owed her about a year and a half off in lieu.

'Anyway, just wanted to say. I've read your recent memo and the figures are excellent,' he said. 'Keep up the good work!' He waved a memo, which was actually the one she'd written over a month ago, under her nose for proof. 'Jolly good show,' he added, sounding like someone from the twenties.

'Thanks, sir,' she said, thinking how typical it was that just as she was smoothing the ground for her great escape Nigel was finally starting to be a reasonable boss.

'That was a turn up for the books,' she said to Ann, once Nigel had disappeared into his office.

'I know,' she said. 'He actually made *me* a coffee this morning! It's some strategy of Will's, I think.'

'A strategy?'

'Yeah, their response to MehToo.'

'Oh.'

'Yes,' Ann met her eyes. 'I probably shouldn't tell you, but when I went in earlier they were having some sort of mind-mapping session. And Will had written "troubleshooting" on his pad.'

'*Troubleshooting*?'

'Yes, as in making sure they covered their backs so we don't start a riot or something in the office, I think!'

'Bloody hell.' Once again, the enlightened duo had completely and utterly missed the point.

'Exactly.'

'Look,' Clare leaned in slightly in case they were overheard. 'Have you given, you know, my proposal any thought?'

Ann nodded. 'Yes,' she said.

'And.'

'And, yes!' Ann said again.

281

'Yes, you'll come?'

'Seriously,' Ann said. 'If you leave me here to watch the whole Nigel and Will show play out I will lose my mind.'

'Leaving early?' Nigel quipped as Clare raced past his room two hours later, clutching Alfie's poor bag, which because she'd overfilled it so frequently was now splitting at the seams.

She ignored him. Troubleshooting my arse! she thought.

For once, she arrived at the church hall early. Letting herself in, she switched on the lights and looked at the little white-washed space that she'd spent so many evenings in recently. Without the boys to fill it, it struck her how small and tatty it seemed.

But she'd miss it all when it ended, she realised. She'd miss rehearsing with Eezee Troupe, admiring their energy and drive – the excitement of it all. Not the nail-biting stress and horror of the upcoming TV finals that kept her awake half the night. Certainly not the strained muscles and sore bottom that she'd had to contend with since they stepped up their rehearsals.

But the comradery. The idea of working towards a shared purpose. And being an important part of a machine, rather than just another cog whirring around unnoticed. Hopefully that was something she could recreate in her new firm, she thought. That feeling of purpose, of moving forward.

She'd also miss writing raps, she realised. Miss actually sharing her thoughts with the world.

A Nissan Micra and a small Citroën pulled into the car park next to the building and she watched out of the window as all thirteen members of Eezee Troupe squeezed their way out of the tiny vehicles. Perhaps they should start performing contortion or magic as a sideline.

282

Legal? No. Dangerous? Yes. But definitely entertaining.

'Clare!' a few of them cried, seeing her standing on her own through the window.

'Someone's early!' Mark said as he pushed open the door.

'Nice to see you!'

'Tomorrow's the big day!'

They bounced past her one by one, grinning, doffing imaginary caps as they did so. 'Hi, everyone,' she said, feeling a bit 'last day of school'ish. Perhaps she should have brought a marker pen to sign everyone's shirts?

'Got the new rap?' Dan asked. He smiled, but she could hear an edge of desperation in his voice. She'd been a bit slow with this one; had wanted to get it just right.

'Yes!' she said, enjoying the look of relief that raced across his features. 'Yes, I have.'

'Great!' He swept her up in his arms and spun her around. There was a moment after he'd set her down, when she'd stood slightly dizzy – looking at him as he looked back at her. A moment of tension when she wondered if she ought to give in, lean forward and kiss the one man in her life who seemed to actually see her.

Then she thought of Toby – the stress he'd been under. The man he'd used to be and hopefully would be again.

'So, let's hear it!' Dan said, smiling.

'Now? Can't I just perform it when you guys dance?'

'No, I think we need to hear it,' Dan reiterated, waving his hand slightly in a way that clearly indicated the rest of them should sit. They did, cutely dropping into assembly-mode and sitting with crossed legs rather than grabbing chairs to perch on.

'Ok,' she replied. Because if she couldn't perform it in front of this funny collection of young men, all of whom were rooting for her to succeed, then she was never going

283

to make it in front of the cameras. Still, it felt more nerve-wracking than it ought to have as she uncrumpled the paper and began to read.

When she finished her performance the room was quiet. She looked up, trying to read into their facial expressions.

Then Dan began to clap, and the others gradually joined in. 'Clare, that was great,' he said. 'Such a brave thing to do.'

'Are you sure? Do you think I might be making a mistake?'

'No, not at all,' he said. 'I think you're doing exactly the right thing.'

Chapter Forty-Five

On the way home, smiling at the memory of the troupe's reaction to her performance, Clare had a sudden jolt of anxiety.

She hadn't heard from Steph.

It wasn't that unusual for the pair of them not to talk for a few days – it wasn't as if they lived in each other's pockets or followed each other around. But after her no-show at the café, surely Steph would normally have rung her to apologise or explain. Or Clare would have rung her.

She felt a sudden pang of worry near her heart. 'Claudia, phone Steph,' she said.

'Phoning Steph.'

The phone rang seven times before the answerphone clicked in again.

'Phone Steph,' she said, again, determined to get through.

This time, the line clicked open to reveal silence.

'Steph?' she said.

'Hi,' came the reply. It sounded like Steph, yet at the same time, it didn't.

'Are you OK?'

Silence.

'Steph, are you OK?' she said, suddenly and instinctively knowing the answer.

Silence.

'Look, I'm coming over,' she said. 'Right now.'

It took ten minutes to get to Steph's house – a modest newbuild at the end of a terraced row on an estate built in the grounds of a Victorian hospital. Lights were on in all the windows, but John's car was nowhere to be seen.

Feeling sick, but not quite knowing why, Clare rang the doorbell. 'Steph?' she called through the letterbox. 'It's me!'

There was a moment's silence, then the sound of someone walking.

When her sister answered the door, Clare barely recognised her. Her hair was greasy and dishevelled and tied up in a messy bun. Her face was swollen from crying; she was wearing a towelling dressing gown that was in need of a wash. But it was Steph's eyes that struck Clare the most. They were expressionless.

'Steph?' she said, stepping into her sister's hallway and hugging her unresponsive body. 'What is it? What's happened?' A sudden fear. 'Where's Wilbur?'

'He's upstairs,' Steph replied, her voice a monotone. 'Don't worry, he's fine.'

'And John?'

'Working.'

'Oh, Steph, why didn't you call me? Why didn't John call me?'

'I don't think he knows what to do.'

'Let me help you,' Clare said. 'What's the matter, are you depressed? Sick?'

Steph let out a hollow laugh but said nothing.

Walking into the kitchen, Clare flicked the kettle on instinctively. Why was it that she always felt problems could be solved with a cup of tea? Probably something about being British.

It took an hour for her to get Steph to open up. How she hadn't been sleeping. How she'd wake up in the night with

286

racing thoughts. How, a few days ago, the feeling of dread that she'd been keeping at bay had descended on her and try as she might she couldn't shift it.

'Oh, Steph,' Clare said, covering her sister's hand with her own. 'You should have called.'

'You're so busy,' her sister shrugged.

'Never. I am never too busy,' Clare said, looking into Steph's eyes for emphasis. 'Do you understand?'

Steph nodded.

'Right. Well, we're going to call the doctor right now and get you an appointment. And until John gets home, I'm going to stay here, OK?'

'OK.' Steph let herself be hugged and even ate a little of the sandwich Clare made.

But the whole time she spent with the shell of her sister; Clare couldn't help feeling that somehow she'd got it all wrong. She'd been wrapped up in her own life, her own petty worries, her own feelings of inadequacy. And she'd let herself believe that everything was OK with her sister – even though there had been signs, even though she'd known, hadn't she, deep down, how hard she had found it herself after Alfie had been born, and that it was possible Steph might go through something similar.

She was going to stop playing games, stop trying to micromanage everything and start getting real with her own life. Stop trying to change the world when she hadn't even got her own ducks in a row.

'I'm sorry, Steph,' she said for the seventh time, looking at her sister. 'I'm so sorry.'

'You don't have to be.'

'We'll fix this, you know. It's not easy, but we can fix this.'

*

For once, Toby noticed something was wrong as soon as Clare got home. And she was grateful. As they cuddled on the sofa for the first time in an age, she remembered those awful days after Alfie's birth when she'd felt as if her world was closing in. And how it had been Toby who'd helped lead her back to life again.

He had been her rock then, and she was determined that whatever had happened to fracture their relationship would be fixed.

Chapter Forty-Six

Clare and Katie were just finishing clearing the table the following evening when Toby opened the front door and shouted a loud 'I'm HOME!'

'Is that Dad?' Katie asked, her face a picture. 'Do you think he's all right?'

'He . . . he seems fine,' Clare replied.

The door was pushed open with such force that it hit the wall, its handle leaving a small dent in the plaster.

'Girls!' Toby trilled, bounding into the kitchen. 'I've got some great news!'

Clare smiled in spite of herself. She'd been feeling sick with worry since she'd realised how ill her sister had become. But Steph was getting help now, and it was hard not to catch Toby's infectious smile, even if she couldn't quite join his over-the-top enthusiasm. 'Go on?' she said, putting her pile of plates next to the sink. 'What is it? You're taking over the TV studios? You've won the lottery?'

'No and no!' he said, still grinning.

'Don't tell me, you're pregnant!' she joked.

'Mum!' admonished Katie, her cheeks reddening.

'No, but close!' he said. 'I've got tickets to watch the *You've Got Talent* live final in London! They were giving them out at work and I grabbed the final four.'

'Really?'

'Wow!' said Katie, seeming genuinely impressed. 'Can I come?'

'I thought we could all go together as a family – it'll be fun!' he continued.

'But Toby,' Clare said, feeling a rising sense of panic, 'you know I'm at that, um, conference again tomorrow.'

'Oh,' he said, his face falling slightly. 'But you could meet us . . . go afterwards?!'

'I'm not sure – it starts pretty early and lasts . . . well, most of the day,' she said, feebly. 'You know, networking. If I'm starting my own firm . . .' She was beginning to hate the lies.

'Oh,' he said, the wind firmly out of his sails.

'I tell you what,' she said. 'Let me see what I can do. The venue's not far from there, so . . .'

He cheered up at this. 'And Katie? You'll come, will you, sweetheart?'

'Definitely,' she said, excitedly.

When Clare was settling down with a well-earned coffee, Toby came and sat with her, holding the tickets. The ink was starting to run in the corner of the top one, smeared by the sweat of his thumb. 'Alfie said no, too,' he said, sadly. 'It seems he's doing something football related.'

'Oh, don't worry about it. Look, you and Katie will have a lovely time. And I'll make sure I'm there,' she said – which wasn't a lie, after all.

'But won't I look a bit of an idiot with empty seats around me?' he asked. 'Like nobody wants to sit with me?'

'They'll put someone else with you I'm sure,' she said. 'You know, move someone from the back to the front. They're not just going to let a prime seat stay empty. Plus, who cares? You're not in it for the positive publicity, and you can't spend your whole life worrying what other people think.'

'You're probably right,' he said. 'Or, maybe I could see if anyone else from work wants it?'

'I'm sure someone will.'

She watched as her husband typed something in on his phone and pressed a button decisively. 'Group text,' he said, as he looked up and met her eye.

Moments later, Toby's phone began to ring. He looked at the caller ID and his eyes widened.

'Hello?' he squeaked. 'Yes. Well, yes, of course. I should have . . . No, you're right. Well, yes it would be. Well, yes, us too! OK, see you there.'

He hung up, his face pale, the red blotches reappearing on his neck. 'That was Hatty,' he said. 'She was . . . rather friendly actually. Seems she's keen on going – to show solidarity to Martha. She didn't get her hands on any of the tickets yesterday . . . and she seemed, well, really nice.'

'That's good, right?'

'Yes. I think.'

Once the kids were in bed and Toby was snoring in front of the news, Clare pulled out Alfie's bag and emptied its contents into a desk drawer. Then, quietly, she went up to her bedroom and began to fill it with the things she needed: Martha B.'s sunglasses, which she'd squirreled away underneath the underwear in her top drawer, and the top and trouser combination Nadia had chosen for her final outfit. Nadia would be bringing the make-up and hair things, but Clare slipped her own make-up bag in too – just in case.

At her laptop, she printed out confirmation of her train ticket, before clearing the cache on her search engine, which would probably only make things seem more suspicious if Toby decided to check up on her. Feeling like someone on the run, she packed everything into the bag and put a folder on top for good measure – just in case someone decided to take a peek.

She knew that Toby didn't believe her story of another property conference in Town; she knew that he was worried, and probably a little suspicious about her motives. But she also knew that she wanted to keep her secret, just for one more day.

He'd started to notice things again, in a way he hadn't for a while. Noticed when she stayed out late or wasn't home on time. Asked questions. Seemed suspicious and interested. In fact, at long last, showing her that he cared. Just with the worst possible timing.

She was relying on the fact that it would all be over tomorrow; and with Toby and Hatty sitting in the front row, it would be over in rather spectacular style. She just hoped that after what she intended to do, Ann stuck with her and came to her new firm. And that she might still be able to find herself a client or two.

She went back downstairs to her husband, who was watching the headlines with one eye open. 'Hi, love,' she said, feeling like a cheating spouse returning after a liaison. 'Everything all right?'

'Uh huh.'

'Nothing on the news we need to worry about?'

'No, seems fine for once.'

'Good. Well, I'm off to bed,' she said, straightening up again. 'Got to make an early start tomorrow.' She'd promised Dan she'd be there by 8 a.m.

'Clare,' Toby said, as she reached the door.

'Yes?'

'Do I need to worry about this thing you're going to?'

'Toby,' she said, with a small smile. 'Seriously, just trust me – it will be fine.'

She just hoped she was right.

Chapter Forty-Seven

Clare practised her breathing in a way that was meant to relax her, according to internet research. She watched her stomach inflate under her sequinned top and then breathed out through her mouth, deflating her belly like a wasted balloon. In, one, two, three. Out, one, two, three. Her legs stretched before her in satin trousers which Nadia had assured her were 'flattering'.

Before the Martha B. episode, Clare had been involved in just two live performances. The first had been a recorder recital when she was five. She and the other grade one recorder students had been forced to stand in front of the whole primary school and play *Frère Jacques* in unison. She'd managed to get through it, but still remembered the humiliation of having to screech out the notes under the judging gaze of her peers.

'Hey, you! Great playing,' a year six boy had said to her afterwards in the playground, playing an imaginary 'air recorder' and laughing.

She'd managed to avoid getting on stage through the rest of primary school. But in secondary, she had joined a drama club simply because two of her friends had, and it was that or spend lunch hours sitting in the classroom on her own. She'd enjoyed it for the most part, but had accidentally thrown herself into some of the improvs with too much gusto and ended up being awarded one of the main parts in the Christmas panto.

It hadn't been a great performance but judging by the fact she'd got called 'Cinders' for the next four years, it had certainly been memorable.

Now she was here – about to rap live to the nation. But although the nerves coursed through her body, she realised she was kind of looking forward to it, too. It was a peculiar kind of excitement – the kind of excitement that comes with actually wanting something and being afraid that it might be taken away.

Her legs still ached from their almost continuous rehearsals. 'Are you all right?' Dan had asked earlier, worriedly. 'You're not limping are you?'

'No,' she'd lied. 'It's fine.'

She hoped it would be. She'd been working on her flexibility – she'd wanted to leave one particular move she'd planned a secret even from Eezee Troupe. Just in case it went wrong.

Dan had looked concerned but had agreed to the mystery part of the performance.

Clare now stood there, using her notes and keeping her voice quiet. 'I'm preserving it,' she told the concerned producer. 'Don't want to get hoarse.'

One of the runners appeared now at her side. 'Everything OK?' he asked. 'Psyched for the performance?'

'Yes, thank you,' she lied.

In truth, she was even more nervous now than she'd been last time. Knowing that Toby and Katie were here, and that even Hatty had come along, made it all the more nerve-wracking. Even now, she could see them on screen looming large in the front row. Hatty was wearing a T-shirt that said

'Team Martha', with '#MehToo' writ large on her forehead with eyeliner.

Dan had started talking about a release on iTunes, and about a producer who kept calling. She had no idea what the future might hold. All she could do was concentrate on the next few minutes. The ink was barely dry on her lease for the offices and she knew she definitely wanted to run her own firm. She'd heard of portfolio careers – but it was unlikely the term was designed to cover being an international rap sensation and a conveyancing solicitor under the same umbrella. *Yo! Yo! Sign da lease, innit?*

The thought of Toby, Katie and even Hatty witnessing her final move first-hand made her even more nervous, but she steeled herself. After all, it wasn't really any different from their watching it at home on TV. It just meant that she'd see their reaction there and then, rather than hearing about it later. Besides, she reassured herself, she couldn't really see into the audience once the lights went up. She'd just pretend they were back in the church hall, rehearsing where nobody could look, no one could judge and there was no fallout no matter how badly it went.

At her side, Eezee Troupe were squatting, flexing, stretching and flipping their way through their warm-up.

'Ready in two,' said a stagehand, appearing by her side in the near-darkness.

Then Clare's stomach gave the obligatory dip and roll as she heard the first notes of their short film intro being played. 'I want to send a message to women out there,' she heard her screen self saying, 'that we all deserve to be seen and valued for who we are.' The music turned up tempo and Dan appeared on screen. 'I grew up on the wrong side of the streets . . .' he said, 'dropped out of school at fifteen. At eighteen, I met a man who changed my life . . .'

Clare tuned out, mentally rehearsing her lyrics for the last time.

'Ladiees and gentlemen,' said the slightly over-the-top voice-over bloke. 'Performing for you live, iiiitttsssss Martha Beeeeee and the Eeezeeeee Troupe!'

And this was it. In three minutes, she reminded herself, it would all be over.

They walked onto the stage with the lights down, then, as the first beat of the music began to play, she felt her body move instinctively. She raised the mic and began:

'I ain't sayin' I'm a rapper, but I speak the truth,
I'm spitting out these lyrics, gonna raise the roof.
Not looking for a fortune, and I don't want your fame,
Just want people to know me, and remember my name.
The Eezee Troupe love dancin', just look at them flip,
They don't need me to front 'em, yo I'll give you a tip.
Just watch out for these boys and their master moves,
They're comin' at ya, gonna get you in the groove.
I'm not just a performer, no, I work in the law,
But my rap is from the heart, yeah, just the same as before.
Take notice of your mother, your girlfriend and ya sister,
The world is for the taking, but not just for you, mister!
I wanted to be noticed, and just look my flow,
But I've got one more surprise before I take off and go.
My real name is Clare Bailey, just an ordinary girl,
I thought I'd try some rappin', that I'd give it a whirl.
It started as a joke, but yo it started workin',
You haven't seen the last of me, the future's uncertain.
A mum of two young people, and boss to a few,
I'm going to put my heart into whatever I do.
I'm bringing you my music, and I'm going to keep tryin',
But I'll work in law as well – man, you wait, I'll be flyin'.

Want to be a good mum and look after my kids yeah,
There's nothing more important, let them know that I care,
   yeah.
I used to be invisible so meh, yeah "mehtoo",
But I'm bringing light to women with whatever I do.
I gotta leave you now, but remember this thought,
That everybody matters, now, I'll see you in court!'

With that, she took off her wig, hurled it into the audience and dropped into her first ever set of splits.

Chapter Forty-Eight

The headache asserted itself the minute Clare opened her eyes and let the tiniest bit of light filter in. She was wrapped in the duvet. The sheets were soft. She closed her eyes to let her spinning head settle then tried to open them again.

And jumped. There was a face – a giant, grinning face – looming over her. Her vision cleared and suddenly she realised who she was looking at. 'Toby?'

'Cup of coffee?' he said. 'Just how you like it?!'

She shuffled up slightly against the pillows. 'Thanks,' she said, reaching for the mug he was holding. She sipped the contents. Black, strong, lukewarm. But two out of three wasn't bad.

She tried to remember the last time that Toby had brought her a coffee. Normally he was up hours before her and racing out of the house before she'd had time to take her first pee of the day. So, it had been a while.

And the smile? Something was up. She remembered him drinking a fair bit last night – usually he'd be curled up in a ball of vomity regret.

'You OK?' she asked, sipping the coffee and feeling her senses gradually start to return. 'Everything all right?' She squinted against the light and his features gradually came into focus.

'I was going to ask you the same question,' he said, sitting on the bed and squashing her toes with his bottom. 'That was quite some champagne you put away last night.'

She remembered it now. The private club. Champagne. The first time she'd drunk more than three glasses in years.

Eezee Troupe taking to the dance floor and putting the clientele to shame. That man with the black hair trying to get her to sign a contract.

'Have you seen the papers?' Toby asked, (ridiculously, as he knew, didn't he, that she hadn't been conscious for the last ten hours or so).

'No? Why?' she played along.

He gently placed a wodge of papers on her lap. The *Sunday Mole* was on top. 'MC Bailey STEALS THE SHOW!' it screamed in capitals. Underneath was a picture of her flinging her wig into the audience. Her hair underneath was a complete and utter mess. She hadn't considered that bit.

Her memory of last night started to come back in the form of brief snapshots. Standing on the stage. The look of baffled surprise on Toby's face when the wig hit him in the chops. Hatty standing up and screaming 'Go Clare!' The rest of the crowd cheering or yelling – had they been pleased? Or appalled?

The minute the competition had ended, Toby had rushed to meet her backstage. 'I can't believe it!' he'd said. 'How . . . how did I not know?'

'Maybe we both need to notice each other a bit more,' she'd shrugged, as he pulled her in for a kiss – despite Katie's embarrassment.

When she'd been changing, Hatty had appeared in her dressing room. 'I wanted to say thank you,' she'd said, sounding less confident than usual.

'Thank you? For what?'

'Well, don't tell Toby. But they've decided to try *Woman's*

World as a two-presenter show. And guess who's been given a chance to be in front of the cameras again!'

'Oh, Hatty!' Clare had stood and given her a hug. 'That's such good news.'

'Yes, but it was *you* wasn't it? That interview with Martha. I mean, I know they didn't broadcast your criticism of the show. But you got them thinking . . . I can't thank you enough.'

'Hatty, it had nothing to do with me,' Clare had said. 'I wasn't doing you a favour – it was genuinely what I thought. And I only suggested a female presenter . . . no names were named. You got this because you're great.'

She'd watched with pleasure as Hatty beamed and went red.

'I'm still buzzing from last night,' Toby said now.

'Yeah,' she said, sipping her coffee.

'It's . . . well, it's surreal.'

Backstage as they waited for the results, Dan had been very unsure about their chances: 'We can't compete with that magician,' he'd said. 'I mean, imagine keeping a pigeon in your pants backstage.'

When their names had been called, he'd grabbed her and swung her around as if she weighed nothing.

Clare looked at Toby's happy, hopeful face now and felt a pang of guilt. She'd been worried that he might be angry at her deception; possibly even embarrassed by the fact that his 'professional' wife was suddenly performing on a TV talent show. How it would look in the papers, whether he'd be derided. She should have just talked to him. Properly.

'But the rap,' he said, his face switching to serious. 'Am I one of them?'

'What, a rapper?'

'No! No. Am I one of those men who aren't listening . . . aren't seeing you?'

'Well, maybe a bit. Or you were. Things are . . . they're getting better now though, aren't they?'

He brushed his fringe out of his eyes. 'Clare, it might not seem like it, but I do love you, you know? I think I've just been so worried about trying to fit in. It's weird, starting something so new, something you just want to get right.'

'True . . .'

'And suddenly there I was, with my own section to present. All this back-patting, but Hatty, well, she was the only person who ever seemed to want to talk to me . . .'

'Honestly, I understand.'

'But there's more.' He looked away from her, towards the blank wall and she realised he was trying to hold back tears. 'I . . . well, I started taking these diet pills – you know, to shift a few pounds. It's so competitive . . . and . . .'

'Diet pills?'

'Yeah. But they kind of made me . . . spaced out. Then, my heart was racing at night, sweating, sick, that kind of thing. I couldn't concentrate – couldn't think. I'd look at you and my eyes – I couldn't focus them.'

Was that why he'd seemed so oblivious to her?

'Why didn't you tell me?'

'I guess I felt stupid . . . I didn't know what to say. And I was scared. I stopped taking them after a little while and recently things have started to feel better.'

'Oh Toby . . .' She squeezed his hand and looked at him. 'Why would you do that to yourself?'

'Too embarrassed, I suppose. Too scared of failing.'

'You can't be embarrassed in front of me!' she said. 'Especially now,' she added, nodding towards the picture of herself on the front of the *Sunday Mole*.

'True,' he grinned, his eyes still glistening.

And suddenly there they were, holding hands and grinning at each other. She felt a connection she hadn't felt for such a long time. Because he'd finally listened to her, and she'd finally listened to him.

Chapter Forty-Nine

Clare hadn't planned on a grand opening.

In fact, the whole thing felt rather embarrassing.

Nevertheless, here she was, with a photographer from the local paper, Toby, Ann, the mayor in full regalia and an assortment of vaguely interested bystanders and hardcore Martha B. fans, snipping a ribbon in front of the door into her new office.

This morning, Katie had rushed into her arms before she left the house. 'I'm so proud of you Mum,' she'd said. 'You know that right?'

'Did Dad put you up to this?'

'No. Seriously, I am. And we women, we need to celebrate each other, right?' Her little girl, with her sweet, serious eyes looked up at her.

'Yes. Yes, we do.'

Even Alfie had wished her good luck, as he brought a pile of last night's plates down from his room. 'Hope it goes well,' he'd said, stacking his crockery in the dishwasher.

'T-thank you,' she'd stammered, wondering if she was living in a strange parallel universe where teenage boys actually picked up after themselves. 'And thanks for doing that.'

'S'no problem. It's my crap, isn't it?'

'Don't say crap.'

'Sorry.'

*

'How does it feel to be striking out on your own?' asked a man in a grey suit now, sticking a recording device in her face.

'Daunting, but exciting,' she replied, trying to smile.

'And is this the end of Martha B.?' a woman with glossy hair asked her.

'Oh, I don't think we've seen the last of her,' Clare said, with a wink. In truth, Dan was in discussions about possibly recording a track on iTunes. And if she could come up with a suitable rap – something longer, less novelty – she was thinking about giving it a go.

Looking past the reporters she could see Toby, his eyes fixed firmly on her. A smile on his face. Her Toby. His blood pressure now in check, he seemed more like himself again.

'I'm so proud of you, you know,' he'd told her this morning before she'd left.

'Thank you.'

He'd looked at her steadily.

'What?' she'd said, checking her hair was more or less in place.

'How on earth,' he'd said, 'did I get so lucky?'

'Steady on, I'm only opening a tiny start-up.'

'Not that, although obviously that's amazing too. And not the Martha stuff – also amazing – but you. My beautiful, clever wife.'

'Oh stop it!' she'd joked, but she'd been pleased.

She smiled at him now and he blew her a kiss of encouragement.

After one last pose for the camera, she walked through the door of her new firm, with Ann at her heels.

'Gawd, talk about OTT,' said her new employee. 'You'd think we were opening some sort of major landmark, rather than a tinpot legal start-up.' She seemed to think twice about

her words after saying them. 'I mean, it is a great thing –
not . . . you know what I mean.'

'Don't worry,' Clare said. 'I know exactly what you mean!'
They looked at each other.

'Shall I put the kettle on?' Ann asked.

'No,' Clare said, firmly. '*I'll* put the kettle on.' She wrapped
an arm around her friend – 'no hierarchy in this firm.'

'And no unitards?'

'*Definitely* no unitards.'

After the furore over her 'big reveal' had died down, Clare
had gone into work where both Will and Nigel suddenly
seemed almost too interested in everything she had to do or
say. 'Can't believe that was you on the TV!' Will had said,
with a reverence that could only have come from someone
of his age to whom achievement was almost solely measured
in the number of likes and clicks.

'Yep. That was me!' she'd said.

'The phone's been ringing off the hook!' Nigel had said,
greedily. 'Lots of new clients wanting to work with you.'

'Wonderful,' she'd replied. Feeling a little guilty. But,
well, not too guilty. And a little confused about why people
would want a rap star to do their conveyancing for them.
But whatever brought the business in . . .

Later that afternoon when she'd handed in her notice,
Nigel had begged her to stay. 'Your department keeps this
firm afloat!' he'd said. 'It gives me the space to nurture Will's
talent and build the litigation!'

'Yes,' she'd said. 'But, you know, you have other conveyancers who can take on most of my clients,' (Camberwaddle,
she'd been assured, was going to come with her), 'and while
I appreciate all the work you and Will have been doing
together, I think it's time for me to start something new.'

'But?'

'Plus, you know, I was never quite "corporately sexy" enough,' she'd added.

This last sentence had seemed to resonate, and he'd grudgingly wished her luck, after which he and Will had disappeared into his office for what he'd later termed some 'serious mindmapping'.

Then she'd been free to actually plan the next steps of her new life. Ordering office furniture (well, two desks and a couple of chairs), laptops, commandeering mobile phones for herself and Ann. Thinking about how she wanted to shape her new firm. And even looking through CVs for a junior position she hoped to be able to fill in the near future, provided everything went to plan.

Going back home that evening had been almost like stepping back in time. Toby had had a haircut and suddenly looked much more like his old self. 'I'm going to trade in the Merc,' he'd told her. 'We can't afford to run two expensive cars at the moment.'

'Why don't we trade in both our cars and get a couple of little run-arounds instead?' she'd suggested. He'd hugged her fiercely then, as if she'd told him they'd won the lottery or discovered a cure for middle-aged spread or something.

'Thank you,' he'd said. 'I know how much you love that car.'

'To be honest, I think I'd prefer something more eco-friendly.'

'Yes, and maybe less noticeable?'

'Yeah, after all, we need to be ready for the next protest or scandal.'

'Exactly,' he'd laughed, giving her a squeeze.

Even Alfie and Katie had seemed slightly more attentive than usual once Clare had outed herself. Katie had even asked Clare to pose for a selfie with her, and asked her to actually step through the forbidden school gates when she came to collect her. 'You know,' Katie'd said, in a way she'd probably thought was subtle, but which was anything but, 'I don't mind if you want to say hello – meet my friends. You don't have to wait in the car.'

Clearly, her mother's sudden fame – however bizarre – was scoring Katie a few social points.

'Don't wear the wig though, will you?'

Alfie had been less impressed to find out his mum was a talent show rapper. 'It's great,' he'd said, begrudgingly. 'But you know, Sam's mum has a second job as a copywriter. Might be an idea.'

'Sorry, Alfie. Martha ... well, Clare B. is here to stay for a bit at least.'

He'd nodded. 'OK. I mean, it's good. It's just ... kids at school.'

'Maybe I should see if your head teacher wants me to come and do a performance in assembly,' she'd teased, and watched his skin turn grey with horror.

Footsteps on the stairs of the new office reminded Clare now that it must be nearly lunchtime. The door opened cautiously and Steph stepped into their ramshackle space. 'Well,' she said, 'Bailey and Associates, eh!'

'Hey, gotta start somewhere!' smiled Clare. 'No Wilbur today?'

'No, John's taken him for a bit.'

Clare nodded. 'Good. You need a break. And ... how are things?'

'A bit better,' Steph smiled, wryly. 'You know.'

'Good,' she said, leaning forward to give her sister a hug. Once they were in the café, attempting to twirl tagliatelle around their forks, Clare worked up the courage to say what she'd planned.

'Steph,' she said.

'Yes?' her sister replied, shoving a forkful of pasta into her mouth.

'I wanted to ask you something . . .'

'OK?'

Clare took a deep breath. 'Look, I need to take on a few more members of staff – not many at first, we're seeing how it goes. But enough so that I can actually run a firm fairly smoothly.'

'Right?' Steph's voice sounded guarded, sensing that something was coming.

'Well, I wondered . . . Would you like to come on board as a legal PA? You don't need to know anything about the law yet. Ann can help you, and there's a course. If you get on with it you could eventually qualify . . .'

'Thanks, sis,' Steph smiled.

'That's OK. It'll be great, won't it, working together?' she said.

'Hang on,' Steph replied. 'What I was trying to say was: "thanks, sis, but no, I'd rather not".'

'Oh.'

'Hey, it's not you. Or even the idea of working with you – although I can see that being an absolute disaster in the long run, can't you?'

'Well, I suppose . . .'

'There's no suppose about it! We'd be arguing over who made the tea, or whether it was your or my turn to have Mum for Christmas within the first month!'

'I'm sure we could—'

'Anyway, it's not that.'

'It's not?'

308

'No. It's just – I mean, it's really kind of you. But it's not something that I want to do. Law stuff, I mean.'

'Oh.'

'Yeah. I know I complain about looking after Wilbur ... and things haven't been great. But my therapist, she's really helping me to see some possibilities in my future. And I'm hoping, maybe when Wilbur's a bit bigger and I hopefully feel better, that I might get back to the tap dancing.'

'Tap dancing?'

'Yes. Oh, don't worry, I'm not going to start performing, or asking to perform with some young back-up dancers. I mean, that would be embarrassing, right?' Steph grinned, looking more like herself than she had in a while.

'Touché!'

'Well, anyway. I thought I might start running classes. Maybe,' Steph took a deep breath, 'maybe in the long term start a little dancing school.'

'Oh, wow!'

'Yep! And I suppose, not entirely, but a bit of it's down to you.'

'What the Martha B. thing?'

'No, *you*. You starting your own firm. Being frustrated and doing something brave about it.'

'Thank you!' Clare said, feeling her cheeks go red.

'It's true though. Taking a risk, that sort of thing.'

They looked at each other with genuine affection. 'I'm proud of you, sis,' Steph said.

'Right back at ya.'

When Clare got home from her first day, a day full of form-filling and admin, and not at all as glamorous as she might have imagined, Toby was slumped in front of the TV in his habitual pose. Flies undone, shoes kicked off, glass of wine in his hand.

'Hi,' she said.

'Hi. Come and see this,' he said, gesturing to the TV.

She picked up a small glass of wine he'd already poured for her and sat down next to him.

On the TV, Dan from Eezee Troupe was being interviewed. 'Yeah, we're looking forward to it,' he was saying.

'What's he talking about?' she asked.

'Oh, they've been booked to support that other dance act, Street Boyz, on their tour apparently.'

'That's great.'

'Yeah – well done.'

'Oh, I think they did that all by themselves. Pretty talented, those boys.'

'What about you? Or should I say Martha B.?'

'Oh, she's got plans, believe me. I'm still working on the new rap – and I'm hoping the boys will support me. But I think it's important they have their own path, too – they're so talented.'

'That's great, really great. But actually I meant what about you? How was your day?'

And as she told him all about the boring minutiae of her first day as a #girlboss, she realised with a jolt that he was actually listening.

Acknowledgements

Thanks are owed to the wonderful author Nicola Gill who supported me when I had a book related wobble. And to Natalie Hodencq who stepped up to help just when I needed it.

And to Ger Nichol from the Book Bureau, my lovely agent, who is always so amazingly supportive.

Thanks too to Charlotte Mursell, Victoria Oundjian and Olivia Barber at Orion for their editorial support, to Ellen Turner for her hard work on publicity and to all the people who kept the printing presses running in these challenging times.

Thanks as always to my lovely husband Ray Harvey for clocking up nearly 20 years with me and reading drafts and edits without complaint. For always being supportive and giving good advice, most of the time.

To the lovely #writingcommunity on Twitter who've made publishing in 2020/21 more bearable, The D20Authors and Debuts2020/21 groups on Facebook who have helped keep this wobbly show on the road.

To the lovely book bloggers and readers I've connected with in the past couple of years.

And to my kids. Thanks for the cuddles that kept me going (and sorry if I squeezed you a bit too hard).

Credits

Gillian Harvey and Orion Fiction would like to thank everyone at Orion who worked on the publication of *Perfect on Paper* in the UK.

Editorial
Charlotte Mursell
Olivia Barber

Copy editor
Kate Shearman

Proof reader
Laetitia Grant

Audio
Paul Stark
Amber Bates

Contracts
Anne Goddard
Paul Bulos
Jake Alderson

Marketing
Tanjiah Islam

Design
Debbie Holmes
Joanna Ridley

Editorial Management
Charlie Panayiotou
Jane Hughes

Finance
Jasdip Nandra
Afeera Ahmed
Elizabeth Beaumont
Sue Baker

Production
Ruth Sharvell

Publicity
Ellen Turner

Rights

Susan Howe
Krystyna Kujawinska
Jessica Purdue
Richard King
Louise Henderson

Sales

Jen Wilson
Esther Waters
Victoria Laws

Rachael Hum
Ellie Kyrke-Smith
Frances Doyle
Georgina Cutler

Operations

Jo Jacobs
Sharon Willis
Lisa Pryde
Lucy Brem